OBSTRUCTION of JUSTICE

In Loving Memory, Kitty Bronstein

ALSO BY BRUCE BRONSTEIN

NONDISCLOSABLE

FULL DISCLOSURE

DEN of THIEVES

REVERSAL of JUSTICE

FRAUDULENT INTENT

ISBN :9780983934226

Designed and formatted by Jamison Hyman

Published by Bruce Bronstein and Jamison Hyman

Printed by CreateSpace

OBSTRUCTION of JUSTICE

Prologue

Thirty Years Ago

The little boy was only eight years old when his father died. His father's body was discovered behind the desk in his study. When the police were called to the house, they discovered an empty bottle of pills on the top of the desk, which led them to conclude that his death was a suicide.

Harvey Watkins was thirty eight years of age at the time of his death. Harvey Watkins had been happily married for eleven years and seemed to have a promising career at the Internal Revenue Service. A revenue officer his entire career, Harvey had always approached his job with passion for the case assignments and compassion for those taxpayers who found themselves delinquent with their tax obligations.

In spite of his strong work ethic, Harvey Watkins found himself in trouble when a disgruntled taxpayer of questionable character accused him of accepting a twenty five thousand dollar bribe. Despite adamant denials that he never accepted a bribe, Harvey Watkins was forced to endure a series of confrontational interviews with the Inspection Division of the IRS. These interviews later became heated and adversarial when the investigators disclosed that a large deposit had been made to Harvey's bank account around the time period in question.

Confident that a deposit of more than forty two thousand dollars included the alleged twenty five thousand dollar bribe, the investigators were about to recommend that Harvey be fired and prosecuted. When Harvey explained that this deposit represented the net proceeds from the sale of his late parents' house and produced the Settlement Statement to corroborate this, the investigators were forced to re-evaluate the investigation. While there was no documentary evidence to support the allegation that Harvey accepted money from a taxpayer, IRS officials tended to believe that it was theoretically possible.

For almost six months following the time the accusation was made, Harvey felt as if he were living in a fishbowl as his integrity was called into question. Being accused of a crime was a personal affront to Harvey's character. However, the fact that some IRS officials would question his vociferous denials hurt more than the allegation itself. Sensing that IRS officials were more interested in finding him guilty rather than determining the truth, Harvey retreated into his own world and became a recluse.

Throughout this time, Harvey thought back to his dealings with the individual who claimed having paid Harvey twenty five thousand dollars in exchange for recommending that his outstanding tax liability be written off as uncollectible. An internal review of the taxpayer's account showed that the unpaid tax liability was not written off, thereby supporting Harvey's assertion that he did nothing wrong. However, it was the taxpayer's accusation that he paid Harvey twenty five thousand dollars that could neither be proven nor disproven.

Harvey did not want to burden his wife with the dilemma he was under so he attempted to reassure her that everything was fine. In truth, Harvey suspected that he would be subject to some type of disciplinary action regardless as to whether a review panel exonerated him of the allegations.

What Harvey did not expect was a letter advising him that a decision had been made to refer the accusation to the US Attorney's Office for further investigation in spite of the fact that the allegation was without foundation. This meant a possible criminal prosecution based on the oral testimony of a disgruntled taxpayer with a grudge against the IRS and Harvey Watkins in particular.

As word had circulated throughout the Federal Building that Harvey Watkins was under a criminal investigation, his friends and co-workers treated him as if he were a refugee from a leper colony. Harvey was virtually shunned by everyone other than a few secretaries who believed in Harvey's innocence. There were no longer any invitations to join his co-workers for a cup of coffee, offers to go out to lunch, or invitations to socialize on week-ends.

When office meetings were held, no one wanted to sit next to Harvey for fear that the stench of his perceived guilt would rub off on them. This made going to work as enjoyable as drinking a bottle of paint thinner. However, with the accusation that he accepted a bribe still under review, IRS management did not want to allow Harvey to work collection cases. Thus, Harvey was told that he would be temporarily assigned administrative work in the office until further notice.

When a federal employee is told "until further notice," that means whatever it is could be indefinite. In Harvey's case, it could be as long as Harvey is still employed by the IRS.

Harvey had considered trying to find another job in the federal government. However, with an investigation that was still ongoing, no other division within the IRS would agree to accept Harvey on a transfer. Nor would another federal agency accept Harvey in light of the Justice Department's pending investigation.

Ashamed that he could lose his job and conceivably go to prison, Harvey felt that such a result would be a terrible miscarriage of justice. Sensing that he had already lost his job and the respect of his family, friends and neighbors, Harvey decided to end his life. Sobbing in his study while his wife Carol was helping their young son with his homework, Harvey swallowed several dozen sleeping pills and waited to die.

Alone in his thoughts, Harvey reflected on his life. He thought back to his childhood and what it was like to grow up near Druid Hill Lake. As a teenager, Harvey often worked in his parents' grocery store after school. Harvey derived tremendous personal satisfaction from assisting his parents with their grocery store and often dreamed of someday taking over the store when his parents retired. However, once Harvey graduated from college, he was encouraged by his parents to work for the federal government so that he wouldn't have to work fifteen hours a day six days a week.

Finally, Harvey reflected on his marriage to Carol and wiped away the cascade of tears streaming down his face. Although his wife and young son meant more than anything to him, he was willing to surrender his life rather than have to endure the shame of losing his job and be subject to a malicious prosecution.

Aware that he has precious few moments left, Harvey has taken pen in hand to compose a letter to his loved ones. With his eyesight blurry and his thought process betraying him, Harvey found that he was unable to articulate his last words. Finding himself laboring to share his final thoughts, Harvey barely managed to tell his wife and son how much he loved them and that he would miss them. Only seconds after signing the note, Harvey passed on.

Ironically, on the day of Harvey's death, the Justice Department had issued a report declining to accept the case for criminal prosecution because there was no credible evidence that Harvey had accepted a bribe. While the declination memorandum left open the possibility that IRS officials had discretion to take administrative action against Harvey, an opinion was expressed that there was no basis for the accusation and that the apparent motivation for the accusation was made by an unsavory taxpayer as part of a personal vendetta against Harvey.

During the Justice Department's investigation, an assistant United States Attorney had discovered that several years earlier, Harvey had seized a bar owned by a notorious mob figure. The bar's owner had a history of unpaid income and employment taxes totaling almost one million dollars. After Harvey seized the bar, its owner boasted that he would get even with Harvey. That day eventually came.

The individual who had claimed Harvey accepted a bribe from him was a second cousin of the bar owner. While not notorious like his cousin, this person was of somewhat questionable character, which should have set off bells and whistles to IRS investigators. Apparently the bells and whistles had not gone off at the time of the internal investigation.

At eight years of age, Morris was not prepared to go through life without his father. Morris looked up to his father as his role model and best friend. It was Harvey who took Morris fishing on weekends, got him started in sports and insisted that Morris join the Boy Scouts in order to develop good character traits.

When it was time for Morris to go to bed, it was his father who read him bedtime stories. While Morris always enjoyed having his dad read to him before going to sleep, it was really Harvey who derived greater pleasure from doing so.

Without his father by his side, Morris felt denied from having lost his father, friend and mentor. Consequently, this became the sole responsibility of Carol, who in addition to providing for her son's care, would now have to find a job to provide for his financial support.

Carol Watkins, like her late husband, did not have a large family. Carol's parents had recently retired and were living on fixed income. In addition, neither Carol nor Harvey had siblings who could lend a hand when things got tough. Thus, Carol Watkins was forced to now assume the dual role of homemaker and breadwinner.

Carol was able to eventually land a job as a teacher's assistant in the elementary school that her son attended. Although the job did not provide them with financial security, it did allow Carol the opportunity to spend more time with Morris, as she walked him to and from school and made it a point to keep tabs on him whenever she had a break during the day.

Morris liked having his mother look after him at school and was very proud of her. Carol was very popular with her students, which helped Morris feel accepted by his classmates. Finally, life seemed to be gradually getting better for Morris, in spite of having lost his father.

Approximately one year after his father's death, Morris would experience another traumatic incident of unimaginable proportions. His mother was killed in an automobile accident by a drunk driver, who had only recently been released from jail after serving seven days for driving under the influence and without a valid driver's license.

At the age of nine, Morris Watkins became a ward of the state and was placed in a foster home because he did not have a family member who could provide for his custodial support. From the time he was nine until he turned twenty one years of age, Morris had lived in seven different foster homes. While Morris may have had a number of legal guardians responsible for his care, not a single foster parent was a parent in a true sense of the word. These people were merely collecting money from Social Services to provide for the basic needs of a vulnerable child. Yet the most basic need that Morris cherished was never made available to him by his guardians. That need was love. It was something that would have an adverse impact on Morris for the rest of his life.

Chapter 1

Twenty Nine Years Later

"All rise, the Honorable Judge Barton, presiding," announced the judge's clerk as Judge M.L. Barton made his way to the bench.

"You may be seated," the judge said to everyone in the courtroom as he took the files that were handed to him by his clerk.

Judge Barton was recently appointed to fill an opening on the United States Tax Court when one of the sitting judges chose to retire for medical reasons. The youngest of the sitting judges, M.L. Barton looked like a kid compared to the other sitting judges. M.L. is of average height and slender in physique, giving the impression that he spent most of his life in a library. However, the one feature that stands out is his bright smile.

Judge Barton has a warm smile for everyone from court stenographer to the lawyers who will argue cases in front of him. It is almost as if Judge Barton is kind to a fault.

Judge Barton is, in a sense, an enigma. This is his first trial session and for this reason, no one knows what he is like as a trial judge. After serving as a law clerk to a United States District Court judge for two years and then joining a mid-size firm that specialized in civil tax litigation, Barton quickly made partner. As a litigator, Barton achieved notoriety as a lawyer who could mesmerize juries with his oratory skills.

His success in the courtroom brought him to the attention of several United States senators who strongly endorsed him to fill the vacancy on the Tax Court.

As the trial attorneys representing the Internal Revenue Service were somewhat apprehensive of Judge Barton, given the fact that they knew very little about him, they were relatively confident that the cases scheduled for trial on this calendar would be decided in favor of the IRS. Their confidence was predicated on both the facts as well as the law that supported the IRS's position in every case on this docket.

The first case to be heard involved two Motions for Summary Judgment. A Motion for Summary Judgment is a written request for a judgment in the moving party's favor before the case goes to trial where there is no genuine dispute as to any material fact and that the moving party is entitled to judgment as a matter of law.

The trial attorney representing the IRS filed a Motion for Summary Judgment because she believed both the facts and the law clearly supported the IRS's position. The petitioners also sought a judgment without a full trial and filed a similar motion with the court. Both sides have requested to be heard on oral arguments on the respective motions. It is this matter which will be the first case heard by Judge Barton.

"Mrs. Green, are you ready for your opening statement?" inquired Judge Barton in a pleasant tone of voice that was intended to put everyone at ease in his courtroom.

"Yes, Your Honor," Mo Green said as she stepped to her podium. "Good morning, judge. On May 31, 2008, the petitioners purchased property in Baltimore County at a cost of $625,000. The property consisted of a 1,220 square foot brick house on a lot that was more than twenty two thousand square feet. The petitioners purchased the property with the intent to demolish the building and build a new structure to their specifications on the site. The petitioners never resided in the house, nor did they reside on any part of the property at any time in 2008," Mo Green said.

"Prior to the time the petitioners purchased this property, their realtor told them about the Baltimore County Fire & Rescue Department Acquired Structures Program, where a property owner allows the BCFRD to conduct fire training exercises on the property. As part of the exercises, BCFRD destroys the designated building on the owner's property.

"Within a few weeks of purchasing the property, the petitioners contacted BCFRD and obtained information about the requirements for participating in the program. After the petitioners obtained a demolition permit and completed all of the other requirements, they executed documents granting BCFRD the right to conduct training exercises on the property and to destroy the house by burning it during the exercises. Included among the forms that the petitioners signed was a Certificate of Authorization in which the petitioners certified that they were the legal owners of the property and granted the BCFRD permission to use the property for training purposes. In addition, the petitioners declared that they had obtained a permit to demolish the house. Furthermore, none of the documents purported to transfer title to the house or the property, or for that matter, any ownership interest to BCFRD," the trial attorney continued.

"On October 23, 2008, construction of the petitioners' new home began. Construction was eventually completed in July of 2009, whereupon the petitioners obtained a residential use permit and moved into the new house, where they currently reside.

"Prior to its demolition, the petitioners had their property appraised. The appraised value was six hundred and thirty thousand dollars. On their 2008 federal income tax return, the petitioners reported a noncash charitable contribution of three hundred and forty thousand dollars with respect to the donation of the property to the BCFRD.

"The IRS disallowed the deduction on the grounds that the petitioners' donation to the BCFRD was a contribution of a partial interest in property, a deduction which is denied by section 170(f)(3) of the Internal Revenue Code. Your Honor, this code provision specifically denies a charitable contribution deduction for certain donations of partial interests in property and is the operative code section in this case," asserted Mo Green.

"It is Respondent's position that the petitioners merely donated the right to use the property and did not transfer an ownership interest in the house to the BCFRD. Granting a fire department the right to destroy a building while conducting training exercises on the property does not transfer to the fire department all the benefits and burdens of ownership, including title to the building. For example, the fire department does not have the right to keep and use the building in its current condition. Nor can the fire department otherwise sell, dispose of, or encumber the property. In addition, the fire department does not have the right to construct a new structure on the site of the destroyed building. In the case at hand, it is the petitioners who retained those substantial rights," Mo argued.

As she finished this point, Mo Green glanced at Judge Barton to gauge his reaction to her oral arguments. While the trial judge appeared to be listening to what she was saying, Mo sensed that something was amiss. When Mo moved on to her next thought, she wondered if Judge Barton actually had any interest in what she was saying.

"Granting a fire department the right to destroy the building while conducting training exercises on the property is not a conveyance of ownership, title or possession of the building," Mo continued. "Rather, it is a mere license to use the property. It is the destruction of the building that severs it from the land. As the petitioners retained rights to everything that did not disintegrate at the time of severance, there is no property to which title could vest in the fire department.

"Accordingly, it is Respondent's strong belief that the petitioners' grant to the BCFRD of the right to conduct training exercises on their property is a mere license in which no interest in the property has been conveyed. Without a conveyance, there can be no charitable contribution. Thus, we respectfully request that the court sustain the disallowance of the claimed charitable contribution deduction and grant Respondent's Motion for Summary Judgment," argued Mo Green, as she turned to take her seat.

Mo Green is a very accomplished trial lawyer who has a sixth sense about trial judges. As Mo sat down, she had an uneasy feeling that this particular judge would do something that defies logic and not grant her motion.

Turning to the petitioners, who were prepared to argue the case themselves, Judge Barton inquired as to whether they were prepared to present their Motion for Summary Judgment.

"Yes, Your Honor," Mr. Gustafson said as he stood at his podium. Hans Gustafson is a broad shouldered, barrel chested Swede, with a full head of long blond hair that he had wrapped in a ponytail for this proceeding. Standing by his side is his wife, Ingrid, who also has long blonde hair, which she did not bother to tie in a ponytail.

Looking at his wife, Hans is given the nod to speak on their behalf. "Our granting permission to destroy the building conveyed more than a license to use the house. We believe that when we granted the BCFRD the right to destroy the property, we conveyed all rights, title and interest in the property to the fire department. Upon destruction of the building, the property interests transferred to the fire department," argued Hans. "There is no requirement that the land be transferred with the house. As such, we contend that we are entitled to a charitable contribution for the value of the house," added the petitioner, who did a slight bow at the waist as he and his wife returned to their seats.

With both sides seated, it was time for Judge Barton to do something as the ball was now in his court. Taking a few moments to apparently collect his thoughts, the judge shuffled some papers, tugged at the sleeves of his robe and cleared his throat as if to speak. When he finally spoke, he did so with a sense of purpose.

"The court wishes to express its appreciation that both sides presented clear and concise summations for judgment in this case. Having listened to the arguments raised by both sides, I am of the opinion that the fire department's destruction of the house severed it from the land and thus, rendered the structure to be personal property."

Judge Barton continued by saying, "The petitioners ceded every substantial interest they held in the property and retained only insubstantial interests such as ownership of the post-burn debris. They did not expect the structure to be returned to them and it was not. All of the petitioners' substantial property interests in the structure were consumed by the fire department when it destroyed the structure in furtherance of its training objectives," added the judge.

Mo Green has the feeling that a knife has just been used to cut out her heart. The district's best trial lawyer cannot believe what this judge is doing.

"It is my decision that by virtue of the fire department's severance and destruction of the house, the petitioners ceded all substantial property interests they held in the house to the fire department. Once severed, the structure became personal property, whereupon the petitioners were left with only the debris into which it was converted," ruled the trial judge.

"Respondent's argument for judgment is premised on the application of code section 170(f)(3). However, an exception to disallowance under this code provision is made where a taxpayer makes a contribution of an undivided portion of his entire interest in the property," the judge reasoned. "I have therefore determined that the petitioners have satisfied the original congressional purpose behind section 170(f)(3). In view of the fact that the petitioners transferred, in substance, their entire interest in the house to the fire department, section 170(f)(3) does not limit their deduction. Accordingly, Motion for Summary Judgment is hereby granted to the petitioners. Court will recess for ten minutes," Judge Barton declared as he stood to leave the courtroom.

"All rise," the clerk said even though the judge had already exited the courtroom through the back door.

Mo Green was too stunned to stand as she sat at Respondent's table, almost in shock that she had lost the case. It had been a foregone conclusion that Mo would prevail on her motion given the facts and law. Losing this case was not supposed to happen, particularly when one of the IRS's most formidable litigators was handling the case. With this bench decision now a matter of judicial record, explanations are in order to senior executives in Chief Counsel.

Seated in one of the back rows was a junior associate at one of the larger law firms in downtown Baltimore who was sent to observe the trials scheduled for that day. This associate was also stunned when he heard Judge Barton's ruling. Even a relatively inexperienced trial lawyer could deduce that the IRS's position was fundamentally correct from both a factual and legal standpoint. Stepping out of the courtroom and walking down the hallway where he had some privacy, the young lawyer took out his cell phone and called his boss to let him know what had just happened in court.

"Are you kidding me?" said the associate's boss.

"I am not kidding you. This judge ignored the facts and disregarded the law when he ruled in favor of the petitioners. The IRS trial attorney couldn't believe it," remarked the lawyer.

"Who's the lawyer?"

"Maureen Green," said the young associate.

"Jesus Christ. She's probably the best litigator I've seen in the last twenty five years and she lost? I can't believe this!"

Word got out very quickly as to what Judge Barton did in his first case as a judge. Within the hour, several law firms had sent their associates to the courtroom to observe the proceedings. This was now turning into a three ring circus, with the Honorable M.L. Barton serving as the head ringmaster.

Chapter 2

When court resumed, Mo Green stepped to the podium, announced herself and extended the customary salutation to the trial judge. To any observer in the courtroom, this seems redundant when the trial judge knows the IRS trial attorney and was previously greeted with a good morning salutation. However, this is necessary so that the parties arguing the case are identified at the start of the hearing.

Mo Green is still seething over what happened in the prior hearing. However, she must put her emotions aside and focus on the case at hand. As in the prior case, this hearing is a Motion for Summary Judgment and it is Mo who will present the facts.

"Your Honor, the petitioner has filed two claims for a whistleblower award with Respondent under section 7623(b)(4) of the Internal Revenue Code. Respondent has denied both claims because an award determination could not be made under code section 7623(b). As such, the petitioner has failed to meet the threshold requirements for a whistleblower award," argues Mo.

As a general rule, an individual who provides information to the IRS that leads the IRS to proceed with an administrative or judicial action is entitled to receive an award equal to a percentage of the collected proceeds. Thus, a whistleblower award is dependent upon both the initiation of an administrative or judicial action and collection of tax proceeds.

Whistleblower claims are unusual and the Tax Court's jurisdiction in whistleblower cases does not include opening an administrative or judicial action to determine a particular taxpayer's tax liability. In a whistleblower action, the Tax Court has jurisdiction only with respect to Respondent's award determination. Although Congress authorized the Tax Court to review the IRS's award determination, Congress did not authorize the Tax Court to direct the IRS to proceed with an administrative or judicial action. Thus, Respondent's Motion for Summary Judgment should be a routine matter and approved by the judge. However, Judge Barton has now proven to be a formidable foe to the IRS and this hearing will not be a routine matter.

"Respondent has filed an answer to each petition that the petitioner filed. In its answers to the petitioner's claims, Respondent has explained why it does not believe that the tax information provided by the petitioner has merit. Accordingly, Respondent respectfully requests that the court approve its Motion for Summary Judgment," Mo states matter-of-factly.

Standing at his podium, Dan Kavendish loudly objects and does it with such conviction so all in the courtroom can hear him. In opposing the Motion for Summary Judgment, Kavendish is about to make an impassioned speech asking that the court undertake a complete re-evaluation of the facts and take whatever steps are necessary to detect an underpayment of tax.

Some people believe that anything said in a loud tone of voice is more important and truthful than having been said in a softer tone of voice. Dan Kavendish is apparently one of those persons.

In this proceeding, Dan Kavendish is both an attorney and the petitioner. In his capacity as a lawyer, Dan Kavendish was privy to certain financial information. He obtained this information by representing the legal guardian of a purported beneficiary of a Trust. Kavendish later verified the information by examining the public records and the records of his client.

On the basis of the financial information that he obtained, Dan submitted two claims with the IRS, seeking awards for filing whistleblower claims. Dan has alleged in the claims that certain parties had failed to pay millions of dollars in estate and generation-skipping transfer tax.

"Your Honor, in my first claim, I believe that a Trust having more than one hundred million dollars in assets was improperly omitted from the gross estate of Muriel Hathaway, thereby resulting in a possible seventy five million dollar underpayment in federal estate taxes. In addition, I have alleged that in the second claim, Muriel Hathaway impermissibly modified several other Trusts as part of a scheme to avoid the generation-skipping transfer tax." Dan Kavendish has said this loud enough for everyone in the entire federal courthouse to hear.

However, the lawyer with the loud voice is not finished. "Judge, the Tax Court has jurisdiction in a deficiency action to re-determine whether there is any income, estate or gift tax due. On the basis of the facts in this case, I am asking the court to rule as to whether any federal estate or gift tax is due from Muriel Hathaway," Dan declares in both a loud and forceful tone of voice that is less than persuasive considering the motion is ridiculous.

"Your Honor, the Tax Court's jurisdiction in a whistleblower action is different from its jurisdiction to review a deficiency determination," counters Mo. "The petitioner is attempting to use the court to re-determine a tax liability as it would in a deficiency determination. This is clearly improper," the IRS trial attorney adds.

"Mrs. Green, it is not necessary for you to tell me about the court's jurisdiction. I am well aware as to the court's role in whistleblower cases," replied a testy Judge Barton.

Mo has struck a nerve with the judge by making it clear to

him that the court does not have jurisdiction to re-determine a tax liability in a whistleblower case. In essence, if the IRS has concluded that there is no additional tax due, there can be no award. While the petitioner may disagree with the IRS's legal conclusion, the issue of whether there is additional tax due is not a matter for the Tax Court to decide.

Mo decides to give the judge a hard stare as she continues with her arguments. "Respondent reviewed the information the petitioner provided in the whistleblower claims. Respondent forwarded the information to the IRS office with subject matter jurisdiction over the issues raised by the petitioner. After that office reviewed the information provided by the petitioner, Respondent concluded that no administrative or judicial action would be taken against the estate of Muriel Hathaway," Mo asserted.

"Respondent sent the petitioner a letter stating that a section 7623(b) award determination would not be made for either claim because the petitioner did not identify any federal tax issues upon which the IRS would take action. The letter further explained that an award was not warranted for either claim because the petitioner's information did not result in the detection of any underpayments of tax," Mo added. "Consequently, the information that the petitioner submitted to the IRS did not meet the criteria for paying an award."

Pausing for a brief moment to allow the judge to absorb what she just said, Mo concluded by saying, "Respondent moves for summary judgment on the grounds that there are no genuine issues of material fact for trial."

Dan Kavendish is not about to give up without a fight. Sensing that this is his opportunity to challenge the motion, Dan says in a loud voice, "Judge, I disagree. I believe that there are genuine issues of material fact because Respondent failed to properly investigate facts relevant to my whistleblower claims. It is my contention that Respondent failed to apply the correct law in determining the merits of my claims.

Therefore, I ask that the court direct Respondent to undertake an investigation, open a case file and take whatever other steps are necessary to detect an underpayment of tax."

The combatants in this hearing have returned to their respective seats. Savoring the moment to further agitate the IRS trial lawyer, Judge Barton decides to twirl a pen while opposing counsel twiddle their thumbs. Finally, the judge says, "In light of the petitioner's assertions that there is additional estate and gift tax due, I am denying Respondent's Motion for Summary Judgment and will set the matter for trial."

The next case on the trial calendar belonged to Lindsay Cooke, another veteran trial attorney in the Office of the District Counsel. Lindsay, who happened to be seated directly behind Mo Green during the first proceeding, attempted to console her co-worker on her second shocking loss. "I can't believe this happened to you. He totally missed the point on what constitutes a donation of property," offered Lindsay, "as well as not understanding that an award can't be granted where there's no additional tax due."

"I know. Judge Barton's rationale for ruling against me both times makes absolutely no sense. He's misconstrued the statutes. It's almost as if Barton doesn't understand the underlying premise of a gift of property. And for the life of me, I have no idea how he thinks we can somehow resurrect an estate tax. Oh well, I've got to explain this to Warren. Maybe he can make some sense out of this," Mo said as she switched seats with Lindsay. "But first, I'm going to sit through your Motion for Summary Judgment because I'm curious to see what he does in your case."

When Judge Barton was handed the next legal file, he immediately had the case called. "Counsel, are you ready to proceed?"

Lindsay stood at her podium and said, "Yes, Your Honor.

Lindsay Cooke for Respondent."

Standing across from Lindsay was Harold Meekins. "Good morning, judge. Harold Meekins for petitioners."

With a warm smile for the lawyers, Judge Barton said, "Very well, Ms. Cooke, please begin."

"Your Honor, Respondent has filed a Motion for Summary Judgment in the matter of the petitioners having sought review of Respondent's determination to sustain the filing of a Notice of Federal Tax Lien ('NFTL') to collect unpaid federal income taxes. The sole issue for determination is whether Respondent abused his discretion in sustaining the NFTL," Lindsay said.

Lindsay glanced up at the judge before continuing and observed Judge Barton as appearing to be keenly interested in what she had to say. "The petitioners filed a voluntary Chapter 7 bankruptcy case in the United States Bankruptcy Court for the District of Maryland on May 31, 2009 and their debts were discharged in bankruptcy on March 25, 2010. On October 20, 2010, the petitioners filed their 2009 federal income tax return, but failed to pay the tax shown as due which was in excess of forty five thousand dollars," Lindsay continued.

"In November of 2010, the IRS audited the petitioners' 2008 and 2009 federal income tax returns. On February 10, 2011, the IRS sent petitioners an examination report whereby additional tax was due for the 2008 tax year, with a reduction in their tax liability for the 2009 tax year. The petitioners appealed this determination to the IRS's Office of Appeals," Lindsay added.

Before she continued, Lindsay again peered up at Judge Barton, who returned her look with a pleasant smile as if they were the best of friends. "On November 17, 2009, the IRS sent the petitioners an IRS Letter 3172, which is the Notice of Federal Tax Lien Filing and Right to a Hearing pursuant to section 6320 of the Internal Revenue Code with respect to their unpaid self-reported federal income tax liability for 2009. On December 14, 2009, the IRS received the petitioners' timely filed Form 12153 Request for a Collection Due Process ('CDP') or Equivalent Hearing in which they requested a CDP hearing to address whether the IRS should not have filed a tax lien while their 2009 audit was still open. The petitioners did not request that any collection alternatives be considered at the CDP hearing," Lindsay explained.

"Your Honor, I would like to add that at that point in time, the petitioners' 2010 federal income tax return had not been filed and was past due when they submitted their CDP hearing request," Lindsay said for emphasis.

"On June 11, 2112, the petitioners reached a settlement with Appeals and signed Form 870, whereby the petitioners agreed to an increase in tax of three thousand dollars for 2008 and a decrease in tax of twenty five thousand six hundred dollars for 2009. However, after the audit adjustments were agreed upon, the petitioners still had an unpaid balance for 2009.

"On December 27, 2112, Respondent sent the petitioners a Notice of Determination Concerning Collection Actions Under Internal Revenue Sections 6320 and/or 6330, sustaining the filing of the tax lien.

"The parties are in agreement as to the relevant facts in this case. Respondent is seeking summary judgment on the grounds that the petitioners have failed to establish that Respondent abused its discretion by filing a lien," Lindsay said. "Respondent believes that the settlement officer in the Appeals Office properly determined that the requirements of applicable law and administrative procedure were met and concluded that sustaining the NFTL appropriately balanced the need for efficient collection of taxes with the petitioners' concerns regarding the intrusiveness of the lien action," she concluded.

Although Lindsay was finished with her oral argument, she chose not to return to her seat. Standing at her podium, Lindsay wanted to be prepared to quickly address any comments on this matter.

"Mr. Meekins, are you prepared to provide the court with a rebuttal to Ms. Cooke's arguments?" inquired the judge.

"Yes, Your Honor," the portly lawyer said as he waddled to the podium. "I am in agreement with the facts as presented by opposing counsel. However, there is a material fact that Ms. Cooke omitted from her motion argument which needs to be addressed because it is at the very core of this issue.

"The petitioners sent the settlement officer in Appeals a letter that stated that the revenue agent who conducted the audit and the appeals officer who considered their appeal had orally informed them that a lien would not be filed while their 2009 audit was open. It is this fact that is of critical importance because it goes to the very issue of abuse of discretion on the part of Respondent," argued Harold Meekins.

Before Harold had a moment to savor what he believed was a compelling argument, Lindsay interjected by asserting, "Your Honor, no documentation was submitted as to representations made by the revenue agent and the appeals officer that a lien would not be filed. The settlement officer determined that the withdrawal of the NFTL was not warranted."

"Judge Barton, the petitioners dispute this allegation. They have steadfastly insisted that IRS officials informed them that a lien would not be filed. The petitioners accepted this statement as being true. Obviously it wasn't. Accordingly, the petitioners contend that the IRS should be equitably estopped from filing the NFTL," argued the overweight lawyer.

Equitable estoppel is a judicial doctrine that precludes a party from denying his or her own acts or representations which induced another to act to his or her detriment.

Upon hearing that argument, Lindsay immediately shot back by saying, "In order to invoke the doctrine of equitable estoppel, all of the five traditional elements must be satisfied. I don't believe opposing counsel has met his burden."

"Your Honor, I believe that we have," replied Meekins.

"Judge, there must be (1) a false representation or misleading silence by the party against whom the doctrine is to be invoked; (2) an error in a statement of fact and not an opinion or statement of law; (3) ignorance of the fact by the representee; (4) reasonable reliance on the act or statement by the representee; and (5) detriment to the representee. There is no affirmative misconduct or pattern of false promises," argued Lindsay.

As the lawyers apparently had nothing else to add to the subject, Judge Barton raised both his hands and signaled to the attorneys that they could take their seats. Pausing for a few moments to convey the impression that he is contemplating what he is about to say, Judge Barton removes his eyeglasses. The act of removing his glasses before speaking does not impress Lindsay.

"To establish abuse of discretion, the petitioners must show that Respondent's decision was arbitrary, capricious or without sound basis in fact or law. The petitioners claim that IRS officials represented to them that a lien would not be filed while their 2009 audit was open. Even though Respondent insists that there is no documentation to support this claim, I am troubled by the allegation. To summarily dismiss it as not having been said would be unfair to the petitioners. Conversely, it would be inequitable to Respondent to deny its motion and later find out that such representations were never made by the IRS officials," stated the judge.

"Whereas I wish to be fair to both sides, I find it more palatable to rule in favor of the petitioners than to merely dismiss their case out of hand. Therefore, Respondent's Motion for Summary Judgment is denied," ruled Judge Barton.

As this was said, Lindsay slumped backwards in her chair as if she had been smacked over the head by a sledgehammer. The next words she heard were, "Please call the next case," Judge Barton instructed his clerk, as if today is the day IRS trial lawyers will be brought into court, placed into a guillotine and beheaded.

While Lindsay was stunned that she lost, Mo was furious with the judge's ruling. As both women stood to leave the courtroom, Thaddeus Chudzinski made his way to the podium to argue the next case.

By this time, the courtroom was again packed with interested spectators. Many of the courtroom observers had left the courtroom to make phone calls to their offices after the second motion's hearing was concluded. So far, the IRS is zero for three in proceedings where it should be victorious in each case. However, the morning is not yet over.

Chapter 3

As Mo and Lindsay made their way out of the courtroom, Thaddeus Chudzinski took his place at Respondent's table.

Thad's opening statement was brief and to the point. "Your Honor, the petitioner incurred unreimbursed volunteer expenses while caring for foster cats in her private residence. The petitioner's expenses consisted primarily of payments for veterinary services, pet supplies, cleaning supplies and household utilities. The petitioner has claimed a charitable contribution deduction of fifteen thousand dollars with respect to these expenses," Thad said.

"The charitable organization in question is 'Cat Care,' which is recognized as a tax exempt organization pursuant to section 501(c)(3) of the Internal Revenue Code. However, Respondent has disallowed the deduction by reason of the fact that the petitioner did not render services to a qualifying charitable organization under code section 170(c) and that the petitioner failed to substantiate her expenses under section 170(f)(8). Respondent has also asserted in its Notice of Deficiency that the petitioner's expenses have an indistinguishable personal component," Thad added.

Thad had a number of points he wanted to bring to the judge's attention in his opening statement. One such point was that Cat Care's mission consisted solely of "education and sterilization," thereby making the petitioner's services unrelated to the charity's mission. As such, what the petitioner was actually doing did not benefit Cat Care. Thus, fostering cats could not constitute services to the charity, argued Thad. Thad intended to further emphasize this point when he can cross-examine the petitioner, who likes to refer to herself as "The Cat Lady."

Thad also asserted that the petitioner was neither affiliated with the charity, nor did Cat Care initiate or request services from the petitioner. Furthermore, Thad noted that Cat Care neither encouraged nor indirectly oversaw the petitioner's work.

Before concluding his summation, Thad also noted that the petitioner has attempted to deduct cremation services as well as her Costco membership. In addition, Thad noted that the petitioner deducted her vacuum cleaner and household utility expenses. Thad closed by asserting that these expenses were not connected with, and solely attributable to, charitable activities.

Thad's summation addressed the critical points which he will prove through witness testimony. Once The Cat Lady acknowledges that the above assertions are true, Thad plans to show that such expenditures are not deductible.

When it was time for the petitioner to speak, she did so with passion not usually witnessed in Tax Court. "Your Honor, please forgive me if my opening statement is different than what you are accustomed to hearing from lawyers. You see, I'm not a lawyer. I don't even watch those courtroom shows on television. Instead, I'm going to speak from my heart.

"I'm a cat rescue worker. This is something that I've been doing just about my whole life. You see, I love pets and my heart goes out to cats that don't have a home. Can you picture what it's like growing up without family? You're on your own, constantly looking for a safe place to sleep at night, scrounging for anything to eat, not having entitlement to health care. It's awful. I wouldn't wish it on anyone. I'm partial to cats so I have taken it upon myself to provide a foster home for cats that need to be rescued. I'm just a rescue worker who cares about the safety of cats," said the petitioner, who then took a moment to wipe away false tears between sobs.

"I repaired my wet/dry vacuum so that I could easily clean the floors. I incurred higher electricity and gas bills because I laundered more loads of cat bedding and ran a special ventilation system to ensure fresh air. The more frequent laundering also increased my water bills. In addition, my garbage bills increased because of the high volume of cat-related waste.

"I admit that I renewed my Costco membership so that I could buy cat food and cleaning supplies at lower prices. But, I also purchased very large quantities of pet and cleaning supplies at lower overall prices, thereby making the membership fee inconsequential. I also paid most of the veterinary expenses including tests, treatment, vaccines and surgery," The Cat Lady continued.

"I don't really understand all this tax stuff about what's deductible and what isn't deductible. It seems to be a little too technical at times for me. But I can tell you this. In my heart, I know that what I have done to help save homeless cats was the right thing to do," said the petitioner as she then asked the judge for permission to take her seat.

For the next ten minutes, Thad asked the petitioner questions about Cat Care's mission and the services that she was performing. While Thad was able to quickly show that there was no direct correlation between Cat Care's mission and the work the petitioner was doing, it didn't seem to impress the trial judge.

With Judge Barton moving the trial along at a fast pace and encouraging both sides to be brief in their closing arguments, the trial was completed in less than thirty five minutes. All that remained was a decision, which Judge Barton did not have to render at this time. However, Judge Barton seems to be a man who is decisive, particularly when he can rule against the IRS.

"On the basis of the trial testimony and applicable law, I find that the petitioner's foster-cat expenses qualify as unreimbursed expenditures incident to the rendition of services to a charitable organization. Accordingly, such expenses are deductible as charitable contributions," declared Judge Barton, who then called for a ten minute recess.

****

"Boss, you're not going to believe what happened in court this morning," Mo Green said as she and Lindsay walked into Warren Simonsen's office and made themselves at home on the oversized leather sofa with the soft and luxurious seat cushions.

"You came out on the short end to a pro se petitioner. Actually, I should be a little more descriptive and say that you were soundly thrashed. Is that a more accurate account as to what transpired in court?" the District Counsel asked.

"How did you know?"

"I heard about it on the radio. WBAL has reported this story several times already as if it's the feature news of the day."

"Are you kidding me?" asked Mo.

"No, I am not kidding you. And by the way, Ms. Cooke, I don't want you to feel left out so I'll let you know that word has also gotten out as to your performance in court. WBAL has also aired the decision in your case on its noon telecast."

"Jesus," Lindsay muttered under her breath.

Just as Warren was about to say something, Thad entered his

office and leaned against the far wall as if he needed it for support.

"Thaddeus, I'm glad you could make it. Please have a seat and join us," said Warren.

"What in the hell are you doing here? Shouldn't you be in court?" Mo asked her young associate.

"My trial's over," remarked Thad.

"Don't tell me you also lost?" Lindsay asked Thad.

"I'm afraid so," replied Thad, who looked sheepish as he dropped his head almost in embarrassment that he could have lost his case given such a compelling set of facts.

"Trent Stratford was kind enough to call me with the news," said the District Counsel. "One of his junior associates was in court and witnessed this morning's fiasco. Trent has passed along his condolences that we lost three cases we should have won. Now with Thad having lost, we're zero for four.

"We have fourteen more cases scheduled for trial. My guess is that Barton is going to rule against us in each case unless we reach a basis for settlement before it gets called. What I'm going to ask you to do is call as many of the petitioners that you can and see if they will agree to a final pre-trial settlement. If they are receptive, get someone from Appeals to prepare the tax computations without delay. We can't let these cases go forward if we can help it," said the District Counsel.

"What do you want to do about the ones that we've already lost?" Mo asked.

"You mean file motions for reconsideration?" asked the District Counsel.

"Yeah."

In accordance with Rule 161 of the Tax Court's Rules, any motion for reconsideration of an opinion or findings of fact must be filed within thirty days after a written or oral opinion has been served. Pursuant to Rule 162, the IRS has up to thirty days to file a motion seeking to have a decision vacated or revised. The IRS also has ninety days to file an appeal with the United States Court of Appeals.

"We have time to decide whether motions should be filed. I'll defer to Chief Counsel on that. My more immediate concern is this judge," Warren replied.

"Warren, there is something inherently wrong with this judge. He's killing us with his idiotic rulings. If I didn't know better, I'd say he took a bribe to toss each case," Thad remarked.

"I seriously doubt Judge Barton took a bribe. Each case is unrelated and none of the cases are worth that much in tax dollars. No, it's something else. Let's do what we can to resolve whatever issues are in dispute in the remaining cases just to avoid further litigation. I'll deal with the fallout," Warren announced to the troops.

"What about Beverly Baxter?" asked Mo.

"Is Agent Lipschitz set to testify in the Baxter case?" Warren asked.

"Yes."

"Keep Baxter for trial. And let Louie know what's going on so he'll be ready," Warren suggested.

After his staff attorneys left his office, Warren placed a telephone call to his boss, the Regional Counsel for the Mid-Atlantic area to let him know what has happened.

"Let me get this straight, because I'm not sure I heard you correctly. Mo Green lost? You're telling me she lost to a pro se petitioner? Is that right?" asked the Regional Counsel.

"Yes."

"I didn't think it was possible. And Lindsay is no slouch as a trial lawyer. So how is it possible that she could also lose?"

"I don't know. For that matter, Thad also lost. Although he's light in the experience department, Thad is actually pretty good. With the case that he litigated this morning, he was well-prepared and should have won as well. I think we have a problem with a biased judge and should elevate this problem to Chief Counsel."

"Warren, bringing it to Chief Counsel's attention isn't going to accomplish a whole lot. I don't think there's much Chief Counsel can do about it," replied the Regional Counsel.

"I know, but what I'm hearing is that Judge Barton's ignored the facts in each case, disregarded the statutes and law, and has issued rulings that can hardly be considered rational. I've never heard of this type of behavior from any other Tax Court judge."

"OK. I'll pass along your concerns to Chief Counsel and see what they want to do. In the meantime, see what you can do about having your trial lawyers settle the remaining cases," advised the Regional Counsel.

"They're already working on that."

Chapter 4

Alexander Hill had placed a call to opposing counsel to suggest that they meet prior to trial in order to try to reach a basis for settlement. When Cindy Klein heard this, she laughed. "Alex, word has gotten out that this judge doesn't seem to like Respondent's trial attorneys. I would be doing my client a grave disservice if I didn't argue his case before Judge .... whatever his name is, unless you want to concede the case now."

"I'm sorry, Cindy. If you want to win this case, you'll have to argue it in court," replied the District Counsel trial attorney, who sensed that the decision in this case would be in favor of the petitioner. In one hour, Alex Hill would learn the answer.

Alex had been in the District Counsel's Office for almost seven years. During this time, his won/loss record as a trial attorney was quite good. While Alex was not feared by other practitioners as was Mo Green, he was respected as a litigator by opposing counsel and held in high esteem by the trial judges who decided his cases.

When Alex's case was called for trial, he stepped forward as if he were about to face a firing squad. "Mr. Hill, are you ready?" the judge asked.

Thinking that he would be ready in about twenty years, Alex tried to be as confident as possible when he replied in the affirmative that he was quite ready. "Judge, the sole issue in controversy is whether the petitioner was a trader of securities," Alex stated.

The tax consequences to day traders are diametrically

different than the tax consequences to investors. Section 475(f) of the Internal Revenue Code provides that a taxpayer who is engaged in business as a securities trader may elect to use the mark-to-market method of accounting for securities held in a business. Under the mark-to-market method of accounting, a taxpayer generally recognizes at the end of the year, ordinary gain or loss on all securities held in the business as if the securities were sold at the end of the year at its fair market value. Ordinary losses are made available to offset ordinary income and are not subject to the three thousand dollar limitation imposed by code section 1211(b) on the deduction of capital losses in excess of capital gains.

Having framed the issue for the trial judge that this is a day trader case, Alex summarizes the relevant facts by saying, "The petitioner held a degree in economics from Stanford University. During the years in issue, the petitioner operated a ball bearing manufacturing and distribution business. The petitioner has been its sole shareholder, officer and director from the date of its incorporation to the present.

"The petitioner reported W-2 income of twenty eight thousand dollars, forty five thousand dollars and fifty two thousand dollars for the tax years 2007, 2008 and 2009, respectively. The petitioner's corporation reported net income of seven hundred and sixty three thousand dollars, four hundred and eighty five thousand dollars and three hundred and twenty one thousand dollars for the tax years 2007-2009 respectively.

"The petitioner traded securities prior to and throughout 2007-2009. The petitioner made a mark-to-market election under code section 475(f) in 2006 and did not revoke that election through 2009.

"In 2007, the total value of the securities purchased was over twenty million dollars and the total value of the securities petitioner sold was also over twenty million dollars. Based on the petitioner's trading records, he seldom bought and sold the same stock on the same day.

"In 2008, the total value of the securities purchased and sold was one million two hundred and thirty four thousand dollars and one million eight hundred and fifty two thousand dollars, respectively.

"In 2009, the total value of the securities purchased and sold was two million three hundred and forty six thousand dollars and one million seven hundred and fifty six thousand dollars, respectively.

"According to the petitioner's trading records, he engaged in one hundred and eleven transactions over a span of seventy five days in 2007. In 2008, the petitioner participated in only seventy four transactions over a period of eighteen days. In 2009, the petitioner engaged in eighty two transactions over twenty one days.

"The petitioner reported his income, losses and expenses from his sales of securities on Form Schedule C and listed his principal business or profession as "Day Trader," Alex added before he finally paused for a brief moment.

"On his 2007 Schedule C, the petitioner reported a net loss of almost two million dollars arising from the sales of securities and almost one hundred thousand dollars in expenses. The petitioner deducted these losses against his other ordinary taxable income," Alex continued.

"Respondent has disallowed the deductions for ordinary losses beyond the three thousand dollar limit under code section 1211(b) for losses arising from the petitioner's trading of securities during 2008 and 2009, as well as the net operating loss carryover from 2007.

"While the petitioner did manage a large amount of money in 2007, merely managing a large amount of money is not conclusive as to whether his trading activity amounted to a trade or business. The second requirement for classification as a trader involves the petitioner's efforts to profit from short-term savings in the stock market," explained Alex.

"In light of the petitioner's trading activity, Respondent does not believe that the petitioner meets the classification of a trader. Accordingly, Respondent respectfully requests that the petitioner's losses be classified as capital losses, limited to the three thousand dollar capital loss deduction," Alex concluded as he returned to his seat.

Turning to Cindy Klein, the judge asked if she was prepared to offer a rebuttal.

Cindy Klein has been practicing tax law for more than ten years and is well versed in Tax Court rules and procedure. Given what she has heard about this morning's proceedings, Cindy senses that this judge will rule in favor of her client. Therefore, Cindy is of the opinion that she does not have to put on a spirited defense because the judge will find a way to reach a decision in favor of her client. However, this doesn't necessarily mean that Cindy can sleep through this hearing. Some work will be required on her part.

"Your Honor, I have a very brief statement to make. A person who purchases and sells securities falls into one of three distinct categories; that is, dealer, trader or investor. We know that investors typically engage the services of a stockbroker or a financial advisor to buy and sell securities for their own account. The issue in this case is a question of fact," Cindy asserted.

"In determining whether a taxpayer is a trader, there are certain factors to consider. For a taxpayer to be a trader, the trading activity must be substantial. This means that the activity must be frequent, regular and continuous enough to constitute a trade or business. As Mr. Hill alluded to in his opening statement, a taxpayer is required to show that he sought to catch the swings in the daily market movements and to profit from these short-term changes rather than to profit from the long-term holding of investments.

"Based on the petitioner's purchases and sales in 2007, there can be no doubt that this was substantial in every sense of the word," concluded Cindy. "A securities portfolio of twenty million dollars is indeed substantial and should not be dismissed out of hand. Accordingly, we respectfully request that the petitioner be permitted to deduct his losses as ordinary rather than capital."

Cindy wastes no time in having her client take the witness stand. Despite having to acknowledge that he did not engage in a high volume of securities transactions, the petitioner was able to make a convincing argument that his securities portfolio was significant in 2007. Glancing at the judge when he made this argument, the petitioner detected a subtle nod of the judge's head as if he concurred with this assertion.

Cindy picked up on this and decided to wrap up her questions. While Alex was able to show that the petitioner had failed to consistently sell on the same day the securities that he purchased earlier in the day, this critical factor seemed to be of little consequence to Judge Barton.

Upon the conclusion of brief closing arguments, Judge Barton announced that he was prepared to issue a ruling. To no one's surprise, he ruled in favor of the petitioner. Alex Hill stood, turned to congratulate opposing counsel and gave the trial judge a hard stare to let him know that this was not a fair hearing.

Judge Barton didn't seem the least bit fazed that the IRS trial attorneys had taken an immediate dislike to him. Apparently Barton's only concern was in having his trial calendar move at a brisk pace.

As Alex Hill walked out of the courtroom, Lindsay Cooke passed him in the hallway and made the mistake of asking her co-worker how the trial went. "If I had a gun with me, the United States Tax Court would be minus one of its sitting judges," replied Alex.

"Sorry," was about the only thing that Lindsay could say.

"Lindsay, I feel like a lamb having been led to slaughter," Alex said dejectedly.

"I know. He already sabotaged my first case. I don't expect anything different with this one."

As Lindsay was organizing the legal files for her case, Judge Barton returned to the courtroom and wished her a pleasant afternoon. If Lindsay wanted to return the kind thought, she would no doubt wish that Judge Barton be struck down by a lightning bolt this very moment.

"Is counsel ready for oral arguments on Respondent's Motion To Dismiss for Lack of Jurisdiction?" inquired the trial judge.

"Yes, judge. Lindsay Cooke for Respondent." Lindsay is now somewhat apprehensive that she isn't close to being ready.

"Ms. Cooke, please proceed," said the trial judge who was making quite a name for himself with his controversial rulings. In the next few minutes, this judge will earn a few more names.

"Judge Barton, Respondent's Motion To Dismiss for Lack of Jurisdiction, is based on the grounds that the petition was not filed within the period prescribed by Internal Revenue Code section 6213(a). That period ended on January 27, 2011, which is ninety days from the date the Statutory Notice of Deficiency was mailed," argued Lindsay.

"The petitioners moved several times shortly before and after the deficiency notice was issued. At the time the notice was mailed, the petitioners no longer resided at that address. In early October of 2010, the petitioners moved to a new address. While the petitioners were living at the new address, Respondent had issued a deficiency notice. The notice was mailed on October 28, 2010. While residing at the new address, the petitioners received the notice. Indeed, the petitioners have even acknowledged that they received the notice in early December of 2010. That left the petitioners with more than thirty days to file the petition," Lindsay stated.

"However, the petitioners did not file their petition within the requisite ninety day filing period from the date the notice was issued," argued Lindsay. At this point, Lindsay had disclosed all of the relevant facts and made a compelling argument that Respondent's motion to dismiss should be granted. Indeed, it is the correct result by application of statute and by application of the Tax Court's own rules.

The Tax Court is a court of limited jurisdiction. The court may exercise its jurisdiction only to the extent authorized by Congress. The court's jurisdiction to re-determine a deficiency pursuant to code section 6213(a) depends on the issuance of a valid deficiency notice and a timely filed petition. For purposes of section 6213(a), as long as the deficiency notice is mailed, it doesn't matter whether it is actually received by the taxpayer.

Subject to certain exceptions, a petition for the re-determination of a deficiency must be filed with the Tax Court within ninety days from the date a notice is mailed. If a petition is not timely filed, the Tax Court has no jurisdiction to re-determine the deficiency.

It just so happened that Lindsay's opposing counsel is the rather portly Harold Meekins, who was looking forward to winning his second hearing of the day.

"Your Honor, Harold Meekins for petitioners," Harold announces as a formality that is expected of lawyers, regardless of the number of times they have made appearances before the court earlier in the day.

"The petitioners object to Respondent's motion by reason of the fact that the notice was not mailed to their last known address. It is the petitioners' contention that it is irrelevant that they received the notice. The fact that it was sent to the wrong address invalidates the notice," added Harold.

"The petitioners contend that when they moved from their former address, they notified Respondent of the event on a Form 8822 Change of Address," Harold argued. "Upon filing this form with the IRS, the burden to send the notice to the petitioners' new address rested with the IRS. By failing to do so, the notice became invalid."

Lindsay knows that her adversary's legal argument is misguided. Lindsay also feels that every other judge on the Tax Court would have recognized the flaws in Harold's legal conclusion.

"While respondent agrees that the use of a Form 8822 is one of the proper ways to establish a taxpayer's last known address, there is no record that such a document was received before or after the notice was issued," asserted Lindsay.

"Ms. Cooke, am I to understand that the IRS does not have the petitioners' Change of Address declaration on file?" asked Judge Barton.

"That is correct, judge."

"So if the form was filed with the IRS, you would be penalizing the petitioners when the IRS is at fault for failing to update its records and issue its notice to the proper address," said the judge.

"Your Honor, if the Form 8822 had been filed with the IRS, wouldn't it seem likely that the IRS would have received it?" replied Lindsay, who immediately after saying this realized that she shouldn't have posed this question. Lindsay quickly recovered and said, "Your Honor, forgive me, but what I meant to say was that even if the notice was improperly addressed, it should not be considered invalid for purposes of the Tax Court's jurisdiction. I would also ask that you consider that the petitioners still had sufficient time to file the petition."

"Ms. Cooke, I am troubled that the IRS used an improper address on its Statutory Notice of Deficiency. I am therefore of the opinion that the notice is invalid. As such, Respondent's motion to have the case dismissed is rejected. Consequently, the court will retain jurisdiction and the case will be placed on the next trial calendar," ruled Judge Barton.

Upon hearing this, Lindsay merely rolled her eyes as she looked at Harold Meekins, who simply shrugged his shoulders as if he were apologizing for the wrong decision, but willing to accept the decision as a gift.

This ruling only meant that the petitioners would be getting an opportunity to challenge the IRS's deficiency determination in court. Lindsay was hopeful that the trial judge in this proceeding would not be Barton.

Harold Meekins was so pleased that he had prevailed again that he planned to celebrate this evening by having a buffet dinner at one of his favorite restaurants. Had Harold known that this judge was predisposed to rule against the IRS in every hearing, he would have filed more petitions with the court. Harold made a mental note to consider filing more petitions in Tax Court and start a diet tomorrow.

Chapter 5

"Mr. Chudzinski, is this a motions hearing?" inquired Judge Barton.

"Yes, judge." Thad is wondering whether Judge Barton will do something totally unprecedented and rule against his motion before it is argued.

"Very well, please state your basis for summary judgment," instructed the judge.

Taking a deep breath as he stood at his podium, Thad felt as if it didn't really matter what he had to say. On the basis of what has transpired in court, Thad sensed that this misguided jurist would very quickly rule against him and deny his Motion for Summary Judgment.

"Your Honor, the petitioner has sought innocent spouse relief with respect to unpaid federal income tax liabilities for the 2006 and 2007 tax years. As a result of unpaid tax liabilities for these tax years, the IRS filed a Notice of Federal Tax Lien dated September 29, 2008. In response to the Notice of Federal Tax Lien, the petitioner submitted IRS Form 8857, Request for Innocent Spouse Relief. This form was received by the IRS on October 15, 2010," Thad said.

"On January 15, 2011, Respondent issued a determination denying the petitioner relief from joint and several liability under Internal Revenue Code section 6015(b),(c) and (f) because the petitioner failed to meet the statutory requirement for relief under section 6015," Thad added.

"Mr. Chudzinski, on what grounds was relief denied?" asked

the judge.

"The petitioner did not request relief within the two year period following the date of the first collection action," answered Thad.

"Mr. Cabot, did you wish to participate in this discussion?" asked the judge.

Lew Cabot is the petitioner's attorney. A seasoned tax lawyer who is well respected and well liked by his peers, Lew Cabot is aware of what this particular trial judge has been doing of late. If he is going to win a case, the lawyer would like to do it on the merits rather than be handed a gift.

Cabot had once been an IRS trial attorney so he knows what goes into trial preparation. Upon graduation from law school, Lew Cabot went to work for the IRS where he honed his litigation skills. After five years as a government trial lawyer, Lew decided to accept an offer to join a downtown law firm that needed a skilled tax lawyer who could handle litigation work.

Lew is currently the head of his firm's tax litigation practice and its managing partner. Confident that he will prevail given what he has heard about this judge, Lew would like to achieve his anticipated victory with dignity and humility.

Cabot took a few seconds to make his way to the podium. "Judge, I do not take exception to Mr. Chudzinski's factual statements. My client failed to request spousal relief before the two year expiration date. She was late by several weeks. However, my client believes that to summarily dismiss her case from being heard on the merits would be an overly harsh result," the lawyer said without having raised his voice.

Hesitating for a brief moment as if he actually contemplated the arguments raised by each side, Judge Barton said, "Recently, the Tax Court has ruled that the two year limitation period in which to request spousal relief is an invalid interpretation of section 6015. As a consequence, in September of 2011, the IRS announced that it would no longer invoke the two year rule. Are you aware of this, Mr. Chudzinski?"

"I am aware that the two year rule no longer applies to innocent spouse relief that is sought on equitable grounds under section 6015(f). However, the two year rule is still enforceable with regard to the other sub-sections under section 6015," replied Thad.

"You may be right counselor, but not today. Respondent's Motion for Summary Judgment is denied. Mr. Cabot, please inform your client that her trial will be held in this courtroom for later today." Turning to his clerk, the judge said, "Margie, can you schedule the hearing to begin at two o'clock?"

"Yes, judge."

"Gentlemen, I will see you both at 2 PM."

The first thing Thad did was to go to the men's restroom. After Thad soaked his head in cold water, he tried to make sense out of what happened. An invalid interpretation to the other provisions, he muttered to himself as he soaked his face. The next thing he did was call his boss.

"Look Thad, it doesn't really matter, because you're going to have to argue the facts to make the case that Mrs. Keller doesn't qualify for innocent spouse relief," Warren said.

"Boss, he's going to find a way to give this case away," Thad said.

"I know. Just hang in there."

When Gloria Keller arrived in court with her lawyer, she had no idea what to expect. However, Lew Cabot sensed victory in hand but decided not to overplay what he had to say.

On the other side, Thad was worried even though the facts clearly supported his position that Gloria Keller was not entitled to innocent spouse relief.

"Mr. Chudzinski, are you ready?" the judge asked. In truth, Thad was looking forward to this trial with as much enthusiasm as having to consume a bottle of cod liver oil.

"Your Honor, as an administrative matter, Mr. Keller and his lawyer were provided with a Notice of the Innocent Spouse Hearing. Mr. Keller did not intervene, which was his administrative right and has not appeared for trial to be heard in this case," Thad said as the judge nodded his head in acknowledgment.

"The petitioner and Mr. Keller are heavy drinkers. The petitioner worked with Mr. Keller at a brokerage and investment services company. The petitioner was the office administrator and had an ownership interest.

"Mr. Keller and his parents incorporated a consulting practice that structured early retirement plans of teachers. Mr. Keller was instrumental in its profitability.

Thad began his memorialization of the facts by stating, "The petitioner and Mr. Keller jointly purchased a home valued at more than nine hundred thousand dollars. The petitioner was a signatory to the mortgage.

"After being married for twenty years, the petitioner and Mr. Keller became estranged. The petitioner knew that Mr. Keller had a substance abuse problem and that he spent more time frequenting multiple establishments that are commonly referred to as gentlemen's clubs. The petitioner felt humiliated by Mr. Keller's patronage of these clubs. Mr. Keller's excursions would last for several nights and his recovery afterwards would extend for a long period during which he would lie on the couch immobilized," Thad said.

"Mr. Chudzinski, I hope that you are not presenting this

to denigrate someone's reputation, particularly when that person is not in the courtroom," the judge interjected.

"No, Your Honor. I am merely presenting the relevant facts for your consideration. As a matter of fact, it was the petitioner who voluntarily disclosed this to Respondent and has stipulated to it as being an accurate account. It is relevant to this discussion and for this reason, it is being addressed at this time," Thad explained.

"Very well, please continue," Judge Barton said, now that he interrupted Thad's train of thought.

Collecting his thoughts for a second, Thad continued by saying, "Mr. Keller's substance abuse problem had adversely affected his consulting work. This eventually led him to seek medical treatment for his addictions."

Thad is back on track as he says, "Mr. Keller's alcoholism also strained his already tenuous business relationship with his parents. Mr. Keller's parents disapproved of his extravagant lifestyle, for which he failed to reimburse the business for his many personal expenses. This led to Mr. Keller's parents buying him out of the company and structured the buyout as a severance plan.

"Over time, Mr. Keller received hundreds of thousands of dollars each year as severance payments. Although these payments were made to him individually, he reported the payments as income of his corporation. These amounts were significantly greater than what he had earned in his consulting business and constituted most of the income the petitioner and Mr. Keller reported on their 2006 and 2007 federal income tax returns. The petitioner knew of the agreement and the amount of the actual payments in each year.

"Although Mr. Keller deposited the funds in his own bank account, he transferred funds to the joint account whenever the petitioner requested that he do so," Thad added.

"Throughout the marriage, the petitioner was responsible for paying the household expenses. The petitioner paid the monthly mortgage, utilities, automobile payments and college tuition for their children. In addition, the petitioner and Mr. Keller kept a horse training and boarding venture and reported over sixty thousand dollars in losses in 2006 and 2007.

"Despite their substantial income, the petitioner knew she and Mr. Keller faced financial difficulties. Indeed, they had bad credit and had to rely on the corporate credit card to pay their personal expenses.

"The petitioner was responsible for providing information and documents to their CPA and writing the checks to pay their federal income taxes throughout their marriage. In years prior to 2006, the petitioner and Mr. Keller filed joint returns, reporting balances due. To pay those balances, the petitioner signed and remitted checks written against the joint checking account," stated the IRS lawyer.

"For 2006, the petitioner and Mr. Keller filed joint tax returns and reported a balance due of more than one hundred and seven thousand dollars, of which most of the liability was attributable to Mr. Keller's severance payment. However, neither the petitioner nor Mr. Keller set aside any of the severance payment to pay the tax due. In other words, no estimated tax payments were made during the calendar year," asserted Thad.

"For 2007, the petitioner and Mr. Keller again failed to pay the balance due on this return, which was not timely filed. The 2007 return was filed four months late. The unpaid liability exceeded one hundred thousand dollars and no estimated tax payments were made at any time," added Thad. "I would like to point out that at the time the 2007 return was eventually filed, the petitioner knew that the balance due for the 2006 tax year had not been paid."

Thad has presented an overpowering indictment of the petitioner's failure to ensure that the joint tax liability was paid. Given this particular set of facts, Thad has a very strong argument that the petitioner does not meet the elements for spousal relief.

"Thank you, Mr. Chudzinski. Mr. Cabot, I would like to hear from you at this time." What Judge Barton is really saying is that he would like Lew Cabot to come up with a somewhat plausible reason why his client should be granted relief from the unpaid tax liability.

"Thank you, judge. My client has acknowledged that she knew there was a balance due on the 2006 and 2007 tax returns. However, my client signed these returns only when Mr. Keller had agreed to pay the balance due in each year," Cabot said. Whether this is true is open to speculation.

"In 2008, Mr. Keller had a relapse and began to drink again. The petitioner recognized her own alcohol addictions and began to attend AA meetings. Her recovery led her to make a commitment to move out of the marital home.

"In 2009, my client lost her job and did not earn any income for that year. In 2010, my client received money from Mr. Keller to pay their expenses, including their mortgage which was in default.

"My client concedes that she is not entitled to statutory relief under code section 6015(b) and (c). However, my client has sought judicial review of Respondent's denial of equitable relief under section 6015(f) by virtue of the fact that it would be an economic hardship to hold her liable for the unpaid tax liabilities," Lew Cabot argued.

The facts in this case were stipulated prior to trial. As the facts are not in dispute, witness testimony has not been necessary. Thad intends to quickly memorialize several facts before addressing inconsistencies by the petitioner.

"Your Honor, the petitioner either had knowledge or had reason to know that the tax liabilities would not be paid. Petitioner also had actual knowledge of all of the severance payments. The petitioner also failed to ensure that estimated tax payments were made on a quarterly basis during each year. Petitioner cannot prove that it was reasonable for her to believe that Mr. Keller would pay the balances due. Indeed, the petitioner has stipulated that she was the one responsible for handling the family's finances and writing checks in prior years. Given Mr. Keller's drug and alcohol addictions, his extravagant spending habits and his erratic behavior, how could the petitioner possibly believe that he would pay the balances due?" Thad argued.

"The petitioner has admitted that she and Mr. Keller had financial problems that made it difficult to pay their basic household expenses. Given the protracted decline of her marriage, it was clear that the tax liabilities were not going to be paid," Thad concluded.

"Your Honor," Lew Cabot interjected. "My client does not take exception to what Mr. Chudzinski has said. Respondent is certainly correct in this regard. However, my client is financially distressed and is under an economic hardship to pay the outstanding tax liabilities."

Without wasting any time, Thad shot back. "Judge, the petitioner has represented on Form 433-A that her monthly income barely satisfies her monthly expenses. However, Respondent has discovered that the petitioner has bank statements that show that her monthly income exceeds that amount shown on Form 433-A.

"In addition, the petitioner represented on Form 433-A that she did not have any retirement accounts. However, Respondent has discovered an investment portfolio, including a retirement account as part of a brokerage account which petitioner did not disclose.

"Given these misrepresentations, I don't see how the petitioner has met her burden of persuasion that paying these tax liabilities would cause her an economic hardship," countered Thad.

Placing both hands up in the air as if he were about to be robbed at gunpoint, the judge has decided that he has heard enough on the subject. In a hand gesture to the lawyers to let them know that he is about to rule, the judge takes a few seconds before speaking.

"The court appreciates the arguments advocated by both sides. I think there is substantial merit to the arguments raised that the petitioner does not qualify for innocent spouse relief given her knowledge that the outstanding taxes would not be paid. However, what the court must focus on is whether the petitioner is being placed in financial distress if held liable for the unpaid taxes. While true that she derived an economic benefit from not having paid the taxes, if forced to do so, would she be able to meet her reasonable basic living expenses? I think not. Accordingly, the petitioner is hereby granted relief in accordance with the economic hardship test. Margie, please call the next case."

With the sensation that a sharp instrument has just been plunged through his heart by a cruel judge with no sense of fair play, Thad stumbles out of the courtroom, almost in shame that he lost this case. Rushing to catch up to him, Lew Cabot puts his hand on Thad's shoulder to console him.

"Thad, I don't know what to say. I'm truly embarrassed to have won under these circumstances. My client could have lost on the motion hearing as well as on the facts just now. I'm sorry. I don't like to be handed a win when I certainly don't deserve it," admitted the lawyer.

"Do you want to tell that to my boss, because I have to explain this to him," said Thad.

"No. But please give Warren my best."

Chapter 6

Like the weather and the stock market, people have good days and not so good days. A bad day is when a few things that are not expected to go wrong, inevitably go wrong. A really bad day is when a number of things go wrong for no apparent reason. This is something that everyone experiences in their lifetime. However, for several IRS trial lawyers, it's happening to them with this trial calendar.

Warren Simonsen's trial attorneys are getting pummeled in court. They have argued a total of ten cases before Judge Barton and lost all ten cases. They have lost on routine motions that defy logic. They have lost on procedural matters that are nonsensical. They have lost income tax deficiency cases as well as hearings that involve collection issues.

It is one thing to lose a case on its merits. It's an entirely different matter to lose a case because the trial judge is biased or misguided.

With each passing day, Judge Barton's courtroom has been packed with members of the media reporting on the day's events. The press is making this a spectacle of epic proportions. Legal analysts who have been following the proceedings at the request of the media have openly questioned how Judge Barton has arrived at his rulings.

Both the US Attorney's Office and downtown law firms have sent several of its lawyers to the courtroom to observe the proceedings. Every seat in the courtroom is taken and some people have resorted to standing along the wall nearest the entrance doors to the courtroom.

The clerk has now called the case of Beverly Baxter v. Commissioner. As the case was called, Warren Simonsen entered the courtroom, accompanied by Lester Newhouse, the presiding chief judge of the United States Tax Court. Also in attendance was Lawrence Jenkins, the senior aide to United States Senator Sheila Stevens, who was invited to attend the trial at the request of the Chief Counsel of the Internal Revenue Service.

As Senator Stevens was unable to attend the trial because of prior commitments, she asked her senior aide to attend on her behalf and observe the judge's demeanor. If it bordered on conduct unbecoming a member of the bar or violates the letter and spirit of the rules of professional conduct, Senator Stevens wanted a full written report. In this respect, Senator Stevens personally asked the chief judge to sit in the courtroom as a favor to her.

It is highly unusual that a chief judge would observe a trial conducted by another sitting judge. However, unusual circumstances sometimes require unique actions.

Judge Barton immediately recognized Chief Judge Newhouse but does not know Lawrence Jenkins, who is sitting to the left of Warren. It is Lawrence Jenkins that Judge Barton should be wary of because he will be reporting the judge's conduct to his boss, Senator Stevens. If Barton's behavior borders on misconduct, it will be Senator Stevens who, as a ranking member of the Senate Judiciary Committee, will consider impeachment proceedings against the judge.

Judge Barton is so preoccupied with Judge Newhouse sitting next to the District Counsel in the courtroom that he hasn't noticed that Mo Green has started her opening statement. "The petitioner was engaged in the business of providing interior design services to clients. In conjunction with this activity, the petitioner deducted a variety of expenditures which Respondent has disallowed. The grounds for disallowance are (1) the petitioner did not incur such expenses due to a lack of substantiation and (2) if the petitioner did incur the expenses, she has failed to establish that such expenses were ordinary and necessary in carrying out her trade or business activity."

Still furious at Judge Barton for his decisions in the previous cases, Mo gives him a hard stare as she continues with her opening statement. "Respondent has also taken exception to the petitioner's charitable contribution deductions and has disallowed the deductions that relate to Temple Beth Shalom and Caring for Kids.

"Respondent also intends to show that the petitioner has submitted altered documents in a concerted effort to deceive Respondent's investigating agent during the audit. The petitioner's failure to cooperate during the audit and subsequent conduct are noteworthy because it is indicative of fraud," argued the IRS trial attorney.

When Mo used the f word, she could see Judge Barton swallow hard. With a fraud case, the IRS would be presenting evidence of fraudulent conduct. That, coupled with Chief Judge Newhouse in his courtroom, would complicate matters if Barton intended to arbitrarily rule in favor of the petitioner.

Mo spoke for several more minutes and gave the judge another intense look once she took her seat. If looks could kill, Judge Barton would be ready for burial.

When she was called upon to offer an opening statement, Beverly Baxter stood and slowly stepped up to her podium. "Your Honor, I have done nothing wrong," Beverly said. "The IRS is trying to prosecute me when I'm completely innocent of the false charges. Thanks for listening," Beverly concluded as she returned to her seat.

For some inexplicable reason, Beverly had thought that she could handle the audit herself by canceling scheduled appointments, failing to respond to requests for documents, concealing records and telling lies. That didn't exactly work out in her favor.

After the IRS issued its Statutory Notice of Deficiency, Beverly met with Mark Paul Warren, a flamboyant tax attorney who is more flash than he is skillful. As a matter of fact, many tax practitioners will say that Mark Paul Warren is an incompetent buffoon who is all show and no substance.

The incompetent buffoon filed a petition on behalf of Beverly that denied the IRS's allegations that Beverly had substantially understated her taxable income for the years in issue and recklessly filed tax returns that were blatantly fraudulent. Prior to and after filing the petition, the lawyer had foolishly promised his client that he would prevail in court against the IRS. Indeed, the lawyer even boasted that, "On my worst of days, I can run circles around their best lawyer."

When Mo Green filed the Answer in response to the petition, Mark Paul Warren immediately submitted a motion with the court to seek a withdrawal of his Appearance that was on file with the filing of his petition. When Beverly asked her lawyer why he was withdrawing from representing her in court, Mark Paul Warren said, "I'm really good, but I'm not quite as good as Maureen Green. Good luck getting another lawyer."

Mark Paul Warren is not much of a litigator. Throughout his undistinguished career, he litigated a total of four tax cases and lost all four cases. Of these tax cases, he went up against Mo Green on two occasions and was humiliated both times at trial. The thrashing that he received was witnessed by other tax attorneys and was particularly entertaining to those on the IRS's side. After his latest defeat, Mark Paul Warren swore that he would never again set foot in court to oppose Mo Green.

In spite of calling virtually every tax lawyer in Baltimore, Beverly was unable to find an attorney who would represent her in court. When told that the IRS trial attorney would be Maureen Green, every lawyer Beverly spoke with declined to accept her case.

The fact that she couldn't secure the services of a lawyer did not discourage Beverly from going forward. Beverly decided that she had certain things in her favor. She planned on wearing a short skirt to court, hoping to entice the males on her jury to find in her favor. However, what Beverly did not know was that there are no juries to decide cases in Tax Court.

The Tax Court is composed of nineteen presidentially appointed judges who will decide cases. Each candidate goes through an extensive screening process for selection. In Beverly's case, she had better hope that her judge has a weakness for loose women.

Beverly Baxter is in her late twenties and very attractive. Some men may even regard Beverly to be a stunning redhead with curves in all the right places. However, everyone who knows Beverly will say that she is also incredibly stupid. Before the trial is over, Mo Green intends to show that Beverly Baxter is also a pathological liar.

Beverly is dressed in a very stylish designer outfit for today's trial and has chosen to wear extravagant jewelry with her fashionable wardrobe. Unfortunately, this is not a fashion show and petitioners do not get style points on their wardrobe selections. However, with this judge, it seems that a petitioner could be dressed in a burlap bag and still be awarded a favorable decision.

IRS agent Louis Lipschitz is called to the witness stand to testify. Louie has been informed as to Judge Barton's bizarre conduct and intends to get the judge's social security number so that he can start examining his income tax returns.

Louie has many friends in high places. Starting with the President of the United States and continuing with the

Assistant Deputy Attorney General, Louie has racked up some substantial IOU's and intends to call in a debt. If Louie decides to go after a federal judge, he had better have the president in his corner.

"Agent Lipschitz, how many times did the petitioner seek postponements of her audit?" Mo asked her witness.

"There were seventeen separate requests," replied Louie.

"Why so many?"

"First the petitioner claimed that her accountant had her records and would not return them to her. Then she claimed that her computer crashed and her records were on the hard drive. Then, her mother was taken ill. Then, her mother died. Later, her mother was mysteriously brought back to life and was taken ill again. Her car broke down and she didn't have transportation. Her Aunt Ellen got sick. Her dog got sick and had to be taken to the vet. Her niece was performing in her elementary school's dance recital and she wanted to be there. She slipped in the bathroom and injured her foot. She had a scheduling conflict with her dentist, her OBGYN, her ophthalmologist, her chiropractor, and her psychologist. Her Uncle Merton got sick. Her toaster oven caught on fire and she had to replace it. Her ill mother, who was still recovering from her death, needed groceries. She stayed up too late one night and had to stay home for several days to recuperate. She forgot about the scheduled conference. She wanted to hire a lawyer but couldn't find one. I might have left some other excuses out, but that's pretty much what I was getting in the form of excuses."

"Did the petitioner call you with these excuses?" Mo asked.

"No. She sent me fax transmittals and when I attempted to reach her by phone, she did not take any of my phone calls."

"Was she not home when you called?"

"Actually, she was home when I called once."

"How do you know that?" asked the IRS lawyer.

"Because I was sitting in my car outside her house when I called her," answered Louie. "The petitioner has caller ID and would not take my call. I could see her standing in her kitchen staring at the phone on her kitchen wall."

There are people who make it a practice to stare at a telephone as if staring will cause it not to ring. Similarly, people will stare at a toaster oven as if staring will speed up the toasting of a bagel. Louie was about to make a comment at this point about the petitioner continuing to stare at the phone but decided not to press the point with a hostile judge who might want to hold him in contempt of court.

"So the petitioner made a concerted effort to delay the audit. When you finally met with her, what happened?" Mo asked.

"Ms. Baxter would not provide me with documents."

"Did the petitioner give you an explanation as to why the documents would not be provided?"

"First, she claimed that her financial records were confidential and that she had a constitutional right of privacy. When she was informed that the IRS was authorized by law to review financial records, she said that she was concerned that no one at the IRS would understand her books and records because of its complexity." Louie appeared to have difficulty saying this with a straight face.

When taxpayers are asked to submit their financial records to the IRS, it is generally a good idea to do so because withholding relevant information is not helpful. Taxpayers should know that the IRS has the ability to obtain documents through third party summons enforcement. Thus, it is counter-productive to refuse to provide information that can be gathered through a summons. Furthermore, stalling tactics only serve to annoy revenue agents. Pissing off an IRS agent is also not a wise strategic move on the part of taxpayers.

Submitting false documents is also not very smart. If suspicious documents are submitted, it is a relatively simple process for IRS agents to obtain copies from third party sources in order to ascertain the authenticity of documents. It is also relatively easy to distinguish valid documents from those documents that have been altered.

Finally, lying about fraudulent documents is also not in the best interests of taxpayers. Taxpayers who continue to engage in this tactic typically do not fare well.

With Beverly Baxter, she has hit the trifecta by failing to cooperate, engaging in stalling tactics and submitting fabricated documents, which will then be the subject of false testimony.

"Did you have a problem with the petitioner's records?" Mo asked.

"The only problem that I had with her records was that she submitted fraudulent documents that were designed to deceive me," Louie testified.

"Let's start with the petitioner's business records. Please explain why you disallowed the deduction for office supplies in the first year."

"Ms. Baxter combined a variety of categories into office supplies. Ms. Baxter deducted more than sixteen thousand dollars for high-priced designer clothes such as dresses, skirts, blouses, undergarments, shoes and handbags in the first year she claimed to be an interior decorator. She also deducted the cost of perfume, make-up supplies and beauty salon expenses. Furthermore, Ms. Baxter stayed at an exclusive spa and deducted her airfare, lodging, meals and miscellaneous expenses. The total cost of this trip was more than six thousand dollars."

"Agent Lipschitz, I'm a little confused. Did the petitioner include all of these expenses under the classification of supplies?" Mo Green was clearly not confused and intentionally asked this question for the benefit of certain people in the courtroom.

"Ms. Baxter combined these expenses under office supplies. However, she also deducted the out-of-town trip to the spa as well as her perfume and make-up supplies as other expenses. Thus, the same deduction was claimed twice," Louie testified.

"How much was the perfume?"

"Eight hundred and seventy four dollars."

"And the make-up?"

"Three hundred and twenty eight dollars."

"Was there anything special about the clothing?" Mo asked of her witness.

"Other than the fact that it was expensive? No. Ms. Baxter's clothes, while expensive, are adaptable to general wear, as evidenced by the fact that she can wear this type of wardrobe to work as well as to social functions after work."

"Did you obtain a listing of all of the petitioner's meal and entertainment expenses?"

"Yes. Ms. Baxter had continually refused to provide me with receipts as to her purchases. However, I was able to obtain receipts from her credit card purchases through summons enforcement. This amounted to more than five thousand dollars in meal and entertainment expenses each year," Louie stated.

"Were you able to determine if any of the thousands of

dollars in meals were business related?"

"I couldn't tell if any of the meals related to business. Most of the receipts were for general household supplies and groceries."

"What type of household supplies?" Mo questioned her witness.

"Toilet paper, cleaning supplies, various kitchen items, pet food for her dog, that sort of thing."

"I'm sorry, Agent Lipschitz, but did you say pet food?" Mo asked in an incredulous voice as if the petitioner had the audacity to deduct pet food as a business expense in carrying on her interior design work.

"That's correct. She deducted hundreds of dollars in pet food each year."

"Did you say the petitioner also deducted groceries?"

"Yes. She claimed a deduction each year for everything from cereal to ice cream bars," Louie stated.

"You obtained a print-out of the petitioner's itemized expenses?" Mo asked.

"Yes. I ran sub-totals for each type of food, such as juice, cereal, bread, pasta, yogurt, fruit, etc. The petitioner also deducted her membership at Sam's Club as well as meals that she had outside of her home."

"Were you able to trace her meals on a daily basis?"

"Yes. I cross-referenced her meals for each day of each calendar year. The petitioner has claimed deductions for fast food meals where only one meal was purchased. This would suggest that she did not discuss business with another party," Louie stated as a factual conclusion.

"Let's move on to the petitioner's health club membership. Were you able to determine whether the petitioner used her health club in furtherance of her interior design business?" Mo asked.

"Actually, as a matter of clarification, Ms. Baxter did not operate her own interior design business. Ms. Baxter was employed by a design firm, was eventually fired and then hired by another design firm, where she was later dismissed. In fact, she was terminated by a number of design firms throughout the years in issue. In terms of her clients, none were members of her health club."

"Can you explain why her health club expenses are so high?" Mo asked.

"First, there are the monthly membership dues of just over one hundred dollars. On top of that, Ms. Baxter employed a personal trainer who charged her one hundred dollars an hour. The payments that she made to her personal trainer were by check."

"Is one hundred dollars an hour the going rate for a personal trainer at her health club?"

"That depends on what you expect the personal trainer to do. The standard rate per the club is forty five dollars an hour. However, if you want the trainer to have sex with you, the cost is one hundred dollars an hour," Louie replied.

"How do you know this to be true?" inquired Mo.

"Ms. Baxter's personal trainer has been arrested for prostitution on numerous occasions. According to the police reports, he admitted to having charged his clients one hundred dollars an hour to have sex with him."

Mo Green intends to call the personal trainer as a witness and have him testify that the petitioner told him that she didn't mind paying him to have sex because she planned to deduct the payments on her tax returns. By the time the personal trainer is finished testifying on behalf of the government, his reputation as a personal trainer will have taken a serious hit, but will be nothing compared to what is in store for his former client.

"I see that the petitioner has claimed an office-in-the-home each year. Please explain why you disallowed the home-office deductions," Mo prompted Louie.

"According to the interior designers that Ms. Baxter worked for throughout the years in issue, she was instructed by them not to work at home. Each designer preferred to see Ms. Baxter in the office, meeting with clients at the design studio. When necessary, Ms. Baxter was expected to meet with clients in their homes," replied Louie.

Mo has directed Louie's attention to an exhibit. Requesting permission to approach her witness, Mo shows Louie the letters from Beverly's bosses whereby Beverly was directed by each one not to work at home. Louie reads the highlighted portions of the various letters instructing Beverly not to work at home.

"Did you personally interview the individuals who wrote these letters?" Mo asked.

"I did."

"Did you inquire as to the reason why they told the petitioner that they wanted her in the design studio?"

"I did," answered Louie once again.

"And what did they tell you?"

"They said that they did not trust Ms. Baxter and that they had concerns that she was over-billing clients for design services that she did not perform. They wanted her to be visible in the design studio so that they could observe her working. Inevitably, it did not work out and each designer fired her," Louie stated.

At this point, the trial attorney is laying the foundation to further impeach the petitioner's character. In a few minutes, Louie will actually get into the triplicate deductions on Beverly's tax returns. Louie is such a compelling witness that Mo has decided to let him go on at his own pace.

Once Louie has shown that all of the business expenditures claimed by the petitioner are bogus, Mo directs him to Beverly's charitable contributions. This will also prove to be entertaining.

"Please explain why you disallowed the twenty five hundred dollar contribution to Temple Beth Shalom in each of the years in issue," Mo asked.

"Ms. Baxter gave Temple Beth Shalom a check payable in the amount of twenty five hundred dollars in each year. One day before she wrote each check, Ms. Baxter deposited twenty five hundred dollars in her checking account so that there would be sufficient funds available in her checking account. However, several days after the checks cleared, Ms. Baxter sent a letter to Temple Beth Shalom and advised the synagogue that she had made a mistake and had only intended to donate twenty five dollars and not twenty five hundred dollars. The synagogue honored Ms. Baxter's request each time and returned two thousand four hundred and seventy five dollars to her. However, Ms. Baxter reported the donation as twenty five hundred dollars on her tax return in each year," explained the IRS agent.

"What did the petitioner say to you when you brought this to her attention?"

"When I brought the discrepancy to her attention, I sought an explanation. In response, she told me that it was a one-time thing and that it was an honest oversight on her part."

"What was your response to that statement?" asked the lawyer.

"I informed her that it was not an isolated event," replied the agent.

"I informed her that she claimed the same twenty five hundred dollar deduction in the next two years even though Temple Beth Shalom returned all of her money other than twenty five dollars."

"And her response was what?"

"She said she didn't understand the question and asked me to leave," replied the IRS agent.

"OK. Let's turn to the charitable contribution deductions for Caring for Kids. What happened here?"

"It was the same thing. Ms. Baxter wrote a check each year for fifteen hundred dollars. One day before she wrote each check, Ms. Baxter deposited fifteen hundred dollars in her checking account to ensure that she had sufficient funds available to cover the donation. Several days after each check cleared, she complained in writing to the charity that it was a mistake and that she only intended to donate fifteen dollars. Again, Ms. Baxter used the fifteen hundred dollar amount as her charitable contribution in each year," answered Louie.

This type of testimony continues for the next hour. By the time Mo and Louie are finished, Beverly Baxter looks like Public Enemy Number One. The testimony is so devastating that Judge Barton cannot disregard its impact.

Once Mo has taken her seat, Beverly is asked by Judge Barton if she wishes to cross-examine the witness. Nodding tentatively, Beverly stands, attempts to straighten out a slight wrinkle in her short skirt, crosses her arms across her chest in such a way to enhance the contour of her breasts and says,

"No, judge. That man is a liar. I never said those things. He's taken everything I've done out of context. How can I question someone who's telling lies like this?"

Just as Mo had gotten comfortable in her chair, she stood to protest. "Your Honor, I object. The petitioner is now testifying. Furthermore, there's no foundation for her assertion that Agent Lipschitz is lying. If she wishes to challenge Agent Lipschitz's testimony, she should do so based on the facts."

"Relax Mrs. Green," Judge Barton says to pacify the IRS lawyer. "Ms. Baxter is entitled to voice her opinion," the judge said almost in admonishment of the objection.

Glaring in defiance at what was just said, Mo renewed her objection that the petitioner is now testifying and doing so improperly. However, Mo is not quite finished and decides to bait Judge Barton by continuing to assert that there is no foundation for questioning Louie's veracity.

Sensing that the chief judge is going to be all over him, Judge Barton is the first to blink and finally says, "I concur with Respondent. Petitioner will either ask a question of the witness or take her seat."

"Judge, my accountant prepared my tax returns based on all of the records that I had collected during each year. These mistakes were his fault. I shouldn't be held liable for his mistakes." Before Mo can object again, Beverly takes her seat and throws a hand up in the air as if she is finished with this entire sideshow.

After Louie has stepped down, several other witnesses have been called to testify against Beverly. Her former personal trainer has confirmed Louie's testimony that he was paid to have sex with the petitioner and that she boasted to him that this was a business expense which she intended to deduct on her tax returns. Once Mo had finished asking him questions, Beverly declined to cross-examine on grounds that she did not wish to speak to him.

Beverly's former employers also testified that they instructed the petitioner not to do any work at home and confirmed that they had sent directives to her in the form of e-mails. Mo had earlier entered the e-mails into evidence and had the individuals who authored the memos stipulate to having written the e-mails, which they did.

Mo then had officials of the charitable organizations testify as to the petitioner's written requests each year to be reimbursed for the excess cash donations. They confirmed Louie's testimony by authenticating the letters they received requesting that the charity reimburse Ms. Baxter.

Mo still has one more witness to call. It is this person who will tap the final nails in Beverly Baxter's coffin.

"Please state your name," Mo instructed her star witness.

"Donald Aaronson."

"Mr. Aaronson, what is your occupation."

"I'm a CPA. I operate a small accounting firm that specializes in setting up internal accounting systems and preparing tax returns for professionals who are self-employed," answered the CPA.

"Such as real estate agents and interior designers, to name a few?"

"Yes. My firm has prepared tax returns for several interior decorators, including Ms. Baxter."

"Mr. Aaronson, please take a few moments to carefully look at these copies of Ms. Baxter's tax returns and tell me if you prepared them," Mo asks her witness.

After studying the tax returns for only a few moments, the witness shakes his head sideways and emphatically declares,

"Mrs. Green, I did not prepare these tax returns."

"How can you be so certain?" inquires Mo.

"Earlier today, I reviewed my office file copies so that I would be prepared to testify in court. However, my office file copies look nothing like these copies," replied the witness.

Mo turns and walks back to her exhibits and holds up copies of the accountant's office file copies, which had also been entered into evidence. Mo now has the petitioner's tax returns that were filed with the IRS and a copy of each return that had been prepared by her accountant. The CPA is correct when he said that the returns are different.

"Did Ms. Baxter provide you with copies of these canceled checks that purportedly show her paying twenty five hundred dollars each year to Temple Beth Shalom?" Mo asks as she showed the witness copies of the canceled checks.

"No. I was given a schedule that showed the payment in each year as twenty five dollars."

Mo inquires as to the other charitable contributions and each time, she is told that the accountant determined that the donation was for the lessor amount. Mo then moves on to the unreimbursed business expenses and home office deductions.

"There were no unreimbursed employee expenses that I was aware of and there should not have been home-office deductions because to my knowledge, Ms. Baxter did not maintain an office in the home," answered the CPA.

"When did you first learn that Ms. Baxter did not file the tax returns that you had prepared for her?"

"The first time I had learned of this was when Agent Lipschitz met with me and was given copies of my office file copies. Agent Lipschitz provided me with copies of the tax returns on file with the IRS. I could readily see that these were not the tax returns that I had prepared. As a CPA, I certainly know better than to allow a client to deduct dog food and toilet paper as business expenses."

When Mo completed her questioning of Donald Aaronson, Beverly Baxter decided it was time for her to play lawyer.

"Mr. Aaronson, other than myself, have you ever had a client's tax returns questioned by the IRS?"

"Objection," Mo said. "Your Honor, Mr. Aaronson's other clients are not the subject of this proceeding. Furthermore, I think Respondent has already established that Mr. Aaronson did not prepare the tax returns that are the subject of this inquiry. Those returns were prepared either by the petitioner or by a third party at her request. Therefore, the question is irrelevant."

Before Judge Barton could figure out a way to allow the question, the witness said, "Judge, I don't mind answering the question because the answer is an emphatic, NO."

That left Beverly with nothing else to say other than, "Oh. I guess I don't have anything else to ask him."

When it was time for closing statements, Beverly stood and slowly stepped up to her podium. Now pretending to remove a piece of lint from the sleeve of her jacket, Beverly looked about the courtroom and appeared to gather what little thoughts she had. Having said nothing, she is prompted by the trial judge to say a few words on her behalf.

"Judge, I don't know what to say. You see, the problem is, my accountant lied. It was his fault. I gave him all of my records and expected him to prepare my tax returns correctly. He obviously didn't. And when the IRS questioned those tax returns, he then prepared new tax returns based on what the IRS thought the returns should look like," Beverly said. Beverly seems to be making this up on the spot because nothing she is saying makes any sense.

The petitioner, in a desperate move on her part, has thrown her accountant under a speeding train. "I suppose this sounds ridiculous, but how could I have made up these tax returns when I don't know anything about taxes and accounting? And why would I pay someone to prepare my tax returns if I weren't going to file those tax returns with the IRS? It simply doesn't make any sense," argued Beverly.

"I personally don't have any problems paying taxes on my earnings. So, if the deductions that Mrs. Green has a problem with are not allowable, that's okay by me. I'll pay the additional taxes due. But, I've got a real problem with the civil fraud penalty. My accountant should be held personally liable for that penalty," said Beverly.

Beverly has now tacitly consented that the IRS has correctly determined her tax liability. She has also suggested that the fraud penalty is applicable but should be asserted against her CPA. Beverly is now venturing into uncharted water by claiming fraud should be imputed against a witness who did not prepare fraudulent tax returns.

When it was Mo Green's turn, she wasted no time. "Judge Barton, I think the evidence and witness testimony speaks for itself. However, I would like to cite just a few examples in closing."

What Mo was about to say was not for the benefit of Judge Barton. Instead, Mo directed her comments for the benefit of the chief judge as well as the senior aide to Senator Stevens. Mo wanted to let them know how egregious this case was and that it should not be a difficult decision for the trial judge.

"The petitioner has attempted to deduct every type of expense that she may and may not have actually incurred. A CPA would know better than to claim dog food as a business expense, or for that matter, the costs of every type of personal expenditure imaginable. The list of deductions claimed is virtually endless," asserted Mo.

"But, it doesn't end with fictitious business deductions. Let's not forget about her so-called charitable contributions. I think it's worth mentioning that the petitioner made trips to her bank to deposit funds in a checking account so she could write checks that would not bounce. Once she knew that the checks had cleared, she engaged in a systematic pattern to be reimbursed for most of the donations," argued Mo. "Why? I think it's fairly obvious. The petitioner wanted to claim a fictitious donation and what better way to claim such deductions than to produce canceled checks as documentary evidence."

Glancing to the front row where her boss is sitting, Mo gets a nod of approval. "If this isn't a classic case of fraudulent conduct, I don't know what is! In essence, we have all of the critical elements of fraud. There has been a lack of cooperation on the part of the petitioner throughout the entire process. Documents have been altered and falsified by the petitioner. Duplicate, and at times, even triplicate deductions were claimed. The petitioner has engaged in a concerted effort to deceive the investigating agent as well as other IRS officials, including myself," Mo added.

"What I am now hearing is the icing on top of the cake. The petitioner is blaming her CPA for this mess! Let me see if I got this right. Mr. Aaronson, who has testified under oath that he has never prepared a tax return for another client that has been called into question by the IRS, took it upon himself to prepare fraudulent tax returns which he filed without the petitioner's consent. Only later did he prepare other tax returns that the IRS would find acceptable. However, for some inexplicable reason, he did not file these tax returns with the IRS. Is this what the petitioner is asking the court to believe?" asked Mo.

"I, for one, find this absolutely outrageous. I don't think this requires that I say anything else on the subject, other than to assert that Respondent has met its burden in establishing fraud on the part of the petitioner," concluded Mo as she took her seat.

Until this case, Judge Barton had issued rulings from the bench. The issuance of bench decisions is totally within the provenance of the court. Instead of rendering a ruling in this case, Judge Barton announces that he will take this matter under advisement and issue a ruling within ninety days.

While lawyers do not have the right to request a bench decision, Mo Green decides to raise the subject and bait the judge. "Excuse me, Your Honor. In the previous dozen or so cases that you heard, you rendered a bench decision in each case." Mo was about to add, "And each time you ruled against the Respondent," but chose not to say this. "I am puzzled that you are not issuing a bench decision in this trial given the facts in this case," Mo says.

In actuality, Mo knew that the judge would not issue a bench decision because he could not get away with ruling in favor of the petitioner. Therefore, if Judge Barton is going to find for Beverly Baxter, he must justify his decision in writing. This will be impossible to do.

For several moments Mo Green is standing at her podium while she waits for a reply. However, no reply is forthcoming. What the trial attorney is getting in return is a stern glare from an embarrassed trial judge who has been upstaged. With the chief judge having observed this trial, there is no way that Judge Barton can rule in favor of the petitioner. Instead, Judge Barton merely bangs his gavel, announces the trial is over, and storms out of the courtroom with a beet red face.

Chapter 7

By this time next week, Carmine Delgado will officially be a man of leisure. Actually, for the past forty three years, Carmine Delgado has been a man of leisure since he hasn't done an honest day's work as a life-long member of Club Fed. At this stage in his undistinguished career, Carmine is not about to do anything dramatic such as actually working a case.

Today, Carmine will be handling his last case as an IRS agent. In truth, Carmine will do what he normally does and that is, go through the motions and hope that he can get an answer from one of his fellow agents. If not, Carmine will dump the case on another agent as he cleans out his office cubicle for the last time.

Carmine was asked to give his supervisor at least one year's notice before he intended to submit his retirement papers. The reason why management wanted advance notice of one year was because Carmine would need at least ten months to clean out his file cabinets and office cubicle. Thus, management would have to scale back the new case assignments so that Carmine would be able to get his office cubicle cleaned up for the next agent.

Allowing Carmine ten months to get his office cubicle organized was wishful thinking. With all of the junk that Carmine had accumulated over the past forty three years, there was no way that he could accomplish this miracle in only ten months.

Carmine held fast to the rule that nothing in print should be discarded. Accordingly, Carmine kept every piece of worthless paper that was given to him throughout his tenure with Club Fed. This consisted of thousands of internal memorandums that eventually became obsolete because they were so old. It also included memorandums of IRS rules and procedures that were later superseded by other rules and procedures which were later revoked, rescinded or clarified by more recent publications.

No one could figure out why Carmine kept anything because he never read anything that he was given. Instead, Carmine just tossed whatever it was on a chair or the floor and pretended to get to it someday. At one point, Carmine's stack of papers had exceeded the allowable height before it became a fire hazard. When the Fire Marshall did his annual inspection of the Federal Building, he personally instructed Carmine to do something about the problem.

When Carmine asked the Fire Marshall what the problem was, he was told that his stack of papers represented a fire hazard. "You can't be serious," said Carmine to the Fire Marshall, who retorted, "Do I look like I'm joking?"

"What do you want me to do with it?" asked Carmine.

"I'm not your boss. But as the Fire Marshall, I can cite you for a possible fire hazard. Do you want me to issue a citation?"

"Um, I guess not."

"Then do something about this stack of papers immediately. If I see this stack when I return in twenty minutes, you'll be issued a citation," the Fire Marshall ordered.

It wasn't just papers that Carmine kept throughout his IRS career. Carmine kept inanimate objects on his desk, on top of his file cabinets, and on top of his many stacks of paper. These items, while considered to be junk to everyone else, must have had sentimental value to Carmine because he couldn't bring himself to discard anything. The saying, "One man's trash is another man's treasure," applies to Carmine.

There are three cardinal sins that IRS agents must not commit. The first cardinal sin is losing one's IRS credentials. The second sin involves the failure to protect a live statute from expiration. The third sin relates to losing a tax return. The penalty for committing any of these sins could result in severe disciplinary action, including dismissal from government service.

With all the trash that Carmine accumulated in his office, it was a miracle he hadn't lost tax returns on a frequent basis. However, one day he did misplace ten files that contained tax returns. Frantic with a sense of anxiety that he had never experienced before, Carmine was fearful that he had committed an unpardonable sin.

Carmine looked through all of his file cabinets without success. He then asked every agent on the floor to check their respective cubicles and file cabinets. Again, the missing files could not be found.

Normally Carmine has a deep, dark tan. Once he came to the realization that he had lost ten files that contained income tax returns, Carmine's skin color turned white. It also appeared that Carmine had aged considerably in the few days that he had misplaced the files.

At the time the files went missing, Carmine's boss was on vacation. Carmine knew that when his boss returned to the office, he would learn of Carmine's dilemma. Fearing dismissal, Carmine decided to submit his retirement papers, believing that once he formally submitted his papers, the IRS would not fire him.

In a rather ironic twist, immediately after Carmine had submitted his retirement papers, a paralegal in District Counsel brought the missing files to him. "Hey Carmine, I found these files that belong to you. You left them on my credenza when you were in my office last week. How could you have walked out of my office without remembering that you walked into my office carrying so many files?" asked the paralegal.

While Carmine could have withdrawn the filing of his retirement papers, he decided that at his age, it was time to leave Club Fed. Misplacing files was an indication that he should leave voluntarily. Whereas Carmine could leave his job as soon as he wanted, he figured to stay on for another year so that he could spend the next twelve months cleaning out his cubicle.

With one year to go until retirement, Carmine was instructed by his boss to begin the process of filling up burn bags. Oversized burn bags were given to Carmine for incineration. Carmine was told to take all of the papers to one of the industrial size shredders and to place the shredded documents in the burn bags.

"But I can't," Carmine was overheard saying.

"Why can't you?"

"It would be like cutting off my arms. These papers are part of me," replied Carmine.

"Carmine, have you ever read any of the papers that you've kept for the past forty odd years?" asked his boss.

"I've been meaning to read them. It's just that I haven't had a chance," Carmine would say.

"If you haven't had a chance to read anything for the past forty some years, I think it's highly unlikely you're going to read it now. Furthermore, I suspect that everything you've kept is already outdated. Either shred it or take it home with you. But, I want it out of this cubicle. Understand?" retorted Carmine's boss.

Carmine spent the next several months deciding which

materials to shred, which materials to take home, and which materials to give away. However, none of his fellow agents would agree to accept any of the outdated materials Carmine had offered them.

"What about some of my personal souvenirs? Do any of you guys want some of these items?" Carmine so generously offered his fellow agents. In response, the typical answer was "No, we don't want that junk cluttering up our desks."

Unfortunately, the lawyer sitting across the table from Carmine is not about to let Carmine get away with doing nothing on this particular case. Cindy Klein intends to present a compelling argument on behalf of her client and to do so, she must do the near impossible. Cindy must get Carmine to listen to what she is saying.

"Carmine, the Service Center has disallowed my client's refund claim because the statute of limitations has expired. We do not dispute that the period of limitations expired for purposes of filing a refund claim. However, we believe that the IRS should invoke its administrative authority to permit the refund claim under the doctrine of equitable recoupment," the attractive lawyer said.

"I think you lost me," replied Carmine.

"Where did I lose you?"

"When you said something about a doctrine."

"OK, I'll start at the beginning. My client was an investor in various securities with a brokerage firm that is no longer in existence because its managing partner was subsequently found guilty of securities fraud. The various securities in my client's investment portfolio were supposed to have paid dividends to my client on a periodic basis," Cindy said.

"It was not until the SEC conducted an investigation that securities fraud was discovered. By then, most of the investor funds had been misappropriated and spent on a luxury yacht, a waterfront mansion, a membership in an exclusive country club, expensive jewelry and exotic cars. The investors got back very little of their capital investment.

"The investment goes back almost ten years. In each year, my client was issued a false Form 1099 statement which identified the total dividends subject to income tax. My client reported the amounts as shown on each falsified Form 1099 statement in the applicable year," stated Cindy.

Removing a document from her file and handing it to Carmine, she adds, "This is a schedule which identifies my client's capital investment as well as the dividends which he reported in his taxable income. I have duplicate copies of the Form 1099 statements that corroborate these amounts. I would assume that you can access the same information on IRS computers.

"Please look carefully at the amounts that were credited to my client's account balance," the lawyer said as she pointed to the column on the document that she gave to Carmine.

"Why do you say credited?" asked Carmine.

"That's because the dividends were never actually paid. The individual who was the managing partner of the brokerage firm embezzled all of the funds invested in these securities. Thus, there were never any securities that were held for investment. Therefore, dividends were never paid. There was nothing in the investment account. Now do you see where I'm going with this?" asked Cindy.

"I'm not sure," replied Carmine who was totally clueless.

"My client reported the dividends in his taxable income in each year, as required by law. However, he paid tax on phantom income. We are talking about income that didn't exist because the funds that he had intended to invest with the brokerage firm were misappropriated," explained the now exasperated lawyer.

"OK. So we're talking about a theft loss," replied Carmine.

"No. The misappropriation of funds is not an issue in this case."

"Then what's the problem?" Carmine asks. It is readily apparent that Carmine neglected to read Cindy's letter which was attached to her client's refund claim.

Closing her eyes and silently counting to ten, Cindy says, "The problem is that my client paid tax on income that didn't exist. My client can't recover this because the statute of limitations has expired for filing a claim for refund. I had explained all of this in my letter which I attached to the refund claim. Did you not read it before now?"

Ignoring the question and anxious to get this over with so he can take an early lunch, Carmine says, "Why don't you have your client take a deduction in an open year for the income that he didn't receive?"

"On what grounds would my client be permitted by statute to do that?" inquired the lawyer.

"It's phantom income," Carmine accurately replied, but stopped short of answering the question.

"If you're suggesting that the mitigation provisions apply, you'd better re-think that."

"Why wouldn't the mitigation provisions apply?" Carmine asked without a clue as to what the mitigation provisions involve.

"There is no duplication of income, which is required under the mitigation provisions," stated Cindy.

"OK. So what do you want me to do? You said something about a doctrine ……" Carmine inquires of the lawyer.

The doctrine of equitable recoupment is a judicial doctrine that provides equitable relief to a taxpayer where the statute of limitations for purposes of filing a refund claim has otherwise expired. Under this doctrine, which is intended to serve as a remedy to address a barred statute, a taxpayer can circumvent the restrictions on a time-barred tax year under certain circumstances.

The statute of limitations bars the government and the taxpayer from asserting a claim against the other once the period of limitations has expired for a specific tax year. The policy behind such a restriction is not only fairness to the taxpayer but administrative efficiency that is beneficial to the IRS. From the perspective of the IRS, the period of limitations affords the government an opportunity to make a final determination of revenue for a specific period of time. From a taxpayer's perspective, the limitation period eliminates the requirement to maintain records indefinitely.

In order to achieve an equitable result where a taxpayer is time-barred from filing a refund claim, this doctrine can be invoked. In this case, it is the taxpayer who is attempting to convince the IRS that he should be allowed to exclude in all barred tax years, the income which he paid tax on erroneously.

"Carmine, the doctrine of equitable recoupment would provide a remedy to my client otherwise not available to him. Under this doctrine, he should be allowed to recover the taxes that he erroneously paid on phantom income. If you look at the critical elements under this doctrine, you'll see that my client satisfies each requirement," said the lawyer.

Glancing at his watch, Carmine starts to fidget in his seat. This is immediately noticed by Cindy and she asks him if he is feeling okay.

"Yeah. I just have so many last minute details to take care of before I retire," Carmine replies. However, the only thing on Carmine's mind is going to lunch and then concocting an excuse to transfer this case to another agent. Having listened to what the lawyer had to say about barred statutes and equitable remedies, Carmine has no interest in dealing with this type of an issue especially when he is about to retire.

"You're retiring at the end of the week? Good for you. I think you should be able to easily wrap this case up before you leave," Cindy said.

"I'd like to, I really would," Carmine lied.

Sensing that Carmine was full of horseshit, the lawyer said, "I don't think it would be fair to my client to have this case reassigned to another agent because you couldn't make a decision before you leave. My client is entitled to a prompt answer so that he can pursue the options available to him in case his refund claim is not allowed. I am prepared to elevate this matter to the attention of senior IRS officials, if necessary."

Carmine has now been boxed into a corner. This is his last case. He has no other work to do other than finish shredding worthless documents. He cannot talk his way out of working this one last case.

"OK. As soon as I get back from lunch, I will tackle your case. How's that?" suggested Carmine.

"You're leaving for lunch now?"

"Yeah. Why do you ask?"

"It's not even eleven o'clock in the morning and you're going to lunch?" an incredulous Cindy asked in disbelief that a federal employee would leave a meeting to go have lunch in the late morning hour.

"I like to avoid the lunch crowd," replied Carmine.

Upon hearing that, the lawyer decided to stop in the office of Carmine's boss as the soon-to-be retired agent made a hasty exit from the conference room in order to beat the lunch crowd.

Chapter 8

It is a chilly, overcast day in Baltimore. In other words, it is a typical day in Charm City. Tyrelle Jenkins has been pulled over for driving sixty five miles an hour in an inner city residential neighborhood that has a twenty mile an hour speed restriction. The reason why Tyrelle was speeding was because he was late to a drug deal.

While only eighteen years old, Tyrelle is a businessman who likes to be prompt for his clients. Tyrelle believes in providing his clientele with the best customer service possible. In this regard, he does not like to keep his customers waiting.

The two Baltimore City police officers who have stopped Tyrelle for speeding are conducting a search of his luxury BMW road sedan after detecting the scent of marijuana and observing a suspicious package of what appeared to be cocaine that tumbled out of the glove compartment when Tyrelle opened it to retrieve his suspended driver's license he had forgotten was no longer valid.

"OK. Here's what we have, Mr. Jenkins. We clocked you doing sixty five on a twenty mile per hour residential street. It appears that you've been smoking an illegal substance while driving with a suspended driver's license. We also have what appears to be another illegal substance in your possession. We're going to conduct a search of your vehicle. Kindly step out of the car," one of the police officers instructs the young man who will soon be taken into custody.

Although Tyrelle is still a teenager, he is a veteran of the criminal justice system. Upon being told that his car will be searched, Tyrelle objects on the grounds that the cops are precluded from doing so without a warrant.

"Relax Perry Mason, we've got probable cause. Now step out of your car so we can get started," said the other cop.

As Tyrelle gets out of the car that will soon be impounded, he is frisked and placed in handcuffs. He is then escorted to the rear of the police car where he will be a guest of Charm City's Finest.

A search of Tyrelle's luxury car has turned up other goodies, including several unregistered hand guns, a set of brass knuckles and a variety of martial arts weapons which are illegal in most states. In addition, the cops have discovered several boxes that contain approximately two thousand debit cards. A random sampling of the debit cards shows that each card is in the name of a different person. When the cops returned to their patrol car, they informed the guest in the back seat of their car that he is under arrest for having illegal weapons and that other charges may be pending, such as dealing in illegal narcotics.

"C'mon man, what are you talking about? I don't know nothin' 'bout them guns, the brass knuckles and throwing stars. They ain't mine! And the drugs don't belong to me," Tyrelle said emphatically in an impassioned speech where he proclaimed his complete innocence.

"Who said anything about guns, brass knuckles and throwing stars?" one of the cops said.

"You said what it was, remember?"

"No. We just said the weapons were illegal. Tyrelle, you have the right to remain silent. Anything you say ...."

When the cops were finished reading Tyrelle his Miranda rights, they wrote up their report, made a call to their precinct and told their supervisor about what they found in the car.

"Debit cards, huh?" the precinct sergeant said.

"That's right, sarg. Debit cards."

****

"Detective, you should see this," one of the crime scene investigators yelled out to Homicide Detective Bobby Reed, who was the lead detective at the crime scene. Earlier that evening, a well-known drug dealer had been shot twice in the head from close range. It was an execution style murder and it was personal.

"What is it?" Detective Reed said as he walked over to the closet on the far side of the room where the investigator was examining contents in a cardboard box. "Don't tell me you found more drugs?" the detective asked.

"No. It's debit cards."

"Debit cards?"

"That's right. And every single card is in a different name," replied the investigator.

Detective Reed nodded while considering the connection between a drug dealer and an identity theft ring. "What's in the spiral notebooks?" inquired the detective, as he pointed to a stack of approximately a dozen spiral notebooks near the cardboard box.

"Names, social security numbers and birth dates. We also have copies of Death Certificates for people who recently passed away. Someone has been using this information for identity theft purposes. I think we just stumbled on an ID theft ring," said the crime scene tech to the lead detective, who had already figured this out.

"Yeah. But it looks like whoever aced the vic didn't know about the ID thefts," answered the detective.

"Or else they would have taken the spiral notebooks along with the debit cards," the CSI finished the thought.

"That's right."

When Detective Reed finished his examination of the crime scene, he returned to his precinct where he met with the Chief of Detectives, who has been on the job for less than two weeks.

Peter Zitoli, who had been Chief of Detectives, for the past fifteen years, retired several months ago at the behest of the Police Commissioner. This was done at the request of a city councilman whose niece wanted to be the Chief of Detectives. The niece thought that being the Chief of Detectives would enhance her political aspirations when she ran for mayor.

Peter Zitoli had been eligible for retirement and thought that it might be a good idea to retire at this time if the police department was that anxious to replace him with someone who had political connections and no law enforcement experience. Aware that it was only a matter of time before the job got worse, Peter opted to retire. However, before Peter made this commitment, he first needed to clear it with a higher authority. That would be his wife, Millie.

After discussing this with his wife, Peter decided that they should spend their time sailing along the east coast. Unfortunately, the sailboat had difficulty staying afloat and was put out to sea. Dejected over the prospect of not being able to take to the high seas in his beloved sailboat, Captain Pete and his wife sold their home and moved to Ocean City where they have a small condo near the beach.

To keep busy during the day, Captain Pete has taken a part-time job as a senior consultant in the security industry. What this actually involves is sitting in the lobby of a bank which is located several blocks from where Peter lives. The bank is a small branch office and does not do much banking business. Consequently, Peter will spend most of his time reading romance novels while he drinks coffee and eats donuts.

Laverne Kressley is the new Chief of Detectives. Ms. Kressley was selected for this position because her uncle is a member of the Baltimore City Council. In a private meeting with the mayor, it was strongly suggested that the next supervisory position to be filled in the Baltimore City Police Department should go to a female. Grateful at having been told what to do, the mayor passed this valuable information along to the police commissioner.

When word got out that the police commissioner wanted a Hispanic female who had a physical disability to take the job, the city councilman felt it was time to intercede. "We don't want to select a disabled minority. I have someone else in mind for the position," said the councilman to the mayor.

"Who do you have in mind?" asked the mayor.

"My niece."

"Does she have a background in law enforcement?" asked the mayor.

"Not exactly," replied the councilman.

"Then what are her qualifications for the job?"

"She took a criminal justice course in college."

"I see," said the mayor, who was not exactly overwhelmed by this revelation. "But that hardly makes her qualified to supervise several precincts of veteran detectives who have earned their stripes by solving difficult crimes through hard work and determination."

"Laverne watches all those cop shows on TV," the councilman adds as if this would impress the mayor. "Laverne's a big fan of Law & Order. It's her favorite television show."

"So does my thirteen year-old son, but I wouldn't want him directing the police on how to solve crimes."

"She solves the crimes before each conclusion of NCIS. Can you do that?"

"You're talking about a television program. Get real!" exclaimed the mayor.

"Look, she's my niece and this is what she wants. There will come a day when you'll want something from the City Council. I'll remember this favor and be there for you in your hour of need," promised the councilman.

"OK. I'll talk to the police commissioner and let him know that we don't need a disabled minority hire. We have a young, vibrant, highly intelligent person who is anxious to dedicate her life to law enforcement and has a great deal to offer the department," said the mayor. After having said this, the mayor instantly regretted having acquiesced to political pressure.

Bobby Reed didn't care who held the position of Chief of Detectives as long as that person was competent and didn't get in his way. Laverne is playing to mixed reviews. While she is clearly incompetent, she has made it a point not to get in Bobby's way.

"I suspect that our shooter executed our vic over a drug deal that went south. I've got a CI who might be able to give me the perp," Detective Reed told his new boss.

"What's a CI?" asked Laverne with a straight face and no hint of embarrassment. Upon hearing this, Bobby blinked in disbelief, but managed to reply without laughing.

"A CI is a confidential informant," answered the homicide detective to his boss, who nodded her head as if deep in thought.

Laverne is of no help to her detectives. The detectives know this and must investigate without any guidance from their boss. Detective Reed understands that it is up to him to solve this case.

"I'll need you to approve the disbursement of more funds for my CI. I'm also going to need you to coordinate with officials at the IRS," Bobby said.

"How does the IRS figure into a homicide investigation?" asked Laverne.

"We discovered debit cards and other evidence of identity theft at the crime scene. The debit cards indicate that tax refunds have been issued by the IRS as well as the State of Maryland with regard to phony tax returns. So far, we've found more than two million dollars on just the debit cards that were stacked in the box in the closet."

"Exactly what is it that you want me to do?" asked Laverne.

How about staying out of my way, you knucklehead, Bobby thought to himself. "I tell you what," Bobby said to avoid having Laverne involved. "I know some people at the IRS from prior cases. I'll contact them directly."

"That's a good idea," Laverne said as she tried to act like she was busy.

Chapter 9

"I'm confused. Go over that one more time."

"What part did you not understand, El Jefe?"

"Louie, just start at the beginning, okay?" Tom Collins tells his most annoying agent.

"According to the rules governing professional male tennis players, there are different standards by which appearance fees can be paid to tour players by tournament promoters. With respect to the four most prestigious tournaments which are the Australian, French, Wimbledon and US Open Championships, players are barred from collecting appearance fees. However, male players may charge appearance fees at lower tier tournaments," Louie explained.

"Are appearance fees paid under the table by the tournament promoters?" asked Tom.

"Sometimes. It's a cost of ensuring that top players commit to play so that the tournament sells out. Some sponsors will pay top dollar for advertising if the top players agree to play in the tournament."

"OK. So what's the story with Cahill?" Tom asked, as he settled back in his executive leather chair to listen to what the little guy had to tell him.

"Richard Cahill is currently the top ranked American male tennis player and holds the number four ranking in the world, although his grip on this spot seems to be slipping based on his most recent performances. Cahill has been a touring pro for the past seven years, but earns more from endorsements than he does playing tennis. The majority of his commercial endorsements involve aftershave, deodorant and underwear products. In essence, Richard Cahill's career as a spokesman for personal grooming is immensely profitable," Louie explains to his boss, who appears to have lost interest in what his agent is telling him.

While Richard Cahill is a world class tennis player, people are more inclined to watch him play in tournaments because of his celebrity status and good looks. Tournament promoters have long recognized that tennis fans will flock to tournaments in which a top player has made the commitment to play. Consequently, Richard Cahill is considered to be one of the most popular tennis players in the world, even if he is not the best player on the men's tour.

"Cahill arranged to be paid a one hundred thousand dollar appearance fee to play in a tournament in Berlin. According to tournament officials, Cahill intentionally lost his first round match so he could play in another tournament that started the same week in Madrid. Cahill then collected a second appearance fee of one hundred thousand dollars to play the tournament in Madrid," Louie added.

"Jesus! I should have taken up tennis when I was a kid instead of playing baseball. Who knows where I'd be today," Tom said.

"You'd still be here, so stop dreaming," Louie quickly says. "However, Cahill didn't play the tournament in Madrid. He faked an injury and left Madrid before his match. He then flew to Monte Carlo where he played an exhibition match for which he was paid one hundred thousand dollars."

"OK. I got it. Cahill just made three hundred thousand dollars to entertain some rich people by playing a sport that we sometimes do on week-ends, but not very well," Tom remarked.

"The two tournament promoters who paid Cahill his

appearance fees asked Cahill and his representatives to return the money to them because Cahill did not compete in good faith. Cahill refused to give the money back."

"This sounds like a dispute between a tennis player and tournament officials. What does this have to do with the IRS?" the Chief of the Examination Division wanted to know. "And where are you coming up with all this information?"

"I'm getting to it," replied Louie, "and how I get my information is confidential."

"Well get to it soon because I have things to do," Tom said.

"You can talk to your girlfriend after I'm done," Louie shot back.

"Lipschitz, how many times do I have to tell you I don't have a girlfriend?"

"Sorry. I'll re-phrase the question. Does your wife know about your mistress?"

"Just get on with your story," Tom said in exasperation, apparently having given up convincing Louie that he has always been faithful to his wife.

"Where was I? Oh yeah, the money. Cahill kept the two hundred thousand dollars that he was asked to return and the tournament promoters filed official complaints with the Association of Tennis Professionals. The ATP made this public and numerous major newspapers and magazines publicized the story. Cahill's tax returns for the past three years were flagged by the Service Center and sent to us for audit," Louie explained.

"I know," Tom reiterated to his agent. "I'm the one who assigned the returns specifically to you."

"Did you know that Cahill neglected to report the three

hundred thousand dollars in appearance fees?" Louie asked.

"You're sure?" Tom inquired, before realizing that it wasn't necessary to ask Louie if he was sure.

"Not only am I sure, but I suspect that Cahill may have also failed to report other appearance fees in the same year as well as the other two years," Louie answered.

"Does Cahill have anyone handling his representation?"

"Chatsworth Symington, III."

"Are you serious?"

"Yep. With a name like that, he'd better be good," Louie replied.

"I'm sure he is," said the Chief of Exam.

"Let's hope so. I'm running out of challenges," Louie said as he stood to leave. As Louie got to the door, he turned back to Tom and said, "Don't forget to call your mistress."

****

According to the IRS, identity theft is considered the most serious and prevalent tax scam currently practiced by criminals. Nationwide, criminals are filing fraudulent tax returns of people both living and dead, based on stolen personal information using laptops and free Wi-Fi connections. Once the criminal has someone's personal information, phony W-2 statements are prepared, which show excess withholding taxes.

With little income reported on the W-2, a fictitious income tax return is then prepared and filed electronically. A refund is sought based on the excess withholding taxes. The criminals have discovered the flaw in the IRS's internal policy of issuing a tax refund without bothering to cross-reference the W-2 earnings and pre-payment credits.

For years, the IRS has encouraged taxpayers to file their income tax returns electronically. The motivation for filing electronically is that tax refunds can be issued almost immediately. Congress has encouraged this because the majority of taxpayers who file early do so primarily because they cannot afford to wait several months to recover their excess pre-payment credits.

The problem with this process is that by the time the IRS has verified the W-2 amounts with the pre-payment credits, the refunds have already been received by the criminals, who typically use debit cards for this purpose. Once the refund is processed through use of the debit card, the criminal has unrestricted access to the money. Recovering the refunds is a challenge because the criminals have moved on and are usually able to stay one step ahead of the IRS's collection efforts.

This practice of stealing tax refunds has become so popular that it has essentially replaced drug dealing as a crime of profit.

****

Mark Paul Warren, Esq. has been asked to appear in the Office of the Director of Professional Responsibility to discuss allegations that he is not qualified to represent taxpayers. If it is determined that his conduct does not meet the standards expected of tax practitioners, he will be subject to disciplinary action based on the severity of the misconduct.

Mark Paul Warren prefers to use his entire name when introducing himself to people. This can be ingratiating to those who have to listen to him pontificate on subjects he knows nothing about. It will not take long for the lawyer to annoy the gentlemen who will be conducting this hearing.

The lawyer is sitting across from Jack Ellison and Mike Woods.

"Mr. Warren, I see you have a law degree. How long have you practiced?"

"Let's see," he says, hesitating for far too long. Twirling his hands in the air as if that will help him think, the lawyer is about to say about twenty five years when Jack finally interrupts him by saying, "That's okay, we don't really care."

"If you don't care, why did you ask?"

"It's up to us to ask the questions. It's your responsibility to answer the questions," replies Jack. "Besides, we're not going to wait a couple of minutes for you to figure out how long you've been practicing law. We'll move on to other matters."

"According to the appeals officer who conducted a settlement conference with you, there were issues with the quality of your representation. We need to go over that," said Mike.

"You misstated the facts in the Doris Stone case. As a matter of fact, you materially misstated the facts. Prior to your involvement in the case, Mrs. Stone provided the IRS agent with a detailed Affidavit as to what had happened with respect to the funds that had been misappropriated from one of her investment accounts by her former financial advisor. Mrs. Stone attached her financial statements, including her bank account statements to her Affidavit," Mike stated.

"However, when you took over her representation, you stated facts that were diametrically different than what your client orally testified to and provided in writing to the IRS agent. Later, the appeals officer informed you of the inconsistencies in your Protest Letter and asked you to review your factual assertions. You failed to respond to this request," Jack said. "We'd like an explanation."

"I suspect that my client may have misstated the facts to me."

"Your client denies that. Mrs. Stone faxed you a copy of a transcript from a hearing in District Court. The transcript contains the information that she relied upon when she submitted an Affidavit to the IRS agent. She has provided the IRS with a written confirmation that you received her fax transmittal," Jack said.

"And you got the facts wrong," added Mike. "Now how is that possible?"

"I don't know."

"Did you bother to read what your client sent you?" asked Jack.

"I'm sure I read it."

"If you read it, how could you not understand what you read?" asked Mike.

"I don't know."

"Here's our problem. Actually, to be more precise, it's your problem. If you read the document and got the facts wrong, it indicates that you're incompetent. If you didn't read the document and made up your own facts to paint a different picture of your client's case, then that's an indication that your conduct does not meet the standards expected of lawyers," stated Jack.

"Do you understand what we're getting at?" asked Mike.

Without answering the question, Mark Paul Warren slowly nodded his head.

"Let's move on to the Stanley Lustman case. You do remember Stanley Lustman?" Jack inquired.

"I'm not sure I recall that case," the lawyer lied. However, given the notoriety of the Stan Lustman case, anyone involved in this case would easily remember this as one of the more remarkable income tax cases ever prosecuted.

"You're having difficulty recalling the Stanley Lustman case? Are you serious?" said Mike.

"Seriously, I'm drawing a blank," lied the lawyer.

"Allow me to refresh your memory. Stan Lustman lived in a multi-million dollar luxury home, complete with a collection of exotic cars that he stored in a seven car garage. Lustman also had an extensive collection of expensive jewelry, artwork and antiques throughout the mansion that had an appraised value in excess of six million dollars according to the insurance company. In addition, Lustman maintained multi-million dollar residential estates in the Cayman Islands and the Mediterranean. Lustman lived well. In fact, Lustman managed to spend money like a drunken sailor in a topless bar," said Jack.

"Jack, you neglected to mention the private Lear jet that Lustman frequently chartered when he made trips to his other residences," said Mike.

"Mike, I was about to get to that. But, I didn't want to leave out the part about Lustman being able to afford this kind of lifestyle while reporting negligible earnings on his federal income tax returns each year," said Jack.

Stan Lustman began his career as a master criminal at

a relatively young age. In high school, Stan sold drugs to his classmates. In view of the fact that this turned out to be a lucrative business venture, young Stanley quickly expanded his drug operation. With the profits that he made, the young man purchased vending machines for use in commercial office buildings, hospitals, schools and government buildings. In addition, Stan started to buy dilapidated homes in low-income neighborhoods from the City of Baltimore at a cost of one dollar per home. After completing the necessary renovations to the properties and maintaining ownership for the requisite period of time, Stan sold the homes at substantial gains.

Bored with these types of business activities, Lustman decided to pursue other ventures that had the potential to be far more lucrative. While vacationing in Europe, Lustman met a master forger who needed someone to finance his operation. With Lustman agreeing to a fifty/fifty split of the proceeds, the forger handcrafted a variety of fake antiques which they sold at estate sales for millions of dollars. Soon, the two partners graduated from selling fake artifacts to printing phony currency.

The quality of the fake currency was so good that it initially did not raise any suspicions. Accordingly, the presses used to print the money ran almost non-stop. Then, one day this financially lucrative criminal enterprise came to an abrupt stop.

Stanley's partner got drunk one night, started a brawl in public and was arrested by police in a small countryside village outside France. When the forger attempted to bribe the police officers who arrested him, he did so using the fake currency. The counterfeit currency aroused suspicion and led to an international investigation by Interpol agents. Anxious to cut a deal with the investigators, the forger implicated Stan in the counterfeit operation.

When Interpol notified the FBI that Stan Lustman was a

major crime figure, the IRS thought it might be a good idea to examine his income tax returns. At the time the IRS decided to initiate a referral to the Criminal Investigation Division, Lustman had already been indicted by the Department of Justice for his role in operating an international counterfeit ring as well as engaging in other criminal enterprises such as trafficking in drugs and facilitating identity theft.

The day his indictment was announced, Lustman was traveling to the airport to flee the United States with a duffel bag that contained two hundred thousand dollars in cash. Federal agents arrested Lustman just as he was about to board his private jet.

The Justice Department eventually learned that Lustman had maintained foreign bank accounts in nominee entities. Lustman also had in his possession, multiple passports in different names. Also seized was a laptop computer that was programmed to transfer funds from Lustman's domestic bank accounts to his foreign bank accounts in nominee names.

"We have a copy of the Protest that you prepared on behalf of Lustman in order to challenge the Jeopardy Assessment. Let me see if I have this right. You argued that the IRS's filing of a Notice of Jeopardy Assessment was unreasonable because it had failed to show that Stan Lustman had understated his taxable earnings for a single tax year and that he was engaged in illegal activities. Did I get that right?" asked Mike.

"It was all circumstantial," replied the lawyer

"Your client was churning through money like he had a printing press in the basement of his mansion. However, during this time, he reported earning a paltry fifteen thousand dollars a year. And your explanation for this was ......?" asked Mike.

Placing his palms up in the air as if he is about to feign indifference, the lawyer says, "You'd have to ask his accountant about that."

"Why should we ask an accountant when it was you who prepared these tax returns?" Jack wanted to know.

"I prepare a lot of tax returns for clients. I don't recall having prepared Mr. Lustman's income tax returns," the lawyer said in an unconvincing denial.

"Don't you think Mr. Lustman's income tax returns would stand out? Somebody who reports fifteen thousand dollars a year and maintains a lifestyle that Donald Trump would envy! And you don't recall preparing these tax returns?"

As the lawyer is about to say something, Jack interrupts him by saying, "Mr. Lustman was fleeing the country with lots of cash, phony passports and a laptop that shows he had plans to transfer funds overseas. Your client had concealed assets from the IRS and had substantially understated his taxable income in prior years. Mr. Lustman was put on notice that he was the subject of a criminal tax investigation and caught wind of his indictment for carrying on a drug distribution enterprise."

"And you continued to assert that your client was innocent of the charges," said Mike. "That didn't play all that well in court did it?" asked Mike.

Without giving the lawyer a chance to respond, Jack interjected by saying, "We have a transcript of the Jeopardy Assessment hearing in District Court. The judge let you have it pretty good when you tried to deny irrefutable facts. We also have the District Court's ruling in the tax evasion case. That didn't turn out too well either for your client. Nor did the Tax Court's decision in favor of the IRS in the civil fraud case."

"C'mon guys, what's the point in all this? So I made a mistake in representing Stan Lustman. We all make mistakes," the lawyer attempted to downplay the significance of this high-profile case.

"Your mistake is that you did such an inept job in representing your client. It's not that you lost, it's how you went about your representation," said Jack.

"But it was just one or two isolated cases."

"That's not true. There are other instances of incompetence. Would you like to hear about the other examples that were brought to our attention?"

"You argued that Elizabeth Holtzman was entitled to a bad debt deduction for a piece of sculpture that she made for a client who was unable to pay for the sculpture. Do you recall that?" asked Mike.

"Yes," Mark Paul Warren answered with reservations as to how this will turn out for him.

"Please explain your grounds for this deduction," said Jack.

"My client was not compensated for her work."

"How is that a bad debt?"

"She should be entitled to a deduction for not having been paid for providing services to a customer."

"It's not a bad debt. In the first place, Ms. Holtzman never reported income in a prior tax year for the sculpture. Thus, we don't have a situation where income was previously reported and taxed. Accordingly, Ms. Holtzman has nothing to exclude from income in a later tax year. In the second place, Ms. Holtzman never sold the sculpture. According to the agent, when the customer informed your client that she could not afford to purchase the sculpture, Ms. Holtzman made arrangements to donate the piece to charity. A charitable contribution deduction was claimed in the same tax year in which you have argued that your client is entitled to a bad debt deduction," said Mike.

"Oh," the lawyer said with surprise.

"You used to be an IRS agent. Don't you know anything about basic tax accounting rules?" Mike asked.

"I guess I forgot about that stuff. C'mon guys, lawyers like me have to be current with so much stuff, I messed up on a few minor things."

"A competent lawyer would not mess up on stuff like that," Jack said. "You'll have to do better than that."

"And I will. I promise, I will. How do we make this go away?" asked the lawyer.

"It doesn't go away. You do," replied Mike.

"What do you mean?"

"Mr. Warren, we're going to recommend that you be suspended from further practice before the IRS. That's what it means," said Jack.

"You're going to suspend me over some silly factual disputes? Are you guys serious? That's not fair."

"Life isn't always fair. Hopefully, you'll learn from your mistakes and in twelve months, you'll be a better tax lawyer," Jack said.

"That's it?"

"That's it. Enjoy your year off."

Chapter 10

When Mary Beth Phillips graduated from college and entered the business world, she envisioned herself managing a trillion dollar hedge fund for thousands of institutional clients. Mary Beth liked to dream on a grand scale.

Unsuccessful at landing a job managing a trillion dollar hedge fund for thousands of institutional clients, Mary Beth finally accepted a job as a secretary/receptionist in a medical practice. While disappointed that she didn't strike it rich overnight, Mary Beth set her sights on marrying a wealthy doctor who could provide her with all the comforts that she felt she so richly deserved.

The first thing that Mary Beth did when she landed the job was prepare a list of the things that she would need as the spouse of a rich doctor. Included as essential items was a membership in an exclusive country club, a luxury car, an oversized mansion in an upscale neighborhood, as well as an assortment of overpriced designer clothes and jewelry.

Unfortunately, Mary Beth could not entice any of the doctors in the practice to leave their wives. Nor was Mary Beth able to hook up with other doctors beyond one or two dates. The relationships usually dissolved when Mary Beth inquired into her date's realizable net worth and prospective income earning potential.

Mary Beth is an attractive, twenty seven year-old woman who possesses a winning smile to go along with all the right curves. When she smiles, Mary Beth can light up a room. However, behind the smile is someone who will plot and connive her way to instant wealth and is prepared to wield a sharp instrument in case it requires insertion in someone's back.

For the past four years, Mary Beth has worked as an administrative assistant to Drs. Farrell, Deutch, Logan, Samuelson and Myerson. The doctors have one of the most popular ophthalmology practices in the State of Maryland, which keeps Mary Beth very busy.

As the person responsible for collecting co-payments from patients and submitting claims to the insurance companies, Mary Beth is intimately aware as to how much money the medical practice is generating. After four years on the job, Mary Beth has graduated from being responsible for accounts receivable to operating a criminal enterprise.

Each doctor has a separate bank account in his name. It is Mary Beth's responsibility to deposit the fees to each doctor's account. This is not a problem for Mary Beth, because she is quite adept at handling other people's money.

However, Mary Beth has also secretly opened a separate bank account for each doctor. In actuality, these accounts are strictly for Mary Beth's benefit and none of the doctors have been made aware of what Mary Beth has done.

Last year, Mary Beth convinced each doctor to institute a new office policy whereby patients will no longer be allowed to pay their bills by credit card. Thus, payment had to be in the form of cash or check.

Immediately after this change was made, Mary Beth added a new wrinkle to her job. All patients who were in the office to see their doctor were billed for a diagnostic test that was generally not covered by most insurance plans.

When patient files were given to Mary Beth, she reviewed the files to verify whether a refraction test, which is an eye exam that measures a person's prescription for eyeglasses or contact lenses, had been performed. If this test was not performed by the doctor, Mary Beth made an entry in the file so that the test was performed.

Refraction is a process an eye care professional uses to measure a person's refractive error. A refractive error is an optical defect that does not allow light to be brought into sharp focus in the retina, thereby resulting in blurred or distorted vision.

Most insurance carriers will not reimburse eye care professionals for refraction tests, unless it is related to an eye injury or surgery. Aware that any insurance claim submitted will not be honored, Mary Beth sends a bill to each patient requesting payment in the form of cash or check.

Mary Beth decided that if she limited the cost of this diagnostic test to no more than thirty five dollars to each patient, it would probably not be questioned. If a patient gave Mary Beth the requisite amount in cash, that amount would go directly into Mary Beth's pocketbook. If a patient paid the bill by check, Mary Beth would endorse the payment and deposit the funds in one of the secret bank accounts that she had created.

With five doctors seeing as many as thirty patients a day, Mary Beth cleared almost a quarter of a million dollars in the first year of her scheme. This wasn't bad for someone who was earning less than fifty thousand dollars a year whose major responsibility was handling the office's accounts receivable.

Mary Beth's scheme to defraud the medical office's clients has gone undetected for more than one year. For Mary Beth, this was almost as good as managing a hedge fund. Until the day Edna Kravitz showed up to see one of the doctors.

Edna Kravitz is eighty four years of age and in excellent health, both physically and mentally. Edna is a first-time patient of Dr. Myerson and has been referred by another ophthalmologist for purposes of a second opinion. The purpose of the consultation is to discuss a cosmetic procedure that does not require an eye test.

When Edna received a bill for a refraction test, she made a call to her own ophthalmologist to inquire as to whether he asked Dr. Myerson to perform this procedure. After Edna was told that Dr. Myerson did not perform such a test, Edna decided to investigate as to why a bill was sent to her by Dr. Myerson's office.

Before Dr. Myerson could inquire into the matter, Edna had already placed calls to Medicare and Blue Cross to determine if claims had been filed. When told that claims had been filed, Edna contacted the Maryland Medical Society as well as the Maryland Attorney General's Office to file a formal complaint.

Once investigators looked into the matter, they eventually discovered that Mary Beth had falsified the medical records of the five doctors, billed patients for medical tests that had not been performed, and misappropriated the funds that should have been deposited into the bank accounts of her employers. In addition, Mary Beth had filed false insurance claims, thereby defrauding Medicare and other insurance carriers.

Mary Beth was indicted and charged with insurance fraud and embezzlement. Sensing that she might have a legal problem, Mary Beth paid a visit to a renowned criminal defense attorney who happened to live two houses down the street from her.

"Wally, I'm in trouble. I've been falsely accused of committing insurance fraud and embezzlement. Can you help me?" Mary Beth said to her neighbor, while standing outside his front door.

"Of course. That's why God created criminal defense attorneys."

"Good. Can I come in to talk to you?"

This question presented a dilemma for the lawyer because he wasn't quite sure about how to start the clock for billing purposes. This home consultation would certainly not be free under any circumstances. Unsure as to whether the clock started when Mary Beth rang the doorbell or at the time she takes a seat in his cluttered living room to explain her problem, Wallace Shadybrook decided to round the minutes up, double the number and then tell her he was offering her a good neighbor discount. This will be a discount that Mary Beth will never see when she goes off to prison.

Ironically, Wallace escaped a prison sentence by doing something that he is very good at; namely, lying. Previously, Wallace had been implicated as a co-conspirator in Erica Whitman's scheme to defraud Jack Webster out of millions of dollars after Jack had won the Mega Millions Lottery. In addition, Wallace was thought to have been a party to Patty Kirsh's perjured testimony in court. Following Erica Whitman's conviction on the attempted murder charges, the US Attorney considered charging Wallace with an assortment of crimes.

Looking at a possible prison sentence and the loss of his law license, Wallace retained Victor Koslow, one of the best white collar criminal defense attorneys in Baltimore to represent him. While Victor had serious reservations as to Wallace's integrity, honesty and credibility, he vociferously defended Wallace as if he were the victim of an overly zealous US Attorney who was on a crusade to put a slippery lawyer of questionable character in prison.

When asked during the criminal investigation as to whether he knew that Patty Kirsh had lied when she recanted her testimony, Wallace swore on his mother's grave that he had no knowledge whatsoever that Patty had lied in court. In addition, when asked whether he knew that Candice Webster had lied about sexually assaulting Erica Whitman,

Wallace lied again by insisting that he had no knowledge that Candice had lied in court, further citing his desire to swear to the veracity of his oral testimony on his mother's grave.   Had federal prosecutors looked into the death of Wallace's mother, they would have discovered that Matilda Shadybrook currently resided in an assisted living facility where she was about to turn ninety seven years of age.

Wallace repeatedly swore that he was not a party to the conspiracy that Erica and Candice had manufactured. Wallace denied the accusations so many times that the Justice Department eventually grew tired of asking him questions. However, Jack Webster still had a bone to pick with Wallace and would not agree to withdraw his complaint against Wallace.

With Victor's assistance in negotiating a resolution of the charges, Wallace agreed to waive his right to receive any legal fees with respect to Erica's fifteen million dollar out-of-court settlement that Erica had manipulated with Candice's false testimony. In exchange for this concession, Jack eventually agreed to withdraw the criminal complaint he had filed against Wallace.

At the same time Wallace was the subject of a Justice Department criminal investigation, he was the target of an inquiry by the Maryland Bar Association as to whether he should be disbarred. Victor Koslow also handled this matter and convinced the bar association that Wallace had done nothing wrong.

As no criminal charges were pending against Wallace, he was free to continue practicing law. Having lost almost one year to dealing with the investigations into his conduct as a lawyer, Wallace was determined to make up for lost time by overcharging clients whenever possible.

Wallace is a firm believer in the expression, "Do unto others before they can do unto you."   Wallace intends to put this expression into practice by substantially overcharging his neighbor for subpar legal work.

Chapter 11

"Lipschitz, don't you own a watch?" inquired Tom Collins, the beleaguered Chief of the Examination Division, as Louie casually strolled into his office and plopped onto the leather sofa along the far wall. "I asked you to come up here forty five minutes ago."

"This is what I have to put up with all the time," chimed in Johnnie Walker, who said this tongue-in-cheek.

"I'll have to check to see if this constitutes insubordination," added Dave Darick, who recently succeeded Tom as section chief. Whenever possible, Dave enjoyed giving Louie a difficult time as payback for the difficult time that Louie gave him. The only problem is that Louie was quite capable of responding in kind, which he always did.

"That's good. I think I'll start by working my way up the food chain. JW, you have no idea what I have to put up with in dealing with you. The next case I turn in will have pictures and a box of crayons for your personal use since I don't expect you to understand any of the technical issues. DD, don't use big words like insubordination. It's too taxing on your pea-sized brain. And at your age, the less strain on your mind, the better. That brings me to the final joker in this group of misguided managers who need a show of hands before someone can go to the restroom. TC, your request to see me was put on hold," said Louie.

"You have a good reason?" asked Tom.

"I do."

"Let's hear it," said Tom. "This ought to be good."

"Hold on a second. Let me guess. You had to check in with your probation officer and that took longer than expected," said JW.

"No, that's not it. Louie couldn't tear himself away from watching Judge Judy. Or, maybe you were on the phone with your bookie this whole time," DD interjected.

"I thought Louie's bookie is in jail," Tom chimed in.

"He is," said Dave. "But, that hasn't stopped him from taking bets."

"Do you three clowns really want to match wits with me? The last time I checked, the IRS doesn't provide that type of training for its intellectually challenged managers," retorted Louie.

"Managers get special training that no one knows anything about," said Dave.

"The three of you would need special training. Based on what I've seen, the training you've gotten isn't worth crap," Louie retorted.

"And you would know about our special training?" asked Tom.

"I know. I have friends."

"You have connections. There's a big difference," countered Tom.

"Oh. Are you saying that the president is not a friend of mine?"

"The president is indebted to you. However, I can assure you that you are not on his guest list to attend social functions at the White House," replied Tom.

"And you know this for a fact?" Louie wanted to know.

"Just like the Deputy Attorney General makes it a practice to have you over his house for week-end barbeques?" Tom asked.

"Speaking of barbeques, I'll be at my brother-in-law's house this week-end and I'll be sure to pass along everyone's regards," Louie says. This is followed by complete silence. At the mention of Louie's brother-in-law, no one is about to say anything.

Louie's brother-in-law was once the chief-of-staff to the President of the United States. Prior to holding this lofty position, Dan Goldman, worked as a federal prosecutor and later, in an executive capacity at the Treasury Department. During the time Dan yielded immense power, he was able to expedite the dismissal of several IRS supervisors for cause.

"Did you guys forget that Dan is still tight with executives in the federal government?" Louie said with a sly grin. "And I hope you haven't forgotten how Dan got rid of Chatty Cathy for you."

"I would like to remind you that Dan ordered her firing at your request," Tom added.

"Your Royal Highness, let me remind you that you benefited greatly when the evil witch was forced to leave the kingdom. Dan did what no one else in the Examination Division was either willing to do or had the power to do," Louie reminded Tom.

"OK. Your point, as always, is well taken. Are we finished with the bullshit?" Tom wanted to know.

"Yeah. Tell me why I'm here because I don't like to hang out with management any longer than necessary. I have an unblemished reputation to protect," Louie proudly remarked.

Naturally, a comment such as that drew smirks from all who heard Louie declare that his reputation is beyond reproach. However, Tom had other matters to discuss. "I've got something to share with you that you're not going to find amusing," replied Tom. "Do you remember Detective Reed of the BCPD?"

"Aw shit! Don't tell me there's another murder-for-hire contract out on me?"

"We can only wish," Tom said almost to himself.

"What? I didn't catch what you just said," remarked Louie, whose hearing is quite good and heard every cynical word his boss said.

"As far as we know, you are not the subject of a murder-for-hire contract," Tom said. "What Detective Reed called me about involves the filing of fraudulent electronic tax returns."

"What is it about fraudulent e-filings that makes it a police matter?" asked Louie.

"It seems that in the course of a homicide investigation, the BCPD came across numerous spiral notebooks that contained the names, social security numbers and birth dates of people, some of whom who are now deceased. Also found at the crime scene were boxes of debit cards that indicate tax refunds had been issued to someone who had filed thousands of fraudulent returns electronically," explained Tom.

"The dead body at the crime scene has been identified as a member of a drug cartel. He was shot execution style. At the same time, BCPD also arrested someone for multiple traffic citations. In addition to drugs and weapons the police found in his car, they confiscated about two thousand debit cards. Later, detectives found spiral notebooks at the suspect's apartment where a member of his gang had been murdered.

"Detective Reed is of the opinion that criminals are now

resorting to filing fraudulent tax returns to such an extent that it is unprecedented. He thinks that this may be more lucrative than drug dealing," Tom added.

"OK. What does he want us to do?" Louie asked his boss.

"The evidence that was seized by the police will not be turned over to us at this time because it's part of an ongoing police investigation. However, Detective Reed will be meeting with us next week to fill us in on what is going on. I want you to get started on a project," Tom said to Louie.

"What kind of a project?"

"I want you to find out how many fraudulent electronic tax returns have been filed within the past three years and the total amount paid in fraudulent tax refunds."

The thought of performing a clerical function does not meet with Louie's approval. "Why would you have me do that when I can be making people miserable by auditing their tax returns. The last time I checked, my job description called for me to audit tax returns," declared Louie.

"Actually, if you had read the entire job description, you would know that you are also required to perform other duties and responsibilities, as determined by your supervisors. My directive to you falls within this category," remarked Tom.

"What's so important about this project?" Louie wanted to know.

"I want the IRS to initiate a legislative change that would delay the issuance of quick refunds when taxpayers file electronically," answered Tom.

There is a moment of silence in the room. Finally, Louie says, "Let me get this straight. Are you suggesting that we deep-six electronically filed tax returns?"

"That's not quite what I said. For now, I want to suspend issuing any tax refunds until the IRS can process third party information to verify its authenticity."

"That's pretty ambitious, particularly when it was Congress that encouraged taxpayers to file electronically so that those in need of their tax refunds can get their refund checks as soon as possible. What you are proposing is contrary to congressional intent. Are you sure about this?" Louie questioned his boss.

"I'm sure."

"Suggesting that taxpayers who file electronically can't get quick refunds would be a bold move on your part. It could also derail any further career advancement on your part. You could be booted out of the Executive Development Program. Are you willing to take that risk?" Louie asks in what is a surprisingly sincere concern for Tom's government career.

"It's something that needs to be voiced," Tom replies.

"You're sure?" Louie has asked again.

"Absolutely."

"How do you want me to go about this?" Louie asks.

"I need you to find out how many fraudulent claims for refund were filed within the past three years. I also want you to find out how much money was paid out in fraudulent claims," Tom reiterated for Louie's benefit. "Check for things such as how many tax returns were filed using the same residential address and how many refunds were deposited into the same bank account. That should be compelling evidence of massive fraud."

"OK. But there's a big difference between the fraudulent claims that we know about and the total number of fraudulent claims that we don't know about," countered Louie. "The fraudulent claims that we know about compromise such a small percentage of the total fraud."

"I'm aware of that, Louie. We're talking about billions of dollars that's being paid out each year to criminals. Most of the money will never be recovered. The system isn't working and something needs to be done about it," Tom opined.

The process of enacting legislative change is a slow and tedious action. Once approved by the Chief of the Examination Division, Louie's report would be sent to the Assistant Commissioner for Examination. If approved, it would then be sent to the Commissioner for concurrence. If approved by the Commissioner, it would be forwarded to the Department of the Treasury for its concurrence. If approved by Treasury, the recommendation would be submitted to the Senate Subcommittee on Fiscal Responsibility & Economic Growth. If it passes the sub-committee's scrutiny, the House would then consider it for action.

"Louie, when you prepare your findings, make sure you include the numbers from the criminal groups that have been engaging in other crimes," Tom said.

"Such as?" Louie inquired of his boss.

"The drug gangs, counterfeiters, etc. Detective Reed has evidence of drug dealers doing this. We have other groups of criminals doing this also. So far, there's evidence that the Russian Mob and some Nigerian gangs have been filing fraudulent returns in mass," said Tom.

"Where are you getting this information, Tom?" inquired JW.

"Justice has successfully prosecuted members of these groups. They are now behind bars. But, there's a lot more out there. Louie, I want you to work up numbers to show the impact that it has on revenue," Tom added.

"There's also the problem of actually auditing an e-return. It's virtually impossible to perform a comprehensive audit looking at, what is essentially a transcript," Dave chimed in.

"Congress couldn't care less if auditing an e-return is difficult for us. Our best argument for delaying the issuance of refunds is to show that the system is so flawed that it needs to be overhauled," Tom replied.

"You're the boss," Louie said as he walked out of Tom's office.

"You know something?' That's the first time I've ever heard Lipschitz say that I'm the boss," Tom said as his managers got up to leave.

Chapter 12

Prior to graduating from high school, Morris chose to legally change his last name to conform to the last name of the foster parents with whom he was living. Morris did so because he felt ashamed to be a foster child and did not want his college classmates to know that he grew up in foster homes.

Morris was very bright and distinguished himself in the classroom. Indeed, Morris did so well in school that he graduated one year before his high school classmates. Moreover, Morris completed his undergraduate collegiate studies in three years and went on to law school where he graduated at the top of his class.

While Morris was so focused on his studies, he neglected to interact socially with his classmates at school. This lack of social activity prevented Morris from cultivating new personal relationships. By the time Morris had finished school, he had no friends to speak of except for those who sought him out as a tutor.

As Morris became an extraordinarily accomplished legal scholar, he held the federal government and the IRS in particular, in contempt as a result of what his father was forced to endure. This obsession with revenge drove Morris on a journey that would almost consume his everyday thoughts. For Morris, there would be no redemption for his deceased father. Instead, it would be revenge. As far as Morris was concerned, revenge is a dish that is best served cold. In Morris' eyes, it will be served ice cold.

****

"Yeah, I know how to use a gun. So you want it to look like these two were murdered?"

"No genius, I want it to look like they committed suicide by shooting themselves in the head several times. Of course I want it to look like they were murdered. I want it to look as if they were victims of a robbery that went wrong. Do you think you could manage to do that?"

"Hey pal. I'll do whatever you want as long as I get paid. Just as we previously agreed, you pay me half before, the rest after the hits," said the assassin.

"OK. Half up front, half later," repeated the CPA just to make sure there was no misunderstanding.

"Good. 'Cause, if you don't show up with the money, don't bother showing up. Okay?"

"I'll bring the money," the CPA promised.

"That's a total of one hundred G's for the two hits. I don't take checks and I don't do plastic. No sequential numbered bills, either. Got it?"

"I got it."

With this business out of the way, the CPA got up from the table and walked out of the strip joint into the mid-day sun to return to his accounting practice. The assassin stayed behind for a few minutes so that he wouldn't offend any of the strippers if he left before they finished dancing for him.

"Hey Sweetie, can I get you a beer?" asked one of the barmaids who saw a frequent patron at the strip joint straddle the bar stool opposite where she was tending bar.

"Give me a few minutes," Bobby said, as he was still on duty and therefore, prohibited from consuming alcohol. Instead of checking in with his idiot boss, Detective Bobby Reed placed a call to Tom Collins. "Chief Collins, I'd like to stop by your office next Tuesday to chat with you. I've got 'something interesting' you should know about."

That "something interesting" Tom Collins should know about involves Ralph Elwood, former IRS agent who is now a CPA in private practice. Ralph Elwood had his clients give him a total of eight million dollars for the purpose of paying their estimated federal and state income tax liabilities. Elwood assured them that he would remit payment to the appropriate taxing authorities by the requisite due dates.

However, what Elwood neglected to tell his clients was that he had a serious drug and alcohol abuse problem which had led him to gamble excessively and recklessly. Over time, Elwood lost almost ten million dollars to the Russian Mafia.

Elwood convinced the thugs to whom he was indebted that he would satisfy the debt in full if given time. Elwood explained that he would have access to millions of dollars given to him by his clients for the purpose of paying estimated income taxes.

This concept of making estimated tax payments was lost on the thugs who were owed money by Ralph. Elwood assumed that, unlike the thugs to whom he was indebted, his tax clients would not break his kneecaps if he misappropriated their money.

Ralph Elwood found out that there were two witnesses who could testify against him if he were charged with embezzlement. In order to deal with this problem, Elwood decided to pay an assassin one hundred thousand dollars to murder the two witnesses. With the witnesses dead, Elwood assumed that he would not have a problem for the time being.

Ralph Elwood was a person of interest to the Baltimore City Police Department as well as the target of an ongoing federal criminal investigation that the Baltimore Police Department did not know about. Detective Reed had followed Ralph to the strip joint to see if Ralph's visit was business or pleasure. Judging from the looks of Ralph's table companion, it certainly wasn't pleasure.

Snapping a picture of Ralph's business partner with his cell phone, the detective would soon find out who this person is and what his rap sheet looks like. However, it was Ralph Elwood who would prove to be the bigger catch.

When the IRS and the State of Maryland eventually notifies his tax clients that the payments had not been remitted, Ralph Elwood would claim that the funds must have been credited to the wrong taxpayer accounts. Once this argument fails, Elwood had planned to allege that corrupt tax officials had misappropriated the tax payments for their own financial benefit.

Elwood thought that it might take several years to finally get this problem resolved. By that time, he planned to be living on a sailboat docked near a tropical island in a small corner of the world where Ralph Elwood will never be heard from again.

The only problem with this plan is that the assassin who was hired to kill the witnesses was arrested by the police in a botched liquor store robbery that evening. While sitting in a holding cell on the armed robbery charge, the assassin decided to cut a deal with the police. In exchange for a lenient sentence on the armed robbery charge, the assassin agreed to reveal everything he knew about the murder-for-hire plot concocted by Ralph Elwood.

****

Mark Paul Warren has converted his law practice into an advisory practice. Although Mark Paul Warren thought that the transition was seamless, it has greatly confused his clients.

In order to reassure his clients that he will continue to provide first rate service to them, the non-practicing lawyer has prepared a newsletter that explains the minor cosmetic changes that will impact his practice. Without disclosing that he has been suspended from practicing before the IRS for the next twelve months, the lawyer talks about the sweeping changes in the practice of tax law. By the time he is finished with this horseshit, the lawyer has announced that he is proud to offer advisory services in lieu of representation.

This newsletter will be followed by several more newsletters in which the disgraced lawyer will attempt to sell his clients on his advisory services. Each newsletter will conclude by declaring that this is a new and revolutionary approach to the practice of law, which he believes will be copied in the near future by most law firms that practice taxation.

Mark Paul Warren is very much aware of his bottom line. To compensate for the many clients who will soon ditch him when they learn that he cannot appear before the IRS, he will adjust his fee schedule accordingly. In other words, advisory work will be billed out at a higher rate than his previous billable time for subpar legal work.

When he is asked why he is charging more for advisory work, the lawyer will respond, "Because advisory work is specialized. It requires extensive research. Research takes time. In my position, I can't afford to be wrong. I have a legal, ethical and moral obligation to each client to ensure that I provide the highest quality service."

Some clients will buy into this bullshit. Most other clients will not. Mark Paul Warren does not care as long as he can keep his ship afloat for the next year. Once he is allowed to practice again before the IRS, Mark Paul Warren will concentrate on rebuilding his seedy little tax practice into a seedy powerhouse tax practice. By that time, the practice will revert back to doing representation work before the tax authorities, with the explanation given that his many clients require tax representation in addition to advisory services.

****

Chatsworth Symington, III has requested a meeting with Louie to discuss the examination of Richard Cahill's federal income tax returns. Curious as to Symington's skills as a tax lawyer, Louie has agreed to meet with the lawyer.

"Before we get started, I have to tell you that I don't do tax work, Agent Lipschitz."

"If you don't do tax work, why are you representing Mr. Cahill in this matter?" asked Louie.

"My law practice is pretty much limited to entertainment law. I handle the legal affairs of celebrities and spend most of my time negotiating contracts for my clients. Richard is a valued client of my law firm and I agreed to represent him in this dispute," said Chatsworth Symington, III.

"This isn't a dispute. It happens to be an audit."

"Right. I'm hopeful I can resolve this matter for my client."

"Good. The first order of business involves extending the statute of limitations. We can do that now," Louie was quick to say.

"What exactly is the statute of limitations?" asked the lawyer.

"I'm referring to the period of limitations for assessment purposes."

"To be perfectly honest with you, I'm not familiar with tax statutes," replied Chatsworth.

Louie is of the opinion that a crash course in statutes is necessary. "The Internal Revenue Code has specific provisions that deal with statutes. One such statute allows the IRS to extend the period of assessment by consent. If it appears that additional time is needed to determine a taxpayer's correct tax liability, the taxpayer will be asked to enter into a consent agreement, which I am asking your client to enter into at this time," Louie explained.

"I think I understand. But if my client agrees to give the IRS more time to audit his tax returns, you might come up with more adjustments. This might constitute malpractice on my part," replied the lawyer who was cognizant of his potential liability.

"I think I can alleviate your concern. Without sufficient time to do the audit, there is zero chance that the audit will be resolved by mutual agreement. Should your client decline to extend the current statute of limitations, I would have to issue a deficiency notice," Louie said in anticipation that the next question asked would be with regard to a deficiency notice.

With a blank expression on his face, Chatsworth asked, "What is a deficiency notice?"

"A Statutory Notice of Deficiency is issued under two circumstances as a protective measure. If an agreement has not been reached on a liability determination or the current statute of limitations is about to expire, the IRS will issue this notice. Once issued, a taxpayer then has ninety days to file a petition with the United States Tax Court in order to seek a redetermination of the tax liability."

"Tax Court, huh? What's Tax Court like?"

"It's a lot of fun," Louie casually remarked.

"Regardless as to how much fun it is, I don't believe that it is something my client would want to do. Agent Lipschitz, is it possible that we could wrap this case up quickly by negotiating a settlement?"

"On what basis would you negotiate a settlement if I haven't come close to finalizing the audit adjustments?" Louie asked.

"Well, as soon as you have identified the audit adjustments, we could negotiate," reasoned the lawyer.

"The problem I may have is that there isn't adequate time remaining on the oldest tax year to negotiate a settlement with you," countered the agent.

"Hmmm. I suppose I could convince my client to extend the oldest tax year. Does that help you?" offered Chatsworth as an alternative.

"It's a start. I would prefer that the two oldest years be extended to conform to the statute for the most recent tax year. From an administrative standpoint, that would be most desirable," Louie said in a surprisingly polite and respectful tone of voice. This is a tone of voice that is generally foreign to the pesky little agent who has a knack for annoying everyone he meets.

"OK. I'll talk to my client about that."

When Chatsworth Symington, III left the conference room, he also planned to tell his client to hire a tax lawyer.

Chapter 13

Five days after meeting with the local neighborhood assassin, who happens to be more goon than contract killer, Ralph Elwood has brought fifty thousand dollars with him to the local strip joint in which contract killers gather to work out the finer details of murder contracts. Having made the deposit on the hits, Elwood has been assured that everything will be fine. However, this is coming from a thug who is less than proficient in the art of whacking someone and was captured by a seventy two year old woman who was guarding the front door of her liquor store with a baseball bat that she used to smash against the goon's knees before he was arrested and taken away by the police.

"We'll meet here tomorrow and you can bring me the rest of my money because the deed will have been done," promised the assassin, who was outfitted with a listening device that was carefully concealed in his clothes.

"How can you be so sure that you can take care of this by tomorrow?"

"I know what I'm doing. I know where the two stooges live. This ain't gonna be that tough," said the informant. However, this thug was so incompetent that he probably couldn't find the witnesses if they were standing directly in front of him holding signs that read, "WITNESSES."

"Then why am I paying you so much money?"

"Because you need someone who has the balls to whack somebody," replied the thug. "If your balls were the size of mine, you might be able to do it yourself. But, whacking someone isn't for everybody. Some people can't do it. That's okay. It's why God created people like me."

The police who are listening in on this conversation merely roll their eyes at what the goon is saying. The feeling among the officers is that in spite of the comic relief their informant is providing, the sooner this meeting is over, the better.

"Just don't screw it up," the CPA instructs the informant.

"Just make sure you bring me my money the next time we meet," the goon instructs the CPA.

The following day, Ralph Elwood has received the call he had been anxiously awaiting. Told to bring the rest of the money, Ralph inquires as to whether the terms and conditions of the contract have been fulfilled. When told yes, he is instructed to check his e-mail and download the pdf that was recently sent to him. Once he has reviewed the images, he will be convinced that the job was successfully completed.

The Baltimore City Police Department has arrested a number of people outside The Platinum Showgirls who have engaged in similar murder conspiracies. This neighborhood establishment seems to be the "In Place" to plan murders. In just a matter of moments, Ralph Elwood will be the latest in a long line of less than distinguished members of society to have been arrested for plotting evil deeds.

After Ralph Elwood has given the informant the remaining fifty thousand dollars, he is promptly arrested and read his rights by the police officers who have been anxiously waiting for him. As he is being handcuffed and led away to a police car, Ralph Elwood believes that it is necessary that he say, "Guys, you've made a terrible mistake. I can explain everything. You see, I was just joking around when I said that I wanted to have somebody aced. Everything was taken completely out of context. C'mon guys, I was just kidding," Elwood was heard saying as the cops told him to watch his head as they helped him into the back seat of their police car.

When Ralph Elwood was brought to the precinct, he was immediately booked, finger printed and photographed. Ralph, who was not pleased with his current predicament, did not look particularly photogenic in any of his mug shots. However, Ralph has never really looked photogenic. This may be because Ralph is a skinny, little runt with beady eyes and a tongue that darts in and out of his mouth all too frequently as if he were using it to catch flies.

Ralph has always been undersized. As a young child, Ralph was usually bullied at school. Even while attending elementary school, many of the girls in his class bullied Ralph on a non-stop basis. In junior high school, everyone picked on Ralph because he was such an easy target. In high school, Ralph made a concerted effort to stay out of everyone's way for fear of being ridiculed. By the time Ralph enrolled in college, he had grown to almost five and a half feet tall and weighed almost one hundred and ten pounds.

Ralph did not look particularly happy when he was placed in a holding cell with four other gentlemen who have been arrested on various charges that pale in comparison to Ralph's misdeeds. Anxious to be released on his personal recognizance, Ralph did not waste any time when he asked his jailor, "How soon can I make a phone call?"

"The phone's tied up at the moment. We'll let you know when you can call your lawyer," said one of the cops.

About an hour later, Ralph was allowed to make one phone call. He used the opportunity to tell his personal lawyer who did general legal work to call a criminal defense attorney on his behalf. That person would be needed by tomorrow morning for the Arraignment. However, the services of a criminal defense attorney will not be secured overnight by Ralph's personal attorney.

An Arraignment hearing is the first part of the legal process in a criminal proceeding. At this hearing, the defendant is formally informed of the criminal charge and is afforded an opportunity to enter a plea. As Ralph Elwood has not retained an attorney for this hearing, the court has designated legal counsel for him by appointing a member of the legal profession who happened to be in court at that moment to temporarily represent him in this stage of the process.

"Mr. Elwood, my name is Sally Mohr. I have been appointed by the court to be your attorney and will represent you for this proceeding. Following the hearing, you have the right to retain other legal counsel should you wish to do so. Do you understand the nature of the charge?" asked the youthful looking and quite attractive lawyer who was smartly dressed in a dark blue blazer and matching skirt with a pastel blue blouse.

"Yes. I've been falsely accused of conspiring to have two people murdered," Ralph said as if he thought he could convince his lawyer that he was innocent of the attempted murder charge as well as the other criminal offenses.

"The Baltimore City Police Department has made this allegation against you and the Baltimore City State's Attorney will be prosecuting you for the alleged criminal offense. Under the Rules of Criminal Procedure, you will be read the formal criminal complaint in open court, unless you wish to waive its reading. That's entirely up to you. If you plead not guilty at the hearing, the judge may set a trial date," explained Sally, who when she was working in the Office of the Public Defender, handled a number of murder conspiracy cases.

"Are you with me so far?" Sally asked a somewhat disheveled looking client.

"Yes."

"Good. Because after you have entered your plea to the criminal charge, you'll need to consider a number of things. This is something that we can talk about after the hearing," said Sally.

"Right now, what are my options?" asked Elwood.

"Guilty or not guilty. I would recommend that at this time, you choose not guilty."

Entering a not guilty plea allows the defendant time to consider the respective strengths and weaknesses of his case and to determine the possibility of a favorable outcome in court. In addition, it allows the defendant time to prepare a defense and, in some instances, allows the defendant the right to appeal an adverse decision. This is important because defendants who plead guilty waive their right to a trial, to prepare a defense, and the right of appeal.

"Any chance the judge will consider bail?" asked Elwood.

"I seriously doubt it. The prosecutor will argue that you are a flight risk given the seriousness of the criminal charges and the fact that you are alleged to have plotted to have two witnesses murdered could be a factor for no bail. While I will make the request for bail, I don't see the judge granting any request, regardless of the amount set," replied Sally.

"If denied, is it appealable?" Ralph asked.

"We can appeal an adverse bail decision. However, the scope of the review is limited. The only question for an appellate court is whether the trial court abused its discretion," answered Sally.

"When can we talk about a plea bargain?" asked Elwood.

"That comes later."

"I've got information to trade. I want you to cut a deal for me. No prison time. I want full immunity and I want protection against the people I'm willing to rat out. I need to go into the Federal Witness Protection Program."

"Mr. Elwood, you're not being prosecuted by the federal government," Sally tried to explain to her client.

"I know. But I want the FBI to give me protection from the mob."

"Excuse me?" asked the puzzled defense attorney.

"Don't you see? It's the Russian Mafia that I need to hide from." Ralph Elwood has lost sight of the fact that if the Mafia wanted to find him, it could. Therefore, going into a witness protection program will not guarantee his safety.

"Right."

****

"John, I've been doing some thinking and I've come up with a unique way in which you can shelter your income from taxation and conceal assets from the government. I think it's something you should seriously consider," the legal advisor said to one of his clients.

"Is it legal?"

Scrunching up his face as he struggled with this question, the legal advisor finally said, "Legal is a term of art. What is legal in the opinion of your next door neighbor may not be legal in the eyes of your other next door neighbor," replied Mark Paul Warren, former IRS agent and former practicing tax lawyer who seems to have difficulty with the word, "legal."

"I'm not asking my neighbors if it's legal. I'm asking you if it's legal," said the client.

"John, what I'm about to tell you is perfectly legal. It's what we call tax planning. It doesn't fall within the scope of tax evasion." Although what the lawyer has said is technically true, what he is about to describe falls within the scope of tax avoidance.

Tax avoidance involves civil penalties that could include the imposition of the civil fraud penalty, while tax evasion is a criminal act that is prosecuted as a criminal fraud case. A key distinction between civil and criminal fraud lies in the burden of proof. In a criminal case, the prosecution must prove fraud beyond a reasonable doubt, which is the highest level of proof that the law requires and is synonymous to a moral certainty. In contrast, civil fraud requires only clear and convincing evidence, which is still a higher standard than a mere preponderance of evidence.

"John, here's my thought. You're making big bucks as a physician. You need to shelter your earnings. I want to form an offshore Trust where you can transfer your wealth. Let's assign your earnings from your medical practice to the Trust. We can also have your personal residence and other assets re-titled in the name of the Trust."

"What kind of assets?" the client questioned his legal advisor.

"Stocks and securities, for starters. Your cars and household possessions can be transferred as well. Hell, we can put everything you own in the Trust. You'll draw a salary of two thousand dollars a month, which you'll report on your tax returns."

"Wait a minute! Are you suggesting that I only pay tax on twenty four thousand dollars a year?"

"Yeah. That's your salary," remarked the legal advisor.

"I earn more than seven hundred thousand dollars a year from my medical practice. What about that money?" the client exclaimed.

"You've assigned it to your offshore Trust."

"But, it's money that I earned which I'm required to report as taxable income. I may not be a tax lawyer, but I have enough common sense to know that the earnings are taxable to me, not some offshore Trust in a tax haven country. What in the hell are you trying to do to me? I don't want to go to prison for tax evasion," exclaimed the client.

"Who said anything about tax evasion? Did I say this was criminal?" replied the legal advisor who seemed to have difficulty grasping the idea that he was supposed to provide sound advice to his clients.

"I don't think you know what's criminal and what's not," the client shot back.

"John, it just so happens that what I'm recommending to you is a very popular tax planning technique that is being used by wealthy people like yourself. And I might add, innocent people just like yourself who have done nothing wrong."

"I don't care if every doctor in America is doing this. I don't like it and I'm not about to commit fraud."

"John, don't be so quick to reject this suggestion. I think it's perfect for you," suggested Mark Paul Warren, legal advisor extraordinaire.

"I'll tell you what's perfect for me. Another tax lawyer would be perfect for me."

****

The Arraignment hearing for Ralph Elwood is proceeding along at a rather brisk pace. On the advice of his attractive attorney, Ralph has pled not guilty to the charges of witness tampering, murder-for-hire, solicitation of violence and mail fraud.

"My goodness! Mr. Elwood, I can see you've been quite busy," remarked the judge. Judge Andrew Harrison is now in his mid-seventies but has the energy of someone half his age. Distinguished looking with a full head of white hair, the judge neither requires eyeglasses nor a hearing aide.

Turning to the Assistant District Attorney, the judge asked, "Is there anything else?" to which the prosecutor replied, "No judge, it's just the twelve felony counts."

"Good. Now that we have the defendant's plea, what's the people's position on bail?" asked Judge Harrison, who doesn't waste time in getting to the heart of the matter.

"Your Honor, the people oppose bail. The defendant is a former IRS agent who is currently a licensed certified public accountant. The defendant has been charged with having stolen as much as eight million dollars from his clients. His other crimes involve mail fraud, the filing of false tax returns, social security fraud, identity theft and money laundering," added the prosecutor.

"The District Attorney's Office recently learned that the defendant plotted to have two witnesses murdered. The individual who was paid one hundred thousand dollars to murder the witnesses is presently in police custody.

"The defendant owns a beachfront house in Mexico as well as a condo in St. Thomas. If convicted on all twelve counts, the defendant could be sentenced to a total of seventy five years in prison. There is substantial motivation on the part of the defendant to flee the immediate jurisdiction," concluded the prosecutor.

"Ms. Mohr?"

"Your Honor, while the District Attorney may have visions

of the defendant fleeing the country, my client hasn't been convicted yet of perpetrating any crimes. He is entitled to due process and to impose imprisonment is unfair. My client is a practicing accountant who has clients in need of his professional services. If he is denied bail, his accounting practice would suffer irreparable harm," argued Sally.

"Your Honor, the people contend that the defendant's accounting practice is a criminal enterprise given the severity of what has been alleged," countered the prosecutor.

"Judge, whether my client's conduct has violated the standards for practice is a matter best decided by the State Board of Accountancy and not the District Attorney. My client is a licensed CPA and until he is suspended from practicing accounting, he is entitled to operate an accounting practice. To deny him an opportunity to practice his chosen livelihood is harsh. My client is willing to post bail to balance the state's concern that he might flee with his need to remain available to perform accounting work for his clients," Sally added.

"I take it you're referring to the clients that he hasn't attempted to murder," remarked Judge Harrison. I don't think it would be in the best interests of the public to have Mr. Elwood walking the streets of Baltimore. Bail request is denied and the defendant is remanded to the custody of Baltimore's finest. Please call the next case."

With that, Ralph Elwood will be spending his mornings, afternoons and evenings as a guest of the Baltimore City Detention Center. Disappointed in his lawyer's less than spirited defense, Ralph has decided that he will obtain more high-powered talent to represent him. Sally will not be the least bit disappointed that she will not be handling this case after today.

Chapter 14

Chatsworth Symington, III has been busy working the phones. This is something that he is particularly adept at doing.

Chatsworth has no desire to get involved in a tax audit which is outside his area of expertise and comfort zone. In this respect, Chatsworth has made inquiries as to who are the best tax lawyers in Baltimore.

Calls were placed to the offices of Trent Stratford and Joel Abramowitz, who are generally considered to be the best tax lawyers in the Baltimore metropolitan area. When advised that Louie Lipschitz is the IRS agent conducting the audit, both lawyers quickly declined to accept Richard Cahill as a client and wished Chatsworth better luck in finding someone else.

"What is it with this agent that you don't want to take the case?" Chatsworth asked the lawyers. Each time he was told that they want nothing to do with Louie Lipschitz. "He's not an investigating agent that I'd want to go up against," each lawyer had said to Chatsworth.

"Is he that good?" asked Chatsworth.

"He is the best agent I've ever gone up against and my firm makes it a practice not to accept cases in which Agent Lipschitz is handling the audit," replied Joel Abramowitz.

For his part, Trent Stratford acknowledged that he has given up trying to defend clients who are audited by Louie. "I haven't had any success against him and I make it a point to refer the work to other lawyers," Trent admitted.

Chatsworth spent the next several hours furiously working the phones so that he could have someone replace him. Unable to entice a tax lawyer to accept the case, Chatsworth finally found a CPA who was willing to represent Richard Cahill during the audit.

"You do have extensive audit experience?" Chatsworth asked.

"Of course. I've been a practicing CPA for about ninety five years," replied Myron Kleigman.

"What?" the lawyer exclaimed as if he hadn't heard what was just said.

"Wait. No, that's my age, I think. Um, maybe not. I could be older. Let me see, I've been practicing ...... um, I'm not sure how long because I'd have to subtract something from my age to figure out how long I've been practicing."

"Jesus Christ!" Chatsworth wailed in frustration.

"Wait, I got it. I subtract my age when I got my license to figure out how many years I've been practicing," says the CPA. There is a long pause before he continues. "Only, I don't remember when I got my license. Do you know?"

"How would I know?" replied Chatsworth.

"What's that?" said the CPA.

"You asked me when you got your license."

"Why would I ask you that? If I don't know the answer to that question, why would you know it?" asked the CPA.

Myron Kleigman is in the neighborhood of one hundred years of age and for some remarkable reason, has not been suspended from practicing accounting. This is probably because Myron doesn't really practice anymore. While Myron still holds a valid license, he no longer prepares tax returns and is not asked by anyone to advise them on matters such as tax planning.

No one actually recommended Myron Kleigman as a tax practitioner. Chatsworth came across Myron's name when he went through the Yellow Pages without much success.

Unable to find a CPA who would agree to take the case, Chatsworth started to call the firms that advertise on TV as to obtaining tax relief by negotiating settlements with the IRS for pennies on the dollar. "Am I that desperate that I have to solicit people who advertise like gypsy fortune tellers?" Chatsworth asked himself when he made the call.

"Taxes R Us," answered the perky receptionist when Chatsworth asked to speak with the person in charge.

"Let me see if Mr. Moss is available," replied the receptionist.

Eddie Moss is the office manager of Taxes R Us, a fly-by-night commercial income tax preparation firm. Eddie was formerly an IRS agent who had a very undistinguished career as an auditor. Eddie advanced in the IRS by aligning himself with Wayne Sludgeman, aka "Sludge."

In order to obtain a promotion, Eddie did what any other below-average federal employee would attempt to do. Eddie "kissed up" to Sludge and did so without reservation. In fact, it was so blatant that Eddie lost the respect of his fellow workers. However, the desired result was achieved and Eddie was promoted to supervise a group of field agents.

As soon as Eddie was selected to be Louie's supervisor, he decided to intimidate Louie. Apparently, Eddie believed that if he could intimidate Louie, it would have an impact on the other agents in his group. Eddie also thought that this would be payback for all of the times Louie disrespected him in front of his fellow agents.

What Eddie failed to realize was that carrying out a personal vendetta against someone who disrespected everyone was not a good idea. Louie was without question, the best agent in the district and any efforts to undertake a campaign to discredit him in the eyes of senior management would not be a wise career move because Louie produced results that no other agent could match.

When Louie was put on notice that Eddie intended to give him a difficult time, he decided to take the offensive. Accordingly, it was Louie who initiated steps necessary to have Eddie removed as a manager. A work slowdown was orchestrated by Louie that would make all bargaining unit federal employees proud. When senior management realized that the number of case closings in Eddie's group had substantially dwindled during his tenure as supervisor, Eddie was given a pink slip and told to leave the IRS.

Having no success in obtaining a reputable job in the private sector, Eddie eventually joined forces with Hobart Frutz, another IRS manager who was also asked to step down from his job. Hobart was relieved to have someone with IRS experience assist him in the tax practice that he had recently started. However, Hobart had no idea that Eddie was just as incompetent as he was, which created serious problems when forced to represent clients before the IRS.

In a relatively short period of time, the two of them were charged with misconduct and forced to agree to one year suspensions from practice before the IRS.

When Eddie's suspension period was up, he joined Taxes R Us. At that time, Fred Rawlings, its office manager, was forced out as a result of having been implicated in a massive scheme of willfully filing fraudulent tax returns for clients. Rawlings was also charged with having recklessly filed income tax returns in a tax return preparer project that resulted in the assessment of more than two million dollars in fines against him.

Rumor has it that Fred secretly departed the United States for a foreign country that did not have an extradition treaty with the United States. The owner of Taxes R Us thought that the position of office manager should be filled by someone with IRS experience so as to avoid future compliance problems. When Eddie applied for the job, he was believed to be the savior the company needed.

"This is Mr. Moss. How can I help you?"

Chatsworth is already put off by someone who refers to himself as mister rather than use the first name that he was given at birth. Getting a sense that he doesn't like Eddie already, Chatsworth decides to make this brief.

"Do you do audit representation?"

"We can," offered Eddie in what was an outrageous lie.

"I didn't ask you if you can. I specifically asked you if this is something that your firm does."

Fully cognizant that Taxes R Us does not do audit representation, Eddie qualifies the statement by saying that they do provide this service to clients at an additional cost.

"So you have experienced professionals on staff engaged to perform this function?" Chatsworth was anxious to establish.

"We have people who do this," Eddie says and then decides to further clarify the statement. "We contract out depending on the type of case and issues involved." This embellishment is a blatant falsehood.

"So, if someone came to you with a tax problem, you would provide suitable representation based on the degree of complexity?"

"Of course. That's what we do," Eddie lied again for good measure.

"I have a client who is being audited by the IRS. The audit may involve complex factual and legal questions that might require an expertise in certain areas of taxation. My client needs someone to handle his representation who is also knowledgeable in the rules governing practice and procedure before the IRS. Can you do this?"

"Not a problem. We have the most experienced people on call who deal with the IRS. We are feared and respected by the IRS. We take great pride in knowing that the IRS can't push our clients around. We strive to ensure that our clients get treated with dignity and respect."

When Eddie Moss is finished with his long-winded speech, he is told that Louie Lipschitz is the IRS agent in charge of the audit, at which time he promptly hangs up the phone.

Chatsworth has now decided that he needs to engage the services of a white collar criminal defense attorney with extensive experience dealing with the federal government.

****

"Chief Collins, what can you tell me about Ralph Elwood?" Detective Reed asks Tom Collins in his office at the Federal Building.

"I don't really know much about him. He left the IRS before I got here. Why do you ask?"

"Last week, the Baltimore City Police Department arrested him for attempted murder. He's been charged with conspiracy to have two people murdered, as well as theft of eight million dollars."

"Jesus! What is it with people who practice tax?" Tom wondered aloud.

"That's what I want to know," said the homicide detective.

"What can you tell me about the arrest?" inquired Tom.

"The warrant for his arrest alleges that Elwood stole eight million dollars which he intended to use to pay off the Russian Mafia," said Detective Reed.

"The Russian Mafia?" Tom exclaimed in disbelief.

"From what we were able to gather, Elwood had a serious drug and alcohol abuse problem. Apparently this led to his gambling addiction. Once he ran up millions of dollars in gambling losses which he couldn't repay, he kept the money his clients had given to him that was intended to be deposited with the IRS on their behalf," Detective Reed explained.

"And he used the money to pay off the Russians," Tom surmised.

"Not quite. When we arrested him, we discovered that he deposited the money in an offshore bank account. I doubt that Elwood was going to give the money to his Russian friends."

"Talk about a double cross. What a prick!" exclaimed Tom.

At that moment, Louie Lipschitz happened to stick his head in Tom's office when he heard the word "prick" having been said.

"Who's a prick?" Louie asks.

"Detective Reed has asked me about Ralph Elwood. Do you remember him when he worked here?"

"That prick Elwood?" Louie responds.

"How well did you know him?" the detective asks.

"Well enough that I wouldn't piss on him if he were on fire." Having thought about what he just said, Louie corrected himself by saying, "Let me clarify that remark. Upon further reflection, I would piss on Elwood. What's he done?"

Detective Reed proceeds to fill Louie in on Ralph Elwood's current situation. When he has finished, Louie is almost at a loss for words.

"Holy shit," seems to be the best Louie can say.

"Elwood wants to cut a deal in the worst way," Detective Reed says. "Last week, he dismissed Sally Mohr and insists on negotiating a plea bargain with the DA."

"I'll bet he's working a con," Louie replies.

"No doubt. He wants immunity from prosecution and get this …….. a new identity under the Federal Witness Protection Program. He wants the DA to go to the FBI to make arrangements," the detective says.

"Wait a minute. Has he been charged with a federal crime?" Tom interjects.

"Not that I know of, but maybe Elwood knows more than we do."

"What's he offering?" Louie asks.

"Boris Krushenko," answers the detective.

"The Russian Mob Boss?" exclaimed Tom.

"Yeah."

"Elwood's going to toss Boris Krushenko under the bus?" Louie says as he shakes his head in bewilderment.

"Yeah. To escape a harsh life behind bars, he'll give the feds Krushenko," Detective Reed says.

"Exactly what does he have on Krushenko?" asks Tom.

"I can't go into details with you but he claims to have financial records that implicate Boris Krushenko committing securities fraud, engaging in money laundering, stashing money in offshore accounts under a variety of aliases, as well as a few other crimes."

"Does he claim to know anything about any dead bodies?" Tom is curious to know.

"We haven't gotten to that yet," replies the detective.

"What's Elwood's relationship to Krushenko?" Louie asks.

"According to Elwood, he was Krushenko's accountant and financial advisor for a number of years. It seems that Elwood handled his books and records, prepared his tax returns and sat in on meetings when Boris needed financial advice," Detective Reed replies.

"Detective, if I were you, I wouldn't trust anything Elwood says. He's a pathological liar who would sell his mother into slavery if he could make a buck doing it," Louie said.

"Sounds like your typical tax accountant."

Chapter 15

"Before I let everyone go, I want to say a few words about what's happening with Judge Barton."

Warren Simonsen has called an office meeting with his trial attorneys to discuss several matters. The last item on the agenda is Judge Barton. The attorneys have been told that the matter has been elevated to the Office of Chief Counsel. As with lawyers, judges are expected to comply with the code of professional conduct. If a judge has been found to have violated the code of professional conduct, that person may be removed from the bench through an impeachment proceeding.

"And?" asked Mo Green, who was anxiously awaiting word that Judge Barton will soon be the subject of an impeachment hearing.

As I understand it, this is a situation that has never come up before. It appears that this is going to be a precedential case," Warren said.

"How long is it going to take to have him removed?" Mo persisted. "And please don't say fifteen years," Mo almost pleaded, well aware that Tax Court judges are appointed to fifteen year terms and serve at the pleasure of the Senate.

"I have no idea."

"Maybe we should have Lipschitz film the judge in a compromising position," Alex Hill suggested. Louie's reputation filming IRS officials who were engaged in illicit sexual activities during work hours on government premises has spread throughout the IRS, even though this happened several decades ago.

Louie had suspected that his boss was having an affair with an IRS executive and he wanted to get any illicit conduct on government premises on film. In order to catch the culprits in action, Louie hid on top of the ceiling tiles with a video camera while filming the action from a small space where one tile had been partially exposed.

"Oh, Kyle, I've missed you so much. I want you to take me, right now," said Ruth Mellonhead.

"Sweetheart, I've missed you too. I'm going to start making these trips to Baltimore every week so we can be together. Now get naked for me. We don't have much time," replied Kyle Woods.

In no time at all, these two were frolicking around in their birthday suits as if they didn't have a care in the world. The door to the conference room was locked from the inside and the blinds were drawn so that no one could see in the room. With the exception of Louie De Mille filming from an overhead angle, these two lovebirds had all the privacy they wanted.

Louie had been stretched out in such an awkward position for an extended period of time that his left leg had started to cramp. Desperate to alleviate the cramping sensation in his leg, Louie re-adjusted the position of his body. By doing so, his leg banged against one of the joists Suspecting that he heard a noise, Kyle asked Ruth, "Did you hear that?"

"Hear what?" asked Ruth, who had to remove Kyle's pecker from her mouth in order to speak.

"Babe, didn't you hear something?"

"How am I supposed to hear something with your loud moaning?" Ruth remarked.

After a moment, Kyle agrees and says, "I suppose you're right. It must have been your knees grinding into the floor."

"Next time I'll wear knee pads for you," Ruth retorted. Her partner quickly agreed to this suggestion and replied, "Good, I like it when you plan ahead."

As the meeting came to a climax and the participants got dressed, Kyle asked Ruth about her plans.

"It's what we agreed upon. I'll make a name for myself here by getting rid of the male agents and bringing in female agents. That should get me some EEO points with senior management. In one year, I'll be ready for my next promotion and back in the National Office as your Special Assistant," replied Ruth.

"Good girl. If I can get that Assistant Commissioner position, then I'll give you my job in two years. As long as no one knows about us, you're on a fast track to the top."

You're on a fast track to Hell, Louie mumbled to himself as he continued to record his cinematic masterpiece.

It didn't take long for Kyle Woods and Ruth Mellonhead to be terminated. Although Louie never confirmed or denied that he filmed the sex tape, it was a generally accepted fact that he did.

Shortly after this episode, Louie got to work on another sex tape for the sole purpose of getting rid of his new boss. This time, Louie recruited professional talent to entrap his idiot boss. The professional talent happened to be an attractive stripper who had acting skills.

As she got off the elevator, the sultry looking blonde in the four inch high heel shoes walked to the directory that was posted on the wall to find the office of Ricardo Gomez. Although the forecast did not call for rain that day, the lovely young lady in the high heeled shoes was wearing a raincoat that seemed to show off her shapely figure.

The creative genius behind this cinematic extravaganza is Louie De Mille. Once again, Louie is handling the cinematography work while his body is supported by ceiling tiles and structural beams. The director of this production has extensive experience in this particular genre.

Louie's fellow agents know that Gomez, who is a creature of habit, always leaves for lunch at noon and returns to the office exactly one hour later. Louie has once again commandeered a ladder that he will use to climb up to the ceiling. Given his small body, Louie has positioned his body so that it is supported by the joists and tiles directly above Gomez's desk.

Anne Marie Gillespie, who is otherwise known as Heather, has been paid two hundred dollars to wear nothing but panties and a bra under her raincoat, show up at the Federal Building and then entice Ricardo Gomez to do something stupid. Anne Marie has assured the men who have hired her for this job that she will be able to produce the desired result.

Anne Marie has found Ricardo Gomez's office without too much difficulty and enters without bothering to knock. When Ricardo looks up and sees her remove her raincoat, he appears to have difficulty saying, "Young lady, you're not wearing any clothes."

"That's not quite true. Once I've taken off my bra and panties, I won't be wearing any clothes," replies Anne Marie. Before Ricardo can say another word, Anne Marie has her arms draped around his neck as she pulls him on top of her body. With Gomez on top of her, Anne Marie straddles her legs around his butt so that he can't break free from her.

Louie is working the video camera like he was born to do this. The only things missing are a mustache and beret that are the trademarks of the old-school Hollywood motion picture directors.

Anne Marie has played her role to perfection. Ricardo has been filmed with his pants draped around his ankles, his shirt has been ripped off and his face is smeared with lipstick.

The following day, the tape has made its way to senior management. In only a short period of time, Ricardo Gomez has been ordered to step down as an audit manager.

When asked by senior management if he played any part in this particular film production, Louie merely shrugged his shoulders and placed his palms up in the air as if he didn't have any idea as to what had happened.

Given Louie's track record as a filmmaker, it is only natural that the trial attorneys might want to recruit him.

"We are not sponsoring anyone to engage in pornographic activities," Warren interjected.

"I was just thinking out loud, boss."

"Don't," Warren said with his typical smile and chuckle, although he too was probably thinking that such a video could expedite Barton's impeachment.

"Getting back to Barton, the procedures for removal would require impeachment by the Senate. I have brought this problem to the attention of Senator Stevens, who chairs a sub-committee on judicial appointments. Senator Stevens is very much concerned over what has transpired in court and has asked her staff to prepare a report for her committee. In the meantime, Barton's still our problem."

"So it looks like he's going to be a thorn in our side for a few more trial calendars," said Lindsay Cooke.

"I would think so," agreed Warren.

"Do we have a strategy for our next calendar with him?" asked Thaddeus Chudzinski.

"Yes, we have a strategy."

"Care to share it with us, boss?" asked Mo.

"I think it's safe to say that Judge Barton will rule against us in every case. In light of such a scenario, we're going to take only the worst cases to trial if we would lose those cases anyway," Warren said.

"Why not just concede the cases?"

"If we settle every case we can and concede the others so there's nothing left for trial, word will quickly get out that we're afraid of Barton and caved under pressure. I don't want practitioners to know this."

"But don't they already know this?" asked Lindsay.

"Probably. But we need to hold some cases out for trial and let them know that we're willing to go to trial."

"And you're willing to sacrifice us?" Mo interjected.

"As you leave here, make sure you pick up your swords."

****

"Mr. Barton?" asked the caller.

"Yes. This is Judge Barton," M.L. said to let the caller know that he was talking to a judge and not a mere mortal.

"My apologies, I didn't know you're a judge. My name is Robert Templeton. I'm a financial advisor at Langford & Mullens."

"I'm sorry, Mr. Templeton, but I already have a financial advisor to manage my investment portfolio."

"No. That's not why I'm calling. This is not a solicitation."

"You're not going to ask me to open an account?" said the judge.

"No sir. Nor am I going to invite you to a dinner seminar where a representative of our firm tries to sell you long term health care or put you in a new mutual fund. Actually, if you want to open an investment account with us, that would be fine, but that's not why I'm calling. I had a very difficult time locating you. My office managed to find you using your social security number."

"Why are you trying to find me?" inquired Barton, who was beginning to get suspicious of the caller.

"Thirty years ago, your father purchased a twenty five thousand dollar deferred annuity through a small brokerage firm that was later acquired by Langford & Mullens."

"I don't understand," said a puzzled judge who seemed to be at a loss for words as he thought back to the day his father committed suicide.

"Your father invested twenty five thousand dollars in a non-callable deferred annuity thirty years ago and named you as the designated beneficiary. Apparently several months ago, the annuity matured and the principal amount has been sitting in an escrow account for your benefit."

"This is the first I'm hearing of this," Barton replied.

"Your father passed away shortly after he placed the money in the annuity. Apparently he wanted you to have a nest egg to ensure your financial stability as a young adult. It was a very unselfish gesture on his part because the investment has not paid any interest or dividends prior to its maturity," explained the financial advisor.

"How much are we talking about?"

"The terms of the annuity call for ten percent compounded interest over a period of thirty years. Your total payout is four hundred and thirty six thousand, two hundred and thirty five dollars."

"Is this some kind of a joke?" were the only words that Barton could think of saying.

"Judge Barton, I can personally assure you that this is not a joke. We have the paperwork on file in our office where your father set up this account for you. I can disburse the funds to you however you like, whether it's a wire transfer to another brokerage firm or financial institution. Or, should you wish to open an account with us, we can accommodate this request and make the deposit immediately."

"I can't believe I have more than four hundred thousand dollars in a brokerage account that I never knew existed." Judge Barton has said this with a mixture of surprise and disappointment, as he thought back to the allegation that his father accepted a twenty five thousand dollar bribe that destroyed his career and led to his committing suicide.

"Can you tell me when the annuity was purchased?" Barton asked as if he were holding his breath.

"I don't have the exact date in front of me but I seem to vaguely recall that it was in the late summer so it could have been in August of 1982 by my guess."

Click.

"Hello? Hello. Judge Barton, are you still there?"

Upon hearing that the annuity was purchased in the summer of 1982, Judge Barton hung up the phone and cursed out loud. When he was finished cursing, Barton went on a tirade and threw anything he could get his hands on against the wall in his study. A portion of the investment proceeds will be used to repair the damage to the wall and replacing those items that were demolished.

Chapter 16

Frantically going through file cabinets until he found the folder he was looking for, Judge Barton retrieved the folder and trudged over to his desk. Fortunately, Barton did not have anything remaining on his desk that he could throw against the wall, which had already taken a beating during his tirade.

Barton warily opened the folder and flipped through the report of the witness who allegedly bribed his father. Even though he had read this report many times, Barton carefully read the report one more time to make sure the accusation is consistent with the date the annuity was purchased. When Barton came to the page where the taxpayer was asked when he gave Harvey Watkins the twenty five thousand dollars, he saw in bold letters, the words "I don't know the exact date, but it was sometime during the summer."

"Shit," said M.L. Barton. "I can't believe dad accepted a bribe."

M.L. Barton always regarded himself as an honorable man in spite of his unconscionable actions on the bench. There were many thoughts that were now going through his mind, including what he should do with the perceived ill-gotten gains from his late father's deception. There was also the matter as to how to rescind his judicial decisions which were clearly incorrect. This is not a viable option because the thirty day period for filing Motions for Reconsideration have expired and no motions were filed by the IRS.

"Why didn't the IRS file Motions for Reconsideration?" Barton said out loud. "If the IRS had only filed motions, I could reverse myself and grant new trials, rule in favor of the IRS and justice would be served," Barton exclaimed as if he needed to inform the IRS to follow his advice.

The reason why the IRS did not file Motions for Reconsideration was quite simple. The IRS knew that it would be a waste of time because Barton was not going to reverse himself when he had a clear agenda in mind. Now, this agenda will have to be changed.

****

"I'm not having much success. It appears as if there aren't any tax lawyers or accountants who seem interested in representing you."

"Jesus! I'm one of the most famous tennis players in the world and you can't find someone to handle my tax audit. Where the hell have you been looking? In bowling alleys?" Cahill screamed in frustration.

Chatsworth Symington, III has explained to his client that experienced tax practitioners who have dealt with this particular agent do not wish to be involved in this case. "Is there something going on with your tax returns that I should know about?" asks Chatsworth.

"Nope," answered Cahill.

"Did you report all of your income?" asks the lawyer.

"I thought I did. Look, I give all of my records to my accountant who then prepares my tax returns."

"This agent believes that you haven't disclosed all of your income. He's focused on appearance fees. Did you report your appearance fees?"

"Was I supposed to?" asks the client.

"You didn't?" says the lawyer in astonishment that his client could be this foolish.

"I didn't think appearance fees were taxable. I didn't really earn it. C'mon, all I had to do was show up at a tournament. It's like a gift and I know that gifts aren't taxable. So, what's the big deal?" Cahill asks his lawyer.

"What else have you done that I should know about?" Chatsworth asks but isn't quite sure that he wants to know the answer to this question.

"I buried some personal expenses on my returns and had my accountant classify them as business expenses. Don't worry. The agent will never find it," Cahill said with supreme confidence.

"Don't be so sure," Chatsworth cautioned his seemingly intellectually challenged client. "From what I've heard from a number of people, this agent doesn't miss a thing. He'll find it and anything else you've done wrong."

"You mean the appearance fees are taxable?" Cahill asks.

"What little I know about taxation, I can assure you that appearance fees are taxable," responds Chatsworth.

"Where are you on getting someone to handle the audit?" Cahill asks, now getting a sense that he is in more trouble than he had first thought.

"I think our focus should be on someone who does white collar criminal defense work," replies Chatsworth, who would like to wash his hands of Richard Cahill as soon as possible. Retaining a criminal defense attorney at this time would be wise, unless the lawyer is not up to the task of a criminal proceeding.

****

Louie has completed his audit of Richard Cahill's federal income tax returns for the past three years. In addition to discovering that Cahill received hundreds of thousands of dollars each year in appearance fees which were not reported on his tax returns, Louie also determined that Cahill had several million dollars in foreign bank accounts that were not disclosed to the Treasury Department. Louie also asserted in his audit report that Richard Cahill claimed hundreds of thousands of dollars in questionable business expenses.

Louie did not send a copy of his audit report to Chatsworth Symington, III. Instead, he referred the case to CID for consideration as a criminal tax case.

CID is the Criminal Investigation Division within the IRS. Cases that merit criminal investigation are transferred to CID by other functions within the IRS, with CID responsible for referring the case to the Department of Justice for approval if it is believed that criminal prosecution is warranted.

Because jurisdiction was now formally transferred to CID, Louie was required to notify Chatsworth that his client's individual income tax returns were now the subject of a criminal investigation.

The Criminal Investigation Division is very selective when it comes to accepting referrals for criminal investigation. Most referrals by the Examination and Collection Divisions are declined on grounds that it does not meet the standards for a criminal case. This is because the Justice Department's standards for criminal prosecution are quite high. While there are no specific criteria in terms of dollars involved, CID prefers referrals that are large dollar cases involving notable taxpayers who have committed criminal acts. In other words, the more notable the case is, the better the prospects are for acceptance.

In view of the fact that Richard Cahill is a high-profile celebrity athlete and the understatement of tax is substantial, the essential criteria are met. If CID accepts the case, its special agents will soon be conducting a formal investigation. This will not be a pleasant experience for Richard Cahill.

****

Tom Collins has called a meeting in his office. Invited to attend is Louie. When Louie enters, he makes it a point to plop down on Tom's sofa so that he can stretch out and hopefully drift off to sleep.

"Are you comfortable?" Tom asks sarcastically.

Louie nonchalantly shrugs and responds by saying that he makes a nice living despite being underpaid by his employer.

"Is there anything I can get you? Perhaps you'd like something to drink or some refreshments. Or would you prefer if I called Mary Mervis and have some deli sandwiches sent up? I want you to be happy," Tom adds with a healthy dose of sarcasm.

"Really?" Louie asks in a typically innocent tone of voice a five year-old child would use when told that the child has misbehaved.

"Lipschitz, sit your ass up right now and take your shoes off of my sofa. This isn't a lounge and it's not my job to provide you with food and beverages. The last time I checked, you worked for someone who reports to another manager who reports to me. That makes me higher up on the food chain than you. Are you following me?" Tom says.

"I'm not sure. You're reneging on your offer of food and refreshments. I get that. But what's all this about a food chain?" Louie asks just to further annoy his boss.

"Forget it. Where are you on this e-filing project?"

"I have some information for you that will blow your mind, what little mind you actually have. A single address was used to file more than two thousand separate income tax returns which generated more than three million dollars in refunds. Someone at that single address walked away with over three million dollars in fraudulent tax refunds," Louie said as a matter-of-fact.

"In another instance, almost eight hundred refunds were deposited into the same bank account, totaling more than nine hundred thousand dollars," Louie added.

"OK. Stay on it and see what else develops," Tom encouraged his subordinate.

"See what else develops!" exclaimed Louie. "Did I hear you right?" Louie is about to make a point as to the absurdity of what is taking place but is interrupted when Tom holds up his hand.

"I know."

"Boss, we are up to our eyeballs in fraudulent tax returns, with no end in sight."

"Just stay on it."

"Anything for my glorious leader," remarked Louie with typical sarcasm for his boss.

****

Upon receiving formal notification that his client's federal income tax returns are now the subject of a criminal investigation, Chatsworth Symington, III has made telephone calls to virtually every white collar criminal defense attorney in Baltimore, without success. Starting with the most prolific lawyer by reputation, Chatsworth called Victor Koslow. However, Victor quickly begged off when he was told that Louie was the IRS's investigating agent in this case. Next, Chatsworth spoke with Roger Rice, who informed him that he was not accepting new clients. With a list of names provided by the Maryland Bar Association, Chatsworth spent the rest of the day making phone calls without success.

Chatsworth is a lawyer who enjoys doing transactional work on behalf of his clients. Engaging the services of another lawyer is becoming less and less appealing to Chatsworth. When he spoke to the last attorney on the list, Chatsworth decided to lower his standards in seeking legal representation.

"My client is a prominent professional athlete and international celebrity. He can't have this tax case go to trial. The adverse publicity would do irreparable damage to his sports career as well as his commercial endorsements."

"I understand. Resolving legal disputes without going through litigation is what I do for a living. I'll have a deal worked out before the end of the day," promised the lawyer.

"Please send me the Engagement Letter and I'll have my client sign it and enclose a retainer in the amount of one hundred thousand dollars, Mr. …..."

Before Chatsworth could finish, the lawyer interrupted him by saying, "Please call me Wallace."

Chapter 17

It is Erov Rosh Hashanah and Louie's extended family is about to have dinner as they get ready for the Jewish New Year. Typically, the extended family meets at a different relative's home each year. This year, the meal is being catered at Dan Goldman's home in Bethesda.

After Dan left his job as the president's chief-of-staff, he joined a prominent D.C. law firm where he is currently its managing partner. While Dan is no longer active in politics, he still has access to some of the most influential people in the federal government.

"If I were to advocate that the IRS cease its e-filing program, what do you think Congress would do?" Louie asked his brother-in-law before they sat down to dinner.

"Summarily reject the idea."

"I thought so. What are my options to facilitate legislative change?" Louie asked.

"There are no options that I can see. Congress had this program implemented for a reason. Any reasons that you can come up with that are compelling and of significant merit are of no consequence to Congress. Congress will not allow the IRS to dismantle this program. You'll have to come up with another brilliant idea," Dan suggested.

Before Louie could say anything, his eighteen year-old nephew walked over to him and said, "Uncle Louie, am I too young to incorporate?"

"Nate, do you have a driver's license?"

"I got it last year."

"Then I guess you're old enough to incorporate. Why do you ask?"

"I started this business venture last year and was thinking that I should form a corporation to limit my legal liability. By next year, I'll have a staff working for me. I thought I should look into having a company that does business under a trade name and have all the stuff that companies have. You know what I mean?" replied Nate.

"Nate, maybe I shouldn't ask, but what exactly are you doing?" Louie asked.

"I'm a card promoter, Uncle Louie."

"A what?"

"A card promoter," replied Nate. "Remember when I used to collect business cards?"

"This is what you were doing a few years ago?"

"Right. By the time I finished putting together my card collection, I had the most prestigious business card collection in the western hemisphere. Nobody could touch my collection in terms of its star power," Nate said with pride at his accomplishment.

"Yeah, I remember. You had quite a collection."

"That's right. When word got out, I started doing seminars on how to assemble a collection of notable business cards," Nate remarked.

"And that's what you're doing?" Louie said with skepticism.

"I hired a business agent. She got me bookings on local talk shows, I did some newspaper interviews, and so forth. All of a sudden, I developed a cult following. So my agent suggested that I do seminars for people getting started in the business."

"The business of collecting business cards?" Louie asked as if he couldn't believe he was hearing this.

"Yes. And the business of flipping cards," answered Nate.

"What's with the flipping, Nate?" asked Nate's mother as she walked over to where Louie was standing and placed her arm around his shoulder.

"You first build a collection of cards. You only want notable public figures for your collection. And you want signatures, if you can get them. Personally signed cards are more valuable. Then, you market your collection and either swap it for other cards or sell it to another collector or an investor," Nate explained for his mother's benefit.

"People actually buy celebrity business cards?" Nate's mother asked as she turned to go back into the kitchen, shaking her head in disbelief that her son was wasting his time on this.

"You bet. Prominent executives of Fortune 500 companies, TV personalities, owners of professional sports franchises, politicians, famous lawyers, and so forth. Do you have any idea what one of Donald Trump's gold embossed business cards is worth?" Nate whispered to his uncle as his mother stepped away.

"I have no idea, Nate."

"A lot. Now imagine what that card is worth when you bundle it with Bill Clinton or Bill Gates and package it in a deal for other cards."

"I see your point. You've got people working for you?" Louie inquired.

"I will soon. I'm going to train some friends to help get them started in the business world. Once they've mastered the skills needed to do seminars, they'll take over the seminar part of my business, which will allow me to focus on new ventures."

"You can't be serious."

"Uncle Louie, I heard stories about you selling citrus products to federal employees on your lunch hour. Didn't you also entice your co-workers to rent DVD's for one dollar and deliver pizzas as part of your service? And aren't you peddling appliances on the job?" Nate asked.

"Where did you hear these totally unfounded rumors?" said Louie.

"From me," replied Louie's brother-in-law, who knew all about the things Louie did on the side while working at Club Fed.

"Everything your father has told you about what I do is an outrageous falsehood."

"That's what dad said you would say," Nate retorted.

"And what does your father have to say about your business venture?" Louie was curious to know.

"Don't do anything illegal and don't make false promises," replied Nate.

"Sounds like something your father would say."

"Actually, it sounds more like lawyerly advice," added Nate's mother, who happened to walk by at that moment as she led the way for the servers to carry the food to the serving table along the far wall.

"How much time are you devoting to this enterprise of yours?" asked Louie.

"About ten hours a week."

"Why is it that I hadn't thought of something like this when I was Nate's age, Louie wondered.

****

All organizations have individuals in positions of authority who are ill equipped to supervise their employees. This is relatively common in local, state and federal government agencies. While it is rare in law enforcement, it can happen. Indeed, it is happening at this very moment as Laverne Kressley is meeting with Bobby Reed to discuss the status of his investigation into Boris Krushenko's criminal activities.

"Where are you on the Krushenko case?"

"Right where I was the last time we spoke."

"And when was that?" asked Laverne, who seemed to have difficulty keeping track of her detectives' cases.

"Two days ago."

"You haven't solved the case since then?" Laverne asked.

"Unlike episodes of Law & Order and NCIS, it takes a little longer than forty eight hours to solve homicides," replied the detective.

"How much longer will it take?" Laverne has asked this question as if she were waiting for a prescription to be filled at her neighborhood pharmacy.

"I'm a detective, not a fortune teller. I have no idea how

long it's going to take."

"Give me your best estimate in case the commissioner asks," said Laverne.

"Has the commissioner been inquiring into this particular case?"

"Not that I know of, but just in case ……. give me an estimate."

The detective did not want to commit to a guess that could come back to haunt him so he replied by saying, "My investigations take time. It depends on how long it takes to get information from my CI's. Boris is sharp. He's covered his tracks well."

As it finally became obvious that Detective Reed was not about to tell her when his investigation would be completed, Laverne asked, "Do you need help?"

"No." What the detective really wanted to say was that he didn't need any help from his idiot boss.

"OK. Keep me posted," Laverne said as she gazed out the window as if the answers to solving this case were etched along the skyline.

Chapter 18

Wallace Shadybrook has recently concluded a case for a client. With no other active cases at the moment, this should allow Wallace to focus on Mary Beth's case. However, Wallace will quickly toss Mary Beth under a bus if given the opportunity to do so.

The meeting between Wallace and the youthful looking prosecutor lasted no more than four minutes, with the first thirty seconds consisting of an off-color joke that Wallace tried to tell before he was interrupted. "We don't have time for jokes. Let's get down to business," the female prosecutor told Wallace.

"What can you do for my client?" asked Wallace.

"Absolutely nothing," replied the prosecutor. "I plan on prosecuting her."

Anne Marlowe has been with the US Attorney's office for less than two years. Although Anne is often willing to accept a plea bargain when appropriate, she has taken a number of cases to trial. While Anne is well aware that this is a case that she should win, it does have risks if the case goes to a jury. Nevertheless, Anne is prepared to play hardball with Wallace and insist on no deal.

"C'mon. We don't have to take this to trial," Wallace says as he is fully prepared to grovel for any bones that are tossed his way.

"I think it should be tried. The publicity may discourage others from engaging in similar corrupt schemes," Anne counters.

"My client is an emotionally troubled young lady who exercised poor judgment," Wallace is back to pleading.

"Your client is a devious, scheming individual who operated a criminal enterprise and defrauded innocent people as well as insurance companies out of hundreds of thousands of dollars," replied the young prosecutor who was dressed in a conservative pant suit that conveyed the image of a lady who could be all business at the appropriate moment.

"She didn't understand the ramifications of her actions," Wallace stated in hopes of generating some sympathy from the prosecutor. However, Wallace's contention that his client merits empathy for her predicament is quickly dismissed.

"Don't give me that crap," exclaimed the young prosecutor. "Your client carefully planned each step of her diabolical scheme. She intentionally had her employers change to a cash payment system in order to implement her plan. She secretly opened bank accounts to further facilitate her plot. She knowingly falsified medical records and deliberately submitted false insurance claims. She then billed patients for a procedure that was not performed. If the procedure was performed, she still diverted the payments to a bank account that she controlled. I think that pretty much summarizes her actions."

"I think you're taking this out of context. You're making it worse than it really was," Wallace argued without any conviction.

"If you really believe what you just said, you can argue that in court," Anne shot back.

"Wait. What can you do on sentencing?" Wallace asked as if he were now in a full-fledged begging position.

"If your client's convicted, which is an absolute certainty, she's looking at seven years. I'll tell you what I'm willing to do. If she pleads to all counts, I'll go along with seven years," Anne promised.

"What the hell kind of a deal is that?" Wallace said.

"It's the only deal I'm offering," replied the prosecutor, who knew all about Wallace and his desire to cut a deal as quickly as possible just for the sake of cutting a deal.

"But it's not an offer that I can take to my client," Wallace was back to pleading.

"That's your problem. I'll see you in court, counselor," Anne replied.

When Wallace got up to leave the prosecutor's office, he decided to tell Mary Beth that he was successful in negotiating a plea bargain from thirty years to seven years, based on extenuating circumstances. This is a ploy that Wallace has repeatedly used throughout his undistinguished legal career. "It works every time," Wallace could be heard saying as he got off the elevator.

As Wallace turned the corner, he accidentally bumped into a young couple who were on their way to meet with a prosecutor in the Office of the US Attorney. With loose papers flying in the air, Wallace and the young couple bent down to pick up the various letters and legal notices. When Wallace happened to see that the correspondence had come from the Department of Justice, he said almost apologetically, "I hope you're not in trouble."

"As a matter of fact, we are," the couple said almost in unison.

"I'm sorry. I didn't mean to be intrusive, but I'm a criminal defense attorney. If I can be of any assistance to you, I would be pleased to be of service."

"Have you had dealings with the US Attorney?" asked the attractive female who was getting almost all of Wallace's attention.

"As a matter of fact, my law practice is geared specifically to federal and state white collar criminal defense work. I couldn't begin to tell you how many cases because I've been practicing law for about fifty some odd years. In fact, I'm almost three times as old as many of the young prosecutors that I have to go up against."

"We have something of a problem and we don't have a lawyer," said the man who identified himself as Fred Lawson. "This is my wife, Mona," Fred said as they shook hands with Wallace.

"If I can impart one piece of advice, you shouldn't meet with anyone in the US Attorney's office without a lawyer to advise you. Legal representation is a necessity if you are either the subject of an inquiry or the target of a criminal investigation."

"You're right. We tried to hire a lawyer but no one wanted to take our case," said Mona.

Rubbing his left hand over his mouth as if he were salivating at the prospect of picking up a client at the eleventh hour was too good to be true. Wallace's mind was now exploring all of the possibilities. In essence, Wallace would not be expected to know the facts in the case. Thus, not knowing the facts could not be held against him if he escorted his new clients into the US Attorney's office in the next few minutes. Consequently, Wallace had deniability from accusations that he was ill-prepared for the meeting.

Equally important, Wallace could collect legal fees for essentially doing nothing. The prospect of billing a client for holding their hands for an hour was a gift that he couldn't pass up.

"I make it a practice to limit the number of clients I accept to just a few at a time so I can focus on each client's problem. That way, I can be best prepared should the case go to trial. However, I would prefer to explore all viable alternatives to trial because I find that it is generally in the best interests of all concerned to resolve legal disputes out of court. With that in mind, I would be willing to be of assistance in reaching an out-of-court settlement with the US Attorney."

In no time at all, Fred and Mona have thanked Wallace profusely for his kind assistance. However, before they enter the reception area of the Office of the US Attorney, Wallace has Fred and Mona sign a Power of Attorney form that Wallace miraculously found in his briefcase. In addition, Wallace has informed the young couple that his hourly billing rate is four hundred and fifty dollars, with a four hour minimum for his time. Wallace goes on for a few more minutes addressing certain disclaimers for legal purposes. Finally, Wallace states that he cannot guarantee favorable results and cannot be held responsible for the eventual outcome. To set the stage for discouraging Fred and Mona from pursuing a trial, Wallace adds that his hourly rate in court increases to six hundred dollars an hour.

As Fred and Mona seem to be in an awkward position, they reluctantly agree to Wallace's terms, sign the Power of Attorney and write a check in the staggering amount of eighteen hundred dollars, which Wallace greedily stuffs in the pocket of his suit.

Sitting across the conference room table from Wallace, Fred and Mona is Kate Odom, a veteran of six months as a federal prosecutor. Wallace is very much relieved that the prosecutor sitting across from him is not Anne Marlowe.

When Wallace casually inquired how long Kate had worked in the US Attorney's office, he practically jumped for joy upon hearing the words, "six months." However, in the span of six months, Kate knows far more about criminal law than

Wallace. This will not be a fair fight and Wallace's glee will be short-lived.

"Mr. Shadybrook, I'm looking at your Power of Attorney and see that it bears today's date. If you don't mind my asking, when were you retained as counsel?" Kate asked as she raised an eyebrow in concern that Wallace is not prepared for this meeting.

"Just a few minutes ago," replied Wallace, who rated Kate an improvement over Anne in the looks department by a wide margin. However, this was not a beauty contest and no one anointed Wallace to be the head judge.

"Hmmm. Are you familiar with the facts in this case?" inquired the attractive prosecutor, who was dressed in a fashionable matching jacket and skirt that accentuated her shapely figure.

"I'm afraid not," Wallace replied. This was one of the few true statements coming out of Wallace's mouth.

Leaning forward and placing her forearms on the conference room table, Kate was close enough to Wallace that he could take in the pleasant scent of her perfume. "Perhaps it would be helpful if I briefly summarized the relevant facts so you will know what's going on," volunteered the attractive AUSA. Before Wallace could nod his head, Kate started in by saying, "Approximately four years ago, your client borrowed twenty five million dollars from Chase Bank. The loan documents stipulated that the purpose of the loan was to provide necessary working capital for their business. In case you did not know, Mr. and Mrs. Lawson operated more than thirty five donut shops throughout the State of Maryland," explained the youthful looking prosecutor.

"Chase agreed to loan the money to Mr. and Mrs. Lawson on several conditions. The bank required that they personally guarantee repayment of the loan in the event that their company defaulted on the loan repayments. The bank required that Mr. and Mrs. Lawson, in addition to pledging the company's assets as collateral for the loan, also pledge their personal assets as security. Their personal residence was encumbered, as well as the equity in their luxury cars. Valuable artwork in their residence was also pledged as collateral for the loan. Once Chase was satisfied that sufficient assets were made available as security for the bank loan, the funds were given to your client," Kate added.

"Shortly thereafter, the company declared bankruptcy and all of the donut shops ceased operations. When the Lawsons failed to make the first monthly loan repayment, Chase informed them that they were in default of the loan agreement. After the Lawsons missed the second monthly payment on the twenty five million dollar loan, Chase wasted no time and sent a demand notice insisting that Mr. and Mrs. Lawson comply with the terms of the loan.

"Bank officials reminded the Lawsons that as guarantors, they were personally obligated to satisfy the loan repayments. An attorney retained by Chase sent a letter to the Lawsons explaining that they would be held personally liable for repaying the debt and encouraged them to make repayment arrangements without further delay.

"In response to this letter, the Lawsons sent a letter to Chase and informed the bank that because their company had filed for bankruptcy protection, the matter was an issue for the United States Bankruptcy Court. Apparently Mr. and Mrs. Lawson had forgotten about having personally guaranteed the twenty five million dollar bank note.

"Immediately following this letter, Chase learned that the Lawsons deposited twenty five million dollars into an offshore bank account in the Cayman Islands. Characterizing this as a fraudulent conveyance, Chase undertook efforts to recover the funds," Kate said.

A fraudulent conveyance is a civil cause of action that

typically arises in a debtor/creditor relationship. It is commonly asserted where the borrower has an outstanding debt obligation and attempts to transfer assets to either a third party or place property in nominee name in order to obstruct collection efforts. Typically, the transfer of assets may be designed to leave the debtor financially insolvent. In this particular instance, the Lawsons attempted to deposit the funds in an offshore account at the same time they liquidated their business. This convinced Chase to allege that the transfer was motivated by fraud.

"Chase initiated legal action against the Lawsons, which went on for several years. During this time, the matter was referred to arbitration. When an arbitrator ruled in favor of Chase, the Lawsons filed suit, alleging collusion among other things.

"What is particularly interesting is that during discovery, Chase obtained documents that show the Lawsons inquired into making a substantial cash deposit with their offshore bank prior to borrowing the funds from Chase. Documentation was also obtained that confirms a wire transfer of millions of dollars was going to be made. This paperwork is dated prior to the date the actual loan was made with Chase. Thus, the Lawsons never intended to use the twenty five million dollars for their donut shops.

"When Chase found out about this, bank officials filed a criminal complaint with the US Attorney, alleging bank fraud and theft by Fred and Mona Lawson. Soon thereafter, the Lawsons were indicted for bank fraud, mail fraud and a few other criminal offenses. Although they were granted bail, they were placed under restrictions not to leave the immediate metropolitan area as well as not to engage in any lending or borrowing transactions," Kate added.

Leaning back in her chair, Kate looked directly at Wallace to gauge the look on his face. What she saw was surprising because Wallace was not in the least bit perturbed by his client's guilt. However, without letting on, Wallace was very much concerned that the eighteen hundred dollar retainer would bounce like a basketball once he tried to deposit the funds in his bank account.

Placing the palm of his hand on Fred's shoulder so as to let him know that everything would be okay, Wallace said, "I assume we're here to talk about a dismissal of the criminal charges and work out a restitution agreement with Chase."

"Not exactly. We're here to discuss a plea agreement that would send the Lawsons to prison. Chase insists on full restitution of principal plus accrued interest, as well as the payment of its legal fees," countered the prosecutor.

"That's a bit harsh don't you think," Wallace said simply because he couldn't think of anything else to say. However, Wallace's more immediate concern was cashing a bogus check even though he has done nothing to justify legal fees of eighteen hundred dollars.

"I'm not going to waste any more time on this. At last count, you're the fifth lawyer who has appeared in this office on behalf of the Lawsons. Given the seriousness of the charges and the fact that they carefully concocted a plan to obtain funds under false pretenses, I'm not feeling any sympathy for what they did," Kate shot back.

"What are you offering?" Wallace asked.

"Fred goes to prison for seven years, while Mona agrees to a five year sentence. Full restitution plus the payment of interest must be made to Chase, as well as its legal fees. In addition, they must pay two hundred thousand dollars in fines to the federal government."

"Ouch. That's too harsh."

"I'll see you in court, counselor." Kate very quickly stood to let them know that the conference was over. However,

Wallace still had one more hand to play.

"Can I have a moment to discuss this with Fred and Mona?" Wallace asked.

"I'll be outside," Kate said as she intentionally looked at her watch to let them know that they were on the clock.

Kate gave Wallace two minutes before she came back into the conference room. Apparently there was a heated exchange between lawyer and client as Fred and Mona were not happy about Wallace playing a passive role.

"I've discussed the terms and conditions to a plea bargain with my client. The Lawsons feel that the terms you have demanded are too strict and have asked me to propose a counter offer. My counter offer would take into account restitution equal to ...."

"You can stop right there. I don't want to hear about partial restitution. Full restitution is required. And if you were thinking about sentences less than what I'm offering, you can forget about that also. I'm not playing games. If they don't take the deal, they can take their chances at trial," Kate exclaimed as she started to place her legal files in a box, which was a clue that the meeting was just about over.

Fred and Mona exchanged quick glances that suggested panic while Wallace played with his tie by first curling it and then uncurling it several times. Just as Kate was about to leave the room, Wallace said, "We'll agree to your terms."

"Fine," Kate said as she had pretty much reached her tolerance level with Wallace and his unscrupulous client. "I'll have my paralegal bring the plea agreement in for everyone's signatures."

In the next several months, Fred and Mona will be on their way to separate prison facilities where they will have time to wonder about their choice of a criminal defense attorney whose spirited legal defense seemed to lack some spirit. But, then again, they got exactly what they didn't pay for.

Chapter 19

"Five minutes. How about setting the bet at five minutes?"

"No way, Alex. Four minutes at the most," replied Mo Green.

The IRS's trial attorneys are having lunch in the small cafeteria that District Counsel shares with the employees in the Baltimore Appeals Office. The topic of discussion for the day is how long it will take for Judge Barton to rule against the IRS in Thad's case, which is scheduled to be the first case to be heard on the upcoming trial calendar, which starts on Monday.

"OK. Four minutes," Alex replies. "Who'll wager it takes less than four minutes?"

At that exact moment, Warren Simonsen has entered the room and says, "What should take less than four minutes?"

"Thad's trial," answers Alex.

"Are you talking about Kreempuff?" asks the District Counsel.

"You mean Kreempall," Alex corrects his boss.

"Right, Kreempall."

The Kreempall case involves a petition that was mailed on the ninetieth day, but was not delivered by a designated postal carrier. "Are you placing bets that our favorite trial judge will rule against us in under four minutes?" asked Warren.

"Boss, do you want in?"

With a pained expression on his face, the District Counsel says, "I seem to vaguely recall that conducting a gambling activity on government premises is prohibited by law. As members of our distinguished legal profession, you should know that engaging in such conduct violates the standards of conduct and raises serious concerns as to ethical lapses and poor judgment."

"Boss, do you want in or not?" he is reminded for a second time.

"Put me down for five dollars and I'll take the under," replies Warren, who has no desire to prevent his staff from having some fun at Judge Barton's expense.

"What about four minutes?" asks Thad as he walks into the room, carrying the lunch that his wife has prepared.

"We're placing bets that you're going down in under four minutes. Want in on the action?" asks Mo.

"I'll take that bet. Put me down for a dollar and I'll take the over," says Thad.

"One dollar? Are you sure you can afford to gamble one dollar?" asks Lindsay in jest.

"I wasn't sure if you'd go for anything less than one dollar, but I'm okay with that," says Thad in all seriousness.

"Do you need to talk this over with your wife before you make this commitment?" asks Alex.

Thad reaches into his pocket and pulls out a crumpled one dollar bill, places it on the lunch table and says, "I'm in."

"A fool and his money are so easily parted," says Lindsay.

"I've got a case that I shouldn't lose. The law supports my

position," Thad replies.

"True. But Barton will find a way to rule against you and he won't take long," Warren says as a matter of fact. "As soon as he hears that the petition was mailed on the last eligible day to do so, he'll ignore the fact that it was sent by a non-designated delivery service and justify his decision by saying that it is blatantly unfair to require a taxpayer to use certain designated delivery services."

"I know. But can he rule against me in under four minutes?" asks Thad, who appears to be more concerned with his bet than he is in losing the case.

"Yes. And he'll still have plenty of time to say how harsh and inequitable the IRS's position is on the subject. For that matter, he'll even have time to make a speech that the IRS's administrative pronouncement should be changed in order to alleviate any confusion as to what constitutes a qualified delivery service."

"I'm prepared to cite and read Notice 2004-83," offers Thad.

"Thad, you can stand before that turd and read The Bible, but it's not going to help," Mo points out.

"So am I the only one wagering that I can go over four minutes?"

"Thad, you're on an island all by yourself," Alex replies.

****

Today is the moment of truth for Thad. There is a total of fourteen dollars riding on whether his case will go beyond four minutes. Other than Thad, no one is betting it goes beyond four minutes given Judge Barton's propensity to rule against the IRS.

Standing before Judge Barton and glancing at his watch every few seconds, Thad is nervous even though he has only one dollar at risk. Standing several feet away from Thad are the Kreempalls. Mickey and Alice Kreempall know absolutely nothing about the Tax Court rules and procedures and couldn't care less. For that matter, Mickey and Alice know nothing about federal income tax matters. However, the Kreempalls are supremely confident that they will prevail in court because they believe that the IRS's position is blatantly unfair.

"Your Honor, this is a Motion for Summary Judgment. Respondent's position is that the petition was not timely filed within the requisite ninety day period and, as such, the Tax Court does not have jurisdiction," Thad says.

"Mr. and Mrs. Kreempall, do you understand that the IRS is asking that your petition be dismissed?" Judge Barton asks the petitioners.

"Yes, judge," the Kreempalls respond in unison. "Mr. Chudzinski was kind enough to explain all this to us," Mrs. Kreempall says.

"Very well. Mr. Chudzinski, please set forth your grounds for summary judgment," Judge Barton instructed the young trial lawyer.

Already glancing at the second hand on his watch to see how much time is remaining, Thad decides to drag this hearing out as long as he can. Before Thad begins his introductory comments, Lindsay turns to Alex and says, "I think he's stalling for time."

"No doubt, because he knows he has no chance in hell of getting past four minutes," Alex whispered to his fellow trial lawyer.

"Your Honor, Respondent mailed a Statutory Notice of Deficiency to the petitioners on April 8, 2011. The ninetieth day after Respondent mailed the notice was July 7, 2011, which happened to be a Thursday. The petition was received by the Tax Court and filed on July 12, 2011," Thad said as a matter-of-fact while he took a quick glance at his watch.

"Judge, the envelope in which the petition was received bears a FedEx US Airbill dated July 7, 2011, which the IRS has acknowledged is the ninetieth day following the date of the Notice of Deficiency. The problem is that the delivery service selected on the US Airbill is 'Express Saver Third Business Day,' which is not a designated delivery service," asserted Thad.

In order to spend a few more moments on the subject, Thad adds, "For the benefit of the court, the FedEx Airbill is a standard form completed by persons sending mail via FedEx within the United States." Judge Barton merely nods at this and motions with a slight wave of his hand for Thad to continue.

Sensing that the end is near, Thad decides to stall. Lindsay has picked up on this and says to Alex, "I think he's stalling."

"Your Honor, the Tax Court is a court of limited jurisdiction and may exercise jurisdiction only to the extent authorized by Congress. The court's jurisdiction to re-determine a deficiency is predicated on the issuance of a valid Statutory Notice of Deficiency and the timely filing of a petition. Upon issuance of a deficiency notice, the taxpayer has ninety days from the date the notice is mailed to file a petition." Thad has just wasted precious seconds in court by saying something that the judge already knows.

"Thank you for bringing this to my attention, Mr. Chudzinski," Judge Barton says with the requisite sarcasm as if he didn't know this. "The court would be most appreciative if you would address your grounds for dismissal of the petition."

"Of course, Your Honor. I merely wanted to be thorough," Thad replies, knowing that this will take up a few more precious seconds and will further annoy his fellow trial attorneys. "Judge, a petition that is received by the Tax Court after the expiration of the ninetieth day period is deemed to be timely filed if the date of the US Postal Service postmark stamped on the envelope in which the petition was mailed is within the time prescribed for filing." Thad turns to his co-workers in the audience and smiles because he just used up another fifteen seconds by saying something that did not have to be said. His fellow trial lawyers are not amused by Thad's cheap theatrics and do not smile back.

"Mr. Chudzinski, I believe you just stated the obvious. Is there something that I'm missing?" asked the judge.

"Your Honor, I'm getting to the critical point. Stalling to kill a few more seconds, Thad turns to Mickey and Alice Kreempall and with his left hand extended in their direction, Thad says, "The petitioners did not use the US Postal Service to send their petition to the Tax Court."

"Counselor, as I understand it, FedEx is a designated private delivery service. As such, it would be treated as timely mailing for purposes of section 7502(f)(1) of the Internal Revenue Code," says Judge Barton. "What seems to be the problem?" inquires the judge.

Taking a deep breath to take up more time, Thad responds by saying, "In IRS Notice 2004-83, the IRS updated the list of companies and classes of delivery service that constitute designated private delivery services for purposes of code section 7502. Effective with the 2005 tax year, only FedEx Priority Overnight, FedEx Standard Overnight, FedEx 2 Day, FedEx International Priority and FedEx International First are expressly identified as designated delivery services. The 2004 IRS Notice expressly states that FedEx is not designated with respect to any type of delivery service not expressly identified. Thus, 'Express Saver Third Business

Day' service is not a designated delivery service," Thad finally explained.

Before Judge Barton can say anything, Thad adds, "Judge, I have attached a copy of IRS Notice 2004-83 to my pleadings for your convenience." Thad is hoping that the judge will take the time to read Notice 2004-83. When Thad glances at his watch and turns to look at his compatriots in the row behind him, they each give him a venomous look because Judge Barton has now taken the time to read the notice in its entirety.

Once Judge Barton has finished reading the notice, he announces to the parties that Respondent's motion is granted. Hearing this, Thad is more shocked than Mickey and Alice Kreempall.

"We lost?" asks Mickey.

With a nod, Judge Barton says, "The Tax Court acknowledges that the result may appear harsh. However, the court cannot rely on general equitable principles to expand the statutorily prescribed time for filing a petition."

"That's not fair," exclaims Alice. "If we had used the US Postal Service, it would have been okay. But because we used FedEx, it's not okay? Is that what you're saying?"

"Yes. According to the IRS's requirements, the delivery service that you used has not been designated as a valid service for this purpose," replied the judge.

Thad is stunned because he had assumed that Judge Barton would have ignored the requirements set forth in IRS Notice 2004-83 and justified ruling in favor of the petitioners by concluding that it would have been an overly harsh result to require them to comply with an obscure administrative pronouncement that even he did not know about.

"However, you are not without judicial remedy," adds the

judge. "You may pay the tax, file a claim for refund with the IRS and if the claim is denied, sue for a refund in one of the appropriate federal courts." As there was nothing further that needed to be said, Judge Barton instructs his clerk to call the next case.

As Thad looks at his watch to see how he did with the time, Lindsay, Alex and Mo can't help but laugh. Thad not only won his bet, but also won the case.

Chapter 20

Henry Froehmann has a reputation as a lawyer who enjoys spending time in court. Henry enjoys being in court because he is good at arguing cases. Litigation also pays well.

The trial attorneys at the IRS know Henry by reputation. Henry's reputation is well-earned. He doesn't want to be bothered with pre-trial settlement discussions because he is not interested in resolving any disputes prior to trial. That's because Henry likes to be in court.

Henry Froehmann is a very successful litigator who has been practicing law for more than thirty two years. Henry is more feared than respected. Furthermore, Henry is more respected than he is liked.

Henry's client happens to be a very nice young lady who was the victim of an unfortunate accident. This case is not a case that the IRS had wanted to go to trial. However, with Henry Froehmann, it was a foregone conclusion that this case would go forward in litigation.

Henry is standing at his podium while anxiously waiting for Judge Barton to get to his case. Indeed, Henry can't wait for the case to start. In a matter of minutes, Henry will be called upon to present his case.

Opposing Henry Froehmann is Lindsay Cooke, who has yet to recover from the devastating decisions in the cases that she tried before Judge Barton in his first trial calendar. Anticipating an adverse ruling in this case, Lindsay will put in a token appearance and little else.

As the parties have stipulated to the facts, it is not necessary to call witnesses to testify. This trial will move along very quickly, with each side presenting a brief opening statement and their respective arguments. All bets are on Henry to prevail.

"Your Honor, my client was employed by a pharmaceutical firm from 1990 to 2002. In March of 1997, my client fell from her horse during a stadium jumping clinic and suffered a head injury which caused continuing episodes of severe fatigue, mental apathy, dizziness and nausea. My client's illness resulted in permanent disability and caused her to lose her job in May of 2002," Henry said.

"My client is one of six individuals in the mid-Atlantic region qualified to teach Eventing at the various competition levels. For the benefit of the court, the term 'Eventing' is an Olympic sport made up of three disciplines in which a horse and rider compete in dressage, stadium jumping and cross-country jumping.

"In 2000, my client purchased seventeen acres of land in Maryland in an area well known within the equestrian community for horse boarding, training and lessons. That same year, my client began operating a horse boarding and training facility for profit. Although income from the activities in 2000 was modest, it gradually increased as improvements were made to the property and my client was able to hire additional staff.

"By early 2006, my client had established a limited liability company to operate the property. My client currently earns approximately three thousand dollars per month from her LLC.

"Respondent contends in its deficiency notice that the horse boarding and training expenses are not deductible under section 212 of the Internal Revenue Code. To the contrary, it is my client's contention that these expenses are deductible under code section 212," Henry declares with a great deal of conviction because he is absolutely certain that his position is correct.

Turning to the IRS trial lawyer, Judge Barton inquires as to whether she would like to provide the court with an insight as to the basis for her position.

"Your Honor, Respondent contends that these expenses are non-deductible start-up costs under code section 195(a)." Lindsay pauses for a moment to let the judge ponder this code section.

Under Internal Revenue Code section 195, a start-up expenditure is defined as any amount paid or incurred in connection with any activity engaged in for profit and for the production of income before the day on which the active trade or business begins. In essence, the costs have been incurred in anticipation of such activity becoming an active trade or business.

Before the enactment of code section 195 in 1980, a taxpayer was required to capitalize investigatory expenses and start-up costs of a new business under the pre-opening expense doctrine. This rule was based on code section 162 and the clear reflection of income principle. Under this doctrine, a taxpayer could recover pre-opening expenses only by amortizing them over the life of the asset or deducting them as a loss when the asset is sold.

Noting that code section 195 was ambiguous and caused excessive litigation, Congress amended the statute in 1984. In amending the statute, Congress stated that it did so to avoid the controversy and litigation arising under present law with respect to the proper tax treatment of start-up costs by requiring expenses similar to those allowed to be capitalized. The purpose of the 1984 amendment to section 195 was to bring sections 162 and 212 into parity when determining whether an expenditure has been incurred in a start-up activity.

"It is Respondent's contention that the petitioner anticipated that her income-producing activities would eventually become an active trade or business. Thus, Respondent believes that any expenses paid or incurred in the income-producing activity must be capitalized," Lindsay asserted.

Without waiting for the judge to ask him to respond, Henry Froehmann did so. "Your Honor, Respondent's arguments fail for several reasons," Henry asserted. Without bothering to pause, Henry decided to take the offensive by declaring, "Ordinary and necessary expenses for all income-producing activities, whether under section 162 or section 212, are intended to be on equal footing. This means that the distinction between an ordinary expense and a capital expenditure should be applied in the same manner under both code provisions. Once the petitioner's section 212 activity has begun, the deduction being sought is not precluded by section 195, regardless of whether that activity is later transformed into a trade or business. This interpretation is consistent with section 195 and its legislative history," argued Henry.

Before Henry is finished, he will say the words "congressional intent" eighteen times within a span of two minutes. Henry will also refer to the parity between sections 162 and 212 to further emphasize why his client's horse boarding and training activities are deductible under section 212.

During this time, Lindsay has very little to say because she believes that Judge Barton will rule in Henry's favor.

At the conclusion of arguments by both sides, Judge Barton has issued another stunning ruling by holding in favor of the IRS. Lindsay was so stunned by this ruling that she did not know what to say, so she said nothing. For his part, Henry had quite a lot to say.

"Judge, did you just rule against my client?"

"Yes, Mr. Froehmann, I did. Court is now in recess," Judge Barton announced as he quickly stood and exited the courtroom. Henry grabbed his briefcase, collected his files and made a mad dash for the exit door in order to catch up to Judge Barton, who was already long gone.

Failing to find the judge, Henry returned to the elevator where Lindsay was standing. "Do you believe that?" asked Henry.

"Personally, I'm not shocked by anything that man does," replied Lindsay. "Perhaps he's trying to atone for his prior mistakes," theorized Lindsay.

"Maybe. But if he is, why does he have to do it to my client?"

****

Wallace has readily agreed to represent Richard Cahill in his tax evasion case. Although Wallace doesn't know jack about criminal tax litigation, he is not going to let this stand in his way to make a quick buck at the expense of a client who was foolish enough to hire him in the first place. Besides, Wallace has no intention of actually defending his client in court. It is Wallace's plan to collect his retainer and negotiate a plea agreement as quickly as possible. The less time Wallace has to devote to this case, the better. This is particularly true if Wallace does not have to spend any time going over the facts and getting up to speed on the relevant case law.

****

"Warren, I know that we've discussed this before, but do you really want me to argue the Manning case in court?"

"Lindsay, we all have sacrifices that we have to make throughout our careers. This is one of those sacrifices I'm asking of you."

"You're using me as a sacrificial lamb."

"Your case is a classic example of IRS abuse of discretion. Judge Barton won't waste five minutes on this hearing. I have five bucks riding on it. He'll immediately rule against you, citing abuse of discretion. In the grand scheme of things, it's another ruling against us, but deservedly so. Just keep in mind that it's for the greater good."

"My going down in flames is for the greater good?" Lindsay asked her boss.

"In the grand scheme of things, it is. The cases that we're sending to Barton are the ones that we should lose. We're doing this to get those cases out of the way so that we have a legitimate chance to the win the other cases that we should win," explained the District Counsel.

"Makes perfect sense to me," Lindsay remarked as she returned to her office to pick up the files that she'll need in court.

Chapter 21

Lindsay is about to be called to argue the Manning case. This hearing is a Motion for Summary Judgment which should be denied in record time. Last week, bets were placed that this hearing would not go more than three minutes as this was considered to be the worst case the IRS could ever take to trial. However, with Barton issuing several unexpected decisions in favor of the IRS of late, the betting line is now up to five minutes.

Lindsay had not bothered preparing for this hearing because there is nothing for her to say that could possibly justify the IRS's actions. Making her way into court, Lindsay has the feeling that she will soon be named the worst person on the face of the earth for what she is about to do.

Seated opposite Lindsay is the petitioner, Alicia Manning and the young law student assigned to represent her in court.

Matt Noland is a third year law student who attends the University of Baltimore Law School at night. Matt is enrolled in the tax workshop program for law students and has been given this assignment by the director of this program. It is customary for law schools to offer a tax workshop program where its students can obtain practical experience working on actual cases under the supervision of an experienced attorney whose practice involves tax controversy work. The tax workshop program at the University of Baltimore is designed so that individuals who lack the financial resources to retain the services of a lawyer can obtain legal help at no cost from the law school.

Even though the law students are not members of the bar,

they are specifically permitted by exception to practice before the Tax Court in such cases. As a formality, the supervising attorney will be available to assist each law student when the case is called for trial.

Matt has handled a total of two cases in his brief career. While somewhat nervous due to the fact that he is going up against an experienced and well respected lawyer, Matt has been advised by his law instructor that the facts and law are in his client's favor and that the judge should clearly recognize this. The fact that this particular judge has already demonstrated an overwhelming bias against the IRS in his first trial session is also beneficial to the petitioner.

Once the proper salutations have been made and the parties arguing this hearing have stepped forward, Judge Barton inquires if Matt is ready.

Wasting no time, Matt begins by saying, "Your Honor, this is an incredibly tragic case. Ms. Manning resides in an apartment which she rents for six hundred dollars per month. Ms. Manning previously submitted a Collection Information Statement to the IRS, indicating that she had monthly income of eight hundred dollars and monthly expenses of the same amount. Consequently, Ms. Manning has no net disposable income and a total of fourteen dollars in cash on hand. Furthermore, Ms. Manning owns a 1996 Toyota Corolla with over two hundred and forty three thousand miles and has a fair market value of three hundred dollars."

Matt has intentionally referred to his client by her name rather than saying the words "client" or "petitioner." By doing so, Matt intends to humanize her as best he can.

Matt decides to pause for a moment in order to let the judge absorb the gravity of his client's financial condition. He then adds, "Ms. Manning has been diagnosed with pulmonary fibrosis and is dying. As a result of her poor health, she can only find part-time employment. At the present time, Ms.

Manning is working part-time doing janitorial work at a strip mall where she can take her three year old daughter because she cannot afford day care."

Matt has decided to take a longer pause at this time so that the judge can fully appreciate his client's predicament. At this point in the hearing, Lindsay is silently cursing her boss for ordering her to litigate this case. Lindsay has made a mental note to strangle Warren when she returns to her office.

"Your Honor, I would also like to state for the record that Ms. Manning has suffered domestic abuse throughout most of her marriage. She is now a single parent and responsible for the care and financial support of two young children. Without financial assistance from Social Services, Ms. Manning would be so financially destitute that she would not be able to provide for the basic care of her children."

Upon hearing this, Lindsay wonders how long it will take for Judge Barton to declare that everyone in the courtroom should take out their wallets and give whatever cash they have to Alicia Manning. Cognizant that her boss is not in the courtroom to hear this tragedy, Lindsay is prepared to go over each point with Warren before she strangles him.

"This case is about a levy action that does not have to be taken. It is an abuse of discretion to do so in light of the above facts. Ms. Manning owes the IRS less than ten thousand dollars but is unable to pay this amount. If Ms. Manning's wages are levied on, she will be unable to pay her reasonable basic living expenses. Furthermore, if her car is levied on, she will be unable to work," Matt adds.

If a taxpayer is liable for federal taxes and fails to pay the taxes within ten days after notice and demand, the IRS is permitted by statute to collect the tax by filing a lien or levy. If the IRS has determined that enforced collection action is creating an economic hardship due to the taxpayer's financial condition, the IRS must release its levy on all or part of a taxpayer's property. The rationale for this decision is that a levy would create an economic hardship if it causes a taxpayer to be unable to pay his or her reasonable basic living expenses. Matt intends to hammer this point home.

"Your Honor, Ms. Manning meets the criteria to have her account reported as currently not collectible because of financial hardship. This is in accordance with the Internal Revenue Manual. In addition, I would like to point out that the Income Tax Regulations also require a release of a levy that creates a financial hardship regardless of the taxpayer's compliance with filing required tax returns," Matt emphasizes for good measure.

"Judge, I would like to close by saying that Respondent's Motion of Summary Judgment should be denied because the IRS's decision to proceed with the filing of a levy is wrong as a matter of law. When a taxpayer establishes in a pre-levy collection hearing that the proposed levy would create an economic hardship, it is unreasonable for the IRS to proceed with the levy."

As Matt turns to take his seat, he looks to his law professor who gives him a "thumbs up" sign in admiration for his performance. "Matt, you were excellent. You addressed all of the main points and made extremely compelling arguments. I can't see how we can lose."

As Matt took his seat, Alicia Manning whispered in his ear, "Did we win?"

"Not yet. The IRS trial attorney is about to argue the government's position."

"Then the judge will rule in our favor?"

"That depends on how persuasive the IRS's arguments are," Matt whispered to his client. Although confident that he will prevail, the young law student is not about to declare victory before the other side has presented its case.

"Ms. Cooke?   Would you care to offer a rebuttal?"

"Your Honor, Respondent moves for summary judgment on the grounds that the IRS did not abuse its discretion in rejecting collection alternatives and determining to proceed with levy action because the petitioner was not in compliance with her filing obligations.

"There is no record that the petitioner had filed tax returns for the two most recent tax years.   Respondent issued a Notice of Determination to proceed with enforced collection action when it was apparent that the petitioner had not filed the required tax returns. If a taxpayer is not in compliance with his or her filing requirements, there is no abuse of discretion," added Lindsay as she returned to her seat, fully expecting to lose.

Expressing concern for Alicia Manning's financial and medical predicament, Judge Barton spends the next few moments explaining the rules governing the IRS's collection due process procedures. He then concludes the hearing by ruling in favor of the IRS, thereby shocking every person in his courtroom, including the court stenographer, bailiff and his clerk.

Lindsay is so stunned that she won that she shook her head as if she had been dreaming. "What the hell just happened?" Lindsey mouthed the words to no one in particular.

Alex Hill, who was seated behind Lindsay, said, "I'm not sure what the hell just happened."

That comment was repeated when Lindsay returned to her office and stopped in to see her boss. "Say that again?" Warren said.

"Judge Barton ruled in favor of my motion, which should not have been granted. That poor woman sitting there in court...... I felt so bad for her. She's destitute, dying and has no way to care for two young children. What a tragic life.

And we couldn't grant her relief? I can't believe that we took this pathetic case to trial and walked away with a ruling in our favor. This is awful, Warren."

"I know," exclaimed Warren with a sense of frustration in his voice. "You were not supposed to win. This doesn't make any sense. The cases we should win, we don't. And the cases that we should lose, we wind up winning. Barton's driving me nuts."

"What are you going to do about Alicia Manning? What happened in court isn't fair," Lindsay said.

"I'll call the Chief of the Collection Division and ask him to have Ms. Manning's account placed in uncollectible status. Let her student lawyer know that no collection action will be taken."

"And what about Barton?" Lindsay asked.

Warren simply shakes his head as if he doesn't know what to make of this.

"I have difficulty believing that he's now on our side. Do you think he found out about the investigation being undertaken by Senator Stevens and is trying to weasel out of an impeachment proceeding?" asked Lindsay.

"He couldn't have. According to the senator's senior aide, the investigation hasn't started yet."

"What's taking so long?"

"When I last spoke with Lawrence Jenkins, he advised me that the senator's focus is on other matters that impact national security. Apparently a misguided judge who happens to be somewhat arbitrary doesn't pose a threat to our national security."

"We could tell the FBI that Barton's a homicidal maniac

who's doing a really bad job of impersonating a judge," Mo Green chimed in as she stepped into Warren's office.

"That's a really good thought, Mo," Warren said tersely, as he went back to shuffling papers in a legal file.

"I know."

Chapter 22

CID Special Agents Matthew Birk and Raymond Lewis have been assigned the Richard Cahill case. The investigators have reviewed Louie's audit files and have carefully read his internal memorandums in support of the criminal tax charges.

Before a case is sent to CID, the IRS will have its fraud referral specialist review the file to approve the referral. This person is responsible for making sure that the case has the essential elements of criminality and meets the criteria for criminal prosecution. After the case has been referred to CID, it is further evaluated by its criminal investigators as to whether it should be accepted.

Once CID decides to accept the case and later concludes that the matter warrants prosecution, the files will be sent to the Justice Department. If the Justice Department accepts the case for prosecution, the taxpayer who is the subject of the criminal investigation will be charged with having committed a criminal offense. The charging documents will be in the form of an Indictment or Information.

In light of the levels of review and strict standards for criminal prosecution, only a small percentage of cases are selected for prosecution. Given Richard Cahill's strong desire to evade the payment of tax and Wallace Shadybrook's approach to practicing law, this case will soon be on its way to a federal courthouse.

Special Agents Birk and Lewis are sitting in Wallace Shadybrook's run-down office and wondering why a lawyer would want to work in an office that is in such deplorable condition. However, Wallace has no desire to spend money on a nice office when he has very few clients, of whom none are innocent.

In Wallace's mind, there is nothing wrong with furniture that was purchased from The Salvation Army. In addition, Wallace believes that torn carpeting is a good thing because it is a sign that there is heavy foot traffic in his office. There is no secretary or receptionist on staff because no one will work for Wallace. It is fair to say that Wallace objects to paying someone to perform clerical functions when he can do this himself and charge a client more than four hundred dollars an hour to file papers and print a legal document that any paralegal could prepare.

While the agents wait in the small sitting area outside Wallace's office, the lawyer pretends that he is discussing important legal matters with one of his many clients. In actuality, Wallace is placing bets with his bookie, which takes precedence over anything else.

When Wallace eventually terminates the phone call, he greets the agents as if they are his best friends by offering them refreshments that consist of week-old donuts and stale coffee. Wisely, the criminal investigators decline the generous offer because they do not want to have to write a report that Wallace may have attempted to murder them via food poisoning. Wallace will soon find out that the criminal investigators are not his best friends.

Once the special agents have briefed Wallace as to all housekeeping matters and have made it a point to ask Wallace if he understands what they have just said, Special Agent Birk begins by asking Wallace background questions concerning Richard Cahill's tennis career. Annoyed that the agents are going to ask background questions that will take up his valuable time, Wallace interrupts by saying, "I'm prepared to discuss a plea bargain at this time. Where are we on a range?"

The special agents are stunned by Wallace's suggestion that they discuss terms of a plea bargain. "Sir, we are in the preliminary stage of a criminal investigation. Your client has not been charged with any crimes as of yet. I think it's a little premature to begin discussing a plea bargain. Besides, this type of negotiation would be handled by officials at the Justice Department," Special Agent Lewis said.

"C'mon guys, let's not waste time on this investigation. Between the three of us, we all know my client's got dirty hands," exclaims Wallace. Upon hearing this admission, the agents look at each other in absolute bewilderment that a lawyer would throw a client under the bus at any stage of an investigation.

"Fellas, I don't want to get bogged down in this mess. Just give me a number," Wallace says as if he were standing in a bakery anxious to be waited on by the person behind the counter.

"What are you talking about?" asks Special Agent Birk.

"I want a number I can take to my client."

The special agents are still puzzled as to where Wallace is going so they give him looks as if he needs to elaborate on this theme.

"I want to know how many years my client is looking at," Wallace demanded to know.

"You're asking us about a prison sentence and we haven't even started our inquiry. I think it would be a good idea to wait until we've made a determination as to guilt" Special Agent Lewis suggested.

"Why?"

"This isn't how CID works. We investigate, determine if the subject of our investigation is guilty of a crime, and then we refer the matter to the Department of Justice for concurrence. If the Justice Department accepts the case, then you'll have an opportunity to enter into plea discussions. Until this happens, it's not necessary to pursue this matter," explained Special Agent Birk.

"So you're going to sit here and ask me silly questions about my client's tennis career?" Wallace asked.

Upon hearing this, Special Agent Lewis turned to his partner as if to say, "No. We thought we'd exchange recipes for baking brownies and discuss some of our favorite books, if that's okay with you." Instead, the agents bite their tongues and decide to play this strictly by the book.

"That's correct. We'll need to go over a number of factual matters," remarked Special Agent Lewis.

"A number of factual matters?" Wallace is clearly not happy that this investigation is going to take up his time.

"That's correct. We need to cover quite a bit of ground. This is going to take time," said the investigator.

"Jesus, this is not what I had in mind," replied Wallace.

"What is it that you had in mind?" asked Special Agent Birk out of curiosity.

"Fellas, I just wanted to wrap this up now without getting too involved in this mess. I don't know jack shit about the life of a tennis pro. Whatever my client did, I don't want to know," Wallace said in confidence to the agents sitting across from his desk.

"You're the attorney of record and until your Power of Attorney is rescinded, we have to deal with you. We have a lot of questions for you so let's get started."

For the next twenty minutes, Special Agents Birk and

Lewis practically interrogated Wallace by asking him questions about Richard Cahill's tennis career. The agents alternated asking questions about Cahill's playing career, his endorsements and promotional activities, and the contractual arrangements that he has with corporate sponsors and tennis promoters. The agents also told Wallace that they intend to pursue other matters such as various other commercial endorsements that do not involve tennis.

When it became readily apparent that Wallace didn't know squat about Richard Cahill, the agents turned their tape recorder off and told Wallace that they are disappointed that he is wasting their time.

"You were asked to be prepared to answer questions as to background information. So far, you haven't provided adequate responses to the most basic questions," interjected Special Agent Lewis.

"My sincere apologies," offered Wallace, whose apology was not sincere in the least.

"Call your client and get him on the phone. We need to hear from him," an annoyed Special Agent Birk instructed the lawyer.

"I don't know how to reach him," Wallace said.

"What do you mean you don't know how to reach him? He is your client, right?"

"I'm Cahill's lawyer, but I never dealt with him. I was hired by another attorney," admitted Wallace.

"That would be Chatsworth Symington?" asked Special Agent Lewis.

"Right. Chatsworth is Cahill's personal attorney. He handles Cahill's business dealings. Chatsworth retained me to handle any IRS problems."

"Call Chatsworth now," the agents said in unison.

It took Wallace almost ten minutes to get Chatsworth Symington, III to take his call. Once Wallace explained the urgency in getting Richard Cahill to call him, Chatsworth agreed to track Cahill down and ask him to call Wallace. After almost twenty five minutes had passed, Richard Cahill called Wallace.

"Before you say anything, you're on a speakerphone and I have two criminal investigators from the IRS in my office that want to talk to you," Wallace cautioned his client.

"What do they want to talk to me about?" Cahill asked as if he hadn't a clue that he was the subject of a criminal investigation.

"The agents are looking into whether your income tax returns warrant criminal prosecution. There are questions as to whether you failed to report hundreds of thousands of dollars in appearance fees. The agents want to know about your contractual agreements with tennis promoters as well as other business matters. They also brought up some questions about some business expenses. Apparently they have a lot of questions and I'm not prepared to provide responses to their questions," Wallace said.

"Look, I didn't prepare the tax returns. I'm just a tennis player for crying out loud. The IRS should be asking these questions of my accountant," Cahill said.

"Mr. Cahill, this is Special Agent Birk. We have already interviewed your accountant. At this stage of our investigation, we need to interview you."

"If you've already interviewed my accountant, why is it necessary that you interview me? Don't you have the answers to your questions?"

"In a criminal investigation, it is often necessary to interview multiple parties to ensure that the information that has been provided is correct," replied the investigator.

"Was my accountant not truthful?" asked Cahill.

"We cannot say with absolute certainty whether the information he provided is accurate because we are still attempting to verify the authenticity of documents and corroborate his oral testimony. Is there a problem in talking to us?" asked Special Agent Birk.

Hesitating for far too long, Cahill eventually says, "No, of course not." What Cahill really means is that he has no desire to be interviewed by criminal investigators who believe that his tax returns are fraudulent.

"Good. This is Special Agent Lewis. I suggest that you make yourself comfortable because we have a lot of material to cover."

At this point, Richard Cahill is less than pleased with his lawyer because the investigators intend to ask him questions that will prove to be incriminating. As the interview slowly turns into an interrogation, it is becoming increasingly clear that the subject of this interview will be the target of a criminal prosecution as Cahill is soon indicted for tax evasion.

In stark contrast, Wallace is secretly hoping for an indictment because he is anxious to negotiate a plea bargain and cannot do so until his client has been charged with a tax crime. As the interview moves along at a snail's pace, Wallace is wondering what he can do to speed things up.

Chapter 23

Ralph Elwood senses that his legal difficulties have taken a turn for the better. While sitting in a holding cell with nothing to do until he goes to trial, Ralph has been advised that the DA is transferring jurisdiction of his case to the Department of Justice.

"Does that mean I'll be dealing with the US Attorney?" Ralph asks the prosecutor who is washing her hands of this case.

"A representative of that office plans to stop by and speak with you in the next day or so."

"To cut a deal?" asks Ralph.

"I don't believe so."

"Then what?"

"You'll be informed as to the federal charges and the status of your case. Arrangements will be made to have you taken to a federal detention center and arraigned in the United States District Court of the new charges," explained the Assistant District Attorney.

"So when do they cut the deal with me?"

"I don't believe the US Attorney is looking to cut a deal with you. But, I'm just an Assistant District Attorney so I'm not the best person to ask about these things," said the prosecutor as she left Ralph Elwood to consider his fate.

****

"Amy, what's this?" Robert Templeton yelled out as he picked up a file that was placed on his desk with a post-it note.

"That's an old office file on the Watkins deferred annuity going back thirty years. Now that the annuity has been paid off, what do you want us to do with the file?" asked the statuesque administrative assistant whose perfume today had a more exotic aroma than usual.

"Good question," replied the financial advisor as he started to browse through the paperwork in the folder.

Taking in the exotic scent of his assistant's perfume, he said, "That's odd," as he looked up.

"What's that?" asked his long-legged assistant.

"I was under the impression that the annuity was purchased in August, when in fact, the paperwork indicates that it went into effect in March."

"Oh, you know what must have happened? The number three looks like the number eight and it gets confusing at times," replied Amy.

"I think you're right," Templeton quickly agreed. "Oh well, it's nothing of consequence that I would want to bother Judge Barton about so forget I said anything."

"It's forgotten," replied his assistant.

"Good. As far as I'm concerned, you can shred the file."

Chapter 24

"Dr. Duggleman, please explain your reasons for purchasing the thirty five acre farm in New Market." This question has been asked by Trent Stratford, noted tax lawyer and staunch defender of the wealthy.

"Certainly," replied the client who has taken the witness stand in his tax case. "My wife and I purchased the farmland in 1995 and beginning in 2000, we decided to breed, train and market high quality sport horses by refining and improving Hanovarian style horses by using both traditional and state-of-the-art breeding techniques in a boarding facility where they could train. My wife and I believed that because the farm is located in a classic historic setting, it would enhance the marketability of our horses."

"What was your motivation for engaging in a breeding activity?"

"My wife and I both grew up on farms. Although we both practice medicine, we decided years ago to explore alternatives to the practice of medicine out of concern that the medical profession is being adversely affected by government intervention, managed care and HMO's. After doing extensive research, we concluded that the breeding of horses could be an economically feasible alternative to practicing medicine."

Trent Stratford was able to refrain from laughing at his client's response because he knew the answer to his question. With a straight face, he then asked, "What type of research did you undertake?"

"We started the process by taking several collegiate courses offered at the University of Maryland with respect to the care and breeding of horses and read a number of books on the subject of breeding. The instructor who taught in this program advised us as to the fundamentals of breeding and gave us the names of recognized authorities in the field."

"So your college instructor gave you an insight into the best types of mares to breed and different methods of breeding?"

"Yes. However, he encouraged us to conduct numerous studies in order to first determine which types of horses to breed. We later met with noted veterinarians and breeders to discuss various options. Based on the advice of Dr. Wilhem Schmidt, who is considered to be one of the leading veterinarians in the world, we chose a warmblood horse for breeding purposes. We traveled to Munich to meet with Dr. Schmidt as part of our preliminary investigation."

"Then what did you do?" inquired the lawyer.

"We then traveled to Lucerne and met with Hilda Kleinsdorf, who is a world famous breeder. We discussed the breeds that have the best qualities and characteristics that we felt would be the most cost effective. Ms. Kleinsdorf recommended that a warmblood horse such as the Hanovarian breed is considered most desirable because of its temperament and ease of handling."

"Did you do any further investigative research?"

"Yes. We later met with Della Calloway who is an accomplished trainer in Pennsylvania. We discussed the supply and demand for horses, ease of training and prices for different breeds. Ms. Calloway told us that warmblood horses were the most desirable and that the Hanovarian breed generally wins the most prizes at international horse shows. Thus, these types of horses would generate the highest prices," explained the petitioner.

"What did you do after you met with Ms. Calloway?" asked Trent.

"We did some more research and contacted more trainers and breeders within the Mid-Atlantic area to get an idea as to the approximate breeding costs. The following year, we traveled to Germany in order to attend seminars that were sponsored by professional trade groups that included trainers and breeders on the breeding of Hanovarian horses," explained the petitioner.

"Did you speak with experts while in Germany?"

"Yes. In addition to speaking with the individuals who taught the seminars, we were fortunate to be able to meet with noted authorities in the field of horse breeding. We obtained the names of these individuals from the sponsors of the seminars and met with them following the seminar."

"What advice, if any, were you given?"

"We were advised to purchase high-grade sperm for purposes of artificial insemination. My wife and I then purchased sperm from our Hanovarian breeding source in Germany. Before we returned to the United States, we had to learn how to impregnate our stock with the Hanovarian sperm," the petitioner testified.

"I see. I assume that this process required extensive research," the lawyer prompted his client.

"Most definitely. My wife and I did an exhaustive search as to which veterinarians were best qualified to assist in the breeding process."

"And which veterinarian did you decide to use?"

"We eventually decided on Dr. Tomas Czernik. Based on our research, Dr. Czernik is considered to be one of the most qualified veterinarians in the nation with respect to artificial insemination and embryo transfer. According to the research that we did, Dr. Czernik had written extensively on the subject of artificial insemination and has pioneered the embryo transfer process," answered the petitioner.

"In what respect is Dr. Czernik a pioneer in this field?"

"Dr. Czernik uses a state-of-the-art method in the impregnation process. My wife and I were of the opinion that by using the veterinarian with the best reputation and the best possible sperm for breeding, this would enhance the probability for a successful business venture."

At this point, Trent Stratford was satisfied that his client had set the stage for the argument that the petitioners had thoroughly researched the breeding process and undertaken the appropriate steps to show that they conducted this activity with a bona fide profit motive.

Lindsay Cooke was not particularly keen on litigating this case. However, it was because the petitioners had refused to cooperate with the IRS that it became necessary to do so. Rather than ask questions about the artificial insemination of embryos, Lindsay's trial strategy was to get to the heart of the matter and she did so immediately.

"Sir, did you prepare a formal business plan prior to the time you and your wife started this activity?"

There is a long moment of silence before the petitioner finally admits, "No, we did not. We later prepared a business plan," replied the petitioner.

"Sir, I didn't ask you if you prepared a business plan after you started this activity. My question to you was whether you undertook the preparation of a formal business plan before the activity commenced," Lindsay said to the witness.

"Objection, Your Honor. Counsel is being argumentative. The witness has attempted to clarify his response," Trent

Stratford argued.

"Judge, my question didn't call for clarification," retorted Lindsay.

Placing the palm of his hand in the air to get everyone's attention, Judge Barton turns to the witness and says, "I am going to direct you to answer only the question that is being asked. If additional information is required, your attorney has the right to pursue this on re-direct."

"Did you prepare financial projections prior to starting this activity?" Lindsay asks, fully aware that in addition to not having prepared a business plan, the petitioners failed to prepare financial projections.

"No."

"Did you meet with a financial planner to discuss the economic viability of breeding horses before you started this activity?" Lindsay asked.

After deliberating for far too long, the petitioner finally says, "No." The petitioner does so with an icy glare that does not suggest happiness with the question.

"Did you ask a CPA to prepare a cost/revenue analysis for you?" Lindsay asks the petitioner, well aware that the response should be an emphatic no.

"No."

"Did you use cost accounting techniques in order to make informed business decisions as to the profitability of your horses?"

"No," answered an increasingly unhappy petitioner.

"Did you monitor your expenses or, in the alternative, maintain a budget?"

"No."

"Did you engage the services of an attorney to address what you needed to do to ensure that you would be engaged in an activity motivated for profit?" Lindsay asked.

"No."

"According to your records, you used different trainers on a periodic basis. Why?"

"My wife and I were serious about getting the best available training for our horses. That's why we frequently switched trainers," answered the petitioner.

"Isn't that an indication that you failed to carefully choose qualified trainers before you invested in this business?" Lindsay asked.

"No. I suppose you could infer that but we were constantly trying to upgrade the quality of our breed," answered the petitioner.

"Tell me something, Dr. Duggleman. What efforts did you undertake to improve operations from your horse breeding activity such as cutting costs and generating revenue?" Lindsay inquired.

"I'm sorry, I don't think I understand the question. Could you please re-phrase the question?" asked the petitioner, who was clearly not happy with the question asked of him.

"You and your wife have incurred substantial losses from your horse breeding operation on a yearly basis. What steps did you take to limit your operating expenses where appropriate and what steps did you take to generate more revenue?" Lindsay asked as she stepped back and waited for a response.

"My wife and I employed a sharecropper to farm the land.

We introduced the cultivation of soybeans with corn to reduce fertilizer expenses and improve crop yield. More rows of crops were planted in the available space to maximize crop production. We also considered various planting techniques and methods so as to maximize crop production, based on the theory that increased crop production would generate greater profits. We purchased grain storage bins to store crops when grain prices were low and then re-sold the grain in the spring when grain prices rose," explained the witness.

"What you are describing relates to a farming operation rather than a horse breeding activity. I want to know what you did to make your horse breeding activity profitable," clarified the IRS trial lawyer.

"We couldn't cut our costs because if we did, we wouldn't have the best mares. It's that simple," replied the petitioner.

"I suppose it is that simple. I have no further questions, judge," Lindsay said as she returned to her chair.

"Mr. Stratford, do you wish to re-direct?"

"I have just a few questions, Your Honor."

"Dr. Duggleman, did you obtain information from the experts whom you spoke with as to the financial costs involved in breeding horses?" asked Trent Stratford.

"Yes. Many of the individuals that we spoke to provided us with estimates as to what the costs would be if we used artificial insemination and embryo transfers with regard to high-end Hanovarian horses. These individuals had experience in that area and alerted us to the fact that such a process would be costly."

"Are you referring to those persons that you identified by name in your prior testimony?"

"Yes. Although these individuals are not accountants and

lawyers, they are actively involved in the breeding process as either breeders, veterinarians, or college instructors who teach and write books on the subject. I would think that these people would be far more knowledgeable than a lawyer or an accountant when it comes to operating a breeding operation," answered the petitioner.

"Why did you explore various crop planting techniques and methods as opposed to focusing on the breeding operation?" inquired Trent.

"We never ceased our efforts with regard to the breeding operation. My wife and I had always been committed to maintaining the highest quality of breeding mares. With respect to the planting of crops, we did it to generate greater profits. The additional revenue went towards subsidizing the breeding process. Look, my wife and I did what we could to ensure that the farm property could be used in a productive manner that would assist us to spend more money in breeding high quality mares."

Whereas Lindsay was able to undermine the petitioners' assertions that they took the necessary steps to ensure that they carefully investigated the profitability of operating a horse breeding activity, opposing counsel was successful in showing that the petitioners did not have to rely on a lawyer or accountant for sound business advice. In addition, the petitioners were successful in showing that the farm property was used to generate additional revenue. By the time Trent Stratford had finished asking his client to elaborate on the farming operation, Lindsay was having difficulty in raising doubt as to the manner in which the horse breeding activity was conducted.

Next, Trent Stratford had the petitioners' accountant testify as to how the gains and losses were determined with respect to the sale of the horses throughout the years in issue. Having the accountant testify that the sales proceeds had been reported correctly in each instance seemed to certify the accuracy of the tax returns.

However, Lindsay was able to show that in spite of the gains resulting from the sales, the petitioners still reported huge operating losses in each year. On cross examination, Lindsay had the accountant admit that there had never been a net overall profit.

Before the accountant was dismissed, Lindsay made it a point to ask him whether the petitioners honestly believed that they were going to realize a profit from their breeding activity.

"Of course," replied the accountant.

"Each year the activity was in operation?" Lindsay wanted to know..

"With the possible exception of the first and maybe second years, my client honestly believed that the horse breeding operation would generate a profit."

"A profit which would be subject to self-employment tax?" asked Lindsay.

"Yes," the accountant hesitatingly said. The witness correctly suspected that Lindsay would now be asking questions that might undermine his answer that his clients reasonably believed that their horse breeding activity would be profitable after the second year.

"Then please explain why the petitioners never remitted quarterly estimated taxes in any of the tax years following the first two years of the activity. For the record, this covers six tax years following the first two years in which you claim that the petitioners expected to generate a profit," asked Lindsay.

"I'm not sure I understand the question," the accountant said while shaking his head to emphasize his feigned confusion.

In actuality, the accountant understood exactly what Lindsay had asked him to explain.

Although Lindsay had expected this response, she raised an eyebrow as if to doubt the sincerity of the witness and said, "I'll clarify my question for you. If your client expected to earn a profit from breeding horses, the net gain would be subject to self-employment tax. However, no funds had been set aside to pay self-employment taxes. According to IRS records, the petitioners owed the IRS money in each year in issue. Therefore, my question to you is how could the petitioners have reasonably believed that they would realize a net profit and not set aside estimated taxes during any of the years they operated this activity?"

There is a very long period of silence before the witness finally says, "I don't know."

With that, Lindsay has made a small dent in the petitioners' case. However, with this judge's unpredictable rulings, Lindsay is of the opinion that it may not matter in the end.

Chapter 25

Mark Paul Warren's representation of Stan Lustman was a typical reflection of Mark Paul Warren's legal skills. Stan Lustman was quickly convicted of filing fraudulent tax returns, obstruction of justice and tax evasion. As a consequence, Stan Lustman will be spending the next seven or eight years in a federal penitentiary, depending upon how well he behaves.

It is only fitting that Stan Lustman has been assigned to share a cell with Dean Pappas. These two have a great deal in common and will soon become comrades-in-arms as they grow old together behind bars.

Dean Pappas was once a mega star housing developer who had a reputation for building custom homes in a matter of only a few days. Pappas had close ties to the senior executives at People's Bank & Trust Company, which provided him with the financing that he needed for his construction loans.

An informant provided the IRS with information that Dean Pappas had engaged in bank fraud and obstruction of justice with respect to his home construction activities. According to the informant, Pappas' title company handled the closing on all home purchases. At settlement, the home buyer's check was typically not applied against the mortgage that encumbered the property. Thus, the construction loan that Pappas had taken out to build each house remained in effect. The money that Pappas received at settlement was then deposited in separate accounts that Pappas had at People's Bank & Trust.

One of the purchasers discovered this when she was served

with legal papers advising her that liens had been filed against her home. When she learned that Pappas did not apply her check to pay off the first mortgage on her home, she contacted the Maryland State Attorney General's Office. Immediately after doing so, she wrote a letter to the IRS, which led to the audit of Dean Pappas.

Louie Lipschitz was assigned to handle the audit. At the onset of the audit, Louie examined the books and records of Dean Pappas and reviewed the many bank account statements that Pappas had at People's Bank & Trust. It didn't take Louie long to determine that Dean Pappas had constructive receipt of millions of dollars in his accounts, which had not been reported on his federal income tax returns.

At the conclusion of the criminal investigation, Dean Pappas was indicted for bank fraud and tax evasion. Although Pappas hired Victor Koslow to defend him in court, it was Victor's recommendation that his client enter into a plea agreement. Koslow eventually negotiated a plea bargain with federal prosecutors on behalf of Dean Pappas. The terms of the plea required full restitution and the payment of a one hundred thousand dollar penalty, with a prison term of ten years.

Dissatisfied with a ten year prison term, Dean Pappas decided to take out his frustration on those responsible for his unfortunate circumstances. Pappas conspired to murder the FBI agent who investigated the bank fraud. Not stopping there, Pappas decided to murder the assistant US Attorney who prosecuted his case. Next, Pappas plotted to murder the judge who was selected to hear the case and approved the plea agreement.

The key witness who would have testified against Pappas was Louie Lipschitz. Consequently, it only made sense to have Louie killed if everyone else was supposed to be murdered.

Finally, Dean Pappas decided to have Victor Koslow killed for the role that he played in this fiasco. Had Victor been able to negotiate a plea agreement that allowed his client to remain free with a sentence of only three years' probation, Pappas would have been satisfied that justice was served. However, Pappas felt that his lawyer failed him and for this reason, concluded that Victor Koslow must die.

While plotting to have four federal officials and his lawyer murdered, Dean Pappas confided in the wrong person. Tyrone Johnson, who shared a cell with Pappas, was a notorious snitch who made a career out of snitching on his fellow prisoners in order to obtain an early release. Tyrone passed the incriminating information on to law enforcement officials who were instrumental in Tyrone being granted an early release.

As a result of the information that detailed the conspiracy to have five people murdered, Dean Pappas was indicted while still behind bars. Resigned to the sad fact that he will need legal representation, Pappas hired the last lawyer on his list and blatantly lied by declaring how pleased he was that this person will be defending him against the attempted murder charges.

"You've handled these types of cases before?" Dean Pappas asked the lawyer.

"Of course. Criminal defense work is what I do."

"What's your track record?"

"Young man, it's difficult to quantify this because there are varying degrees of success," replied the lawyer who was not about to answer this question. "No attorney can be expected to prevail in every case. It doesn't happen like that in the real world. With some cases, just getting a sentence reduced to the point that the term is something the client can live with is enough of a victory."

"So what would your strategy be in my case?" asked Dean Pappas.

"If you are found guilty of the murder conspiracy charges, I would surmise that you would probably spend the rest of your life behind bars given the length of the prison term and your age. I find this prospect to be an unacceptable alternative for you."

"You haven't answered my question," replied Dean Pappas.

"To challenge the criminal charges in court would be counter-productive. Just based on what little information I've been given, the prosecution has a confidential informant who overheard you allegedly conspiring to have people murdered. There are witnesses who will corroborate this story, including prison guards who overheard your conversations. The testimony of the prison guards will be a problem for us. Prison officials planted an undercover FBI agent posing as an inmate who was about to be released. The undercover FBI agent has the list of names of people you want killed on a handwritten list that is in your handwriting. A video camera has you giving the handwritten list, which the FBI has analyzed as being your handwriting, to the undercover agent. That will also be a serious problem for us. Have I left anything out?"

"No. I think you've covered the relevant points."

"Good. I think after the FBI agent testifies against you, you'll be fitted for an orange jumpsuit with the words "PRISONER FOR LIFE" in big, bold capital letters on the back. By that time, the trial will be effectively over and your fate is sealed. And what exactly was it you wanted me to argue in court?"

"So you're telling me that I shouldn't go to trial?"

"Only if you want to die an old man in prison," replied the lawyer.

"What do you suggest I do?"

"Let me arrange a plea bargain with the prosecutor. As a precautionary measure, I intend to file a motion to have another prosecutor that you haven't put a murder contract on handle this matter. I also intend to ask the judge to recuse himself so that your case is assigned to a judge that you haven't attempted to have murdered. If you behave yourself in prison, you'll accumulate credits for good behavior so it won't be that bad."

For the next few moments, Dean Pappas said nothing as he stared about the room. He has considered the predicament that he is in and has evaluated his two options. Neither option looks appealing. Pappas also reflects on using this shyster to negotiate a plea bargain on his behalf.

"OK. How soon can you start working on a plea, Mr. Shadybrook?"

"I'm not that old. Call me Wally. And I'll start pressing the prosecutor for a plea agreement right away."

****

Wallace Shadybrook would soon find out that there would be no plea bargain for Dean Pappas. The US Attorney intended to prosecute him for the murder conspiracy charges unless Pappas pled guilty to all counts. In view of the fact that Wallace prefers not to appear in court, he intends to bamboozle his client into pleading guilty to all counts.

"Did you cut a deal like you said you would?" Pappas was anxious to know.

"What I said was that I would undertake my best efforts to

get you a reduction in sentence. I've accomplished that," Wallace lied.

"How much?" asked the client.

"The prosecutor insisted on forty five years on top of your current sentence. I negotiated it down to twenty five years. I seriously recommend that you take it," the lawyer said without any remorse that he had failed to act in the best interests of his client.

"Twenty five years? I'll never get out of here if I have to do twenty five years on top of the ten years already," pleaded Pappas.

"Are you kidding me? You'll do a total of twenty five if you behave. You're forty two years old. You'll be out in time to collect Social Security and Medicare benefits," Wallace argued.

"But I'll be sixty seven years old, if I live that long."

"And if you don't take the plea, you'll be eighty some years old after you've served the full sentence, provided you don't get consecutive life terms. What's it going to be?" asked the shyster.

"I want you to go back and re-negotiate. Get it reduced to fifteen years," Pappas ordered his lawyer, who had no intention of doing such a thing.

"You're asking me to do something that I find morally unconscionable," Wallace said with a straight face. "I negotiated your reduction in sentence in good faith. I finally persuaded the prosecutor to accept my offer, which he was most reluctant to do. After finally agreeing to a sentence of only twenty five years, this prosecutor is not going to accept an even lower sentence. What he will do is formally rescind his offer," said Wallace, who decided to let his client consider that for a few moments before he said anything else.

"Should the prosecutor formally rescind the offer, it is considered revoked. It is null and void and will not be offered again. You can't afford to pass this deal up," Wallace continued.

For the next twenty minutes, lawyer and client argued back and forth. Wallace could not afford to let his client know that there was never an offer of a reduced sentence. With the patience of a saint, Wallace finally convinced his client that the merits of doing twenty five more years outweighed the risk of dying in prison.

"OK. Tell the prick that I'll take the twenty five years," a dejected Dean Pappas instructed his unscrupulous lawyer.

****

After Dean Pappas had disclosed that it was Louie Lipschitz who discovered his income tax returns were fraudulent, Stan Lustman exclaimed, "Holy shit! Both of us are in prison because of Lipschitz. That bastard audited my tax returns."

"Oh yeah?" replied Dean.

"Yeah. I reported net earnings of fifteen thousand dollars a year when I was really raking in more than fifty million a year," Stan tells his cellmate.

"Holy shit!" What were you doing to make that kind of money?"

"I was involved in a variety of business ventures."

"What does that mean?"

"I dabbled in a few things," Stan continued to be vague.

"Like what?" asks a curious Dean Pappas.

"Running an international counterfeiting operation, selling fake antiques, distributing drugs, stuff like that," Stan shrugged as if it were no big deal.

"No kidding. I'm impressed," Dean acknowledges to his new friend.

"But, the one thing that I'm most proud of was my favorite," Stan remarked.

"What's that?"

"ID theft," Stan says.

"Huh? You stole people's identities?" exclaims Dean.

"That's right. Once I obtained names, dates of birth, and social security numbers, I had all of the personal information I needed. I could tap into lines of credit, withdraw money from bank accounts, and so forth. I could even file fictitious tax returns."

"Fake tax returns? You're kidding me!"

"Nope. I was filing close to a hundred tax returns each day for about three months. On average, I got a couple of thousand dollars for each fake return. You do the math. It was better than robbing a bank," Stan announces as if defrauding the federal government out of millions of dollars was an honorable act to which he should be proud.

It takes Dean Pappas almost a minute to do the math in his head, before he says, "You made approximately eighteen million dollars a year filing fake tax returns?"

"No. I actually made about eighteen million dollars in ninety days. I only did this for three months because that's all the time I had. By the end of March, it's too risky to file fake returns.

"But you got caught," Dean says.

"Dean, I got caught for other reasons. I didn't get caught for filing fake tax returns. If that IRS agent hadn't audited me, I'd be sipping martinis on a private beach in Hawaii, with nothing to worry about," Stan replies.

"Hey Stan, I just had an idea. We've got plenty of time to kill. Why not file phony tax returns in prison and have the refunds direct deposited to offshore accounts using nominees. As long as we can disguise ownership of the offshore accounts, the government will never be able to trace the money to us."

"Hmmmm. Maybe we can do that. Dean, I like the way you think."

Chapter 26

Mary Beth Phillips has been brought to her new residence. It is a female correctional institute and Mary Beth has been told that it will be her home for the next seven years. After Mary Beth has been strip searched, given a physical examination that is not covered by insurance, and taken to the showers for good measure, she is escorted by the guards to her cell.

After the guards drop Mary Beth off at her cell, the new inmate looks at her cellmate and says, "Which bed is mine?"

"I prefer to be on top, but we can switch off," replied her cellmate.

Unsure how to take that, Mary Beth merely says, "OK."

Stepping toward Mary Beth, the inmate says, "Here, let me help you with your things."

"That's okay, I can manage," Mary Beth says as she begins to feel extreme discomfort in such close quarters with someone who could have the word "PERVERT" etched on her forehead.

"I don't mind at all," says the cellmate as she places the palm of her hand on Mary Beth's ass and gives it a not so gentle squeeze.

Startled, Mary Beth tries to take a step back but is cornered by her taller and stronger cellmate. A reassuring hand is gently placed on Mary Beth's delicate shoulder. Before long, the hand is on Mary Beth's perfectly round breast. "You'll like it here," says Mary Beth's cellmate, as she returns to her bunk.

Resigned to the fact that she will be behind bars for the next seven years and sharing a bunk with this nymphomaniac, Mary Beth introduces herself.

"That's a nice name, Mary Beth," replies her cellmate. "I'm Erica. Erica Whitman."

After a few minutes of casual chit chat, Mary Beth asks Erica what type of crime she committed. Told that it's a long story, Mary Beth says she has seven years to hear it.

"First, I was sent to prison for conspiracy to defraud the federal government. I was convicted of accepting bribes when I was working for the IRS. When I was later tried for tax evasion, I was acquitted because my co-conspirator recanted her testimony in the first trial. As a result, I was given a new trial and acquitted of the original conspiracy charge," explains Erica.

"If you were found not guilty, why are you in prison?" asks a confused Mary Beth.

"I wanted to sue the federal government for sending me to prison."

"Because you were innocent," Mary Beth says.

"Actually, I wasn't really innocent," acknowledges Erica

"I don't understand. I thought someone lied and later told the truth so you were found not guilty."

"No. My co-conspirator didn't lie in the first trial. She lied when she testified in the second trial so I would be found not guilty," explains Erica.

"Why?" asks Mary Beth, who seems more confused than she was a moment ago.

"So I wouldn't have to spend the next ten years behind bars. Unfortunately, my plan didn't work out the way I had hoped," says Erica.

"What plan?"

"While I was in prison awaiting my trial on tax evasion charges, the warden asked me for some personal advice," explains Erica.

"Personal advice?" an even more confused Mary Beth asks.

"The warden's husband won a hundred million dollars in the lottery. The dipshit put the money in some kind of a bullshit Trust that she couldn't touch. They were experiencing some marital problems and if she divorced him, she'd walk away with next to nothing. So, I came up with what I thought was a brilliant idea," Erica says with pride in her voice and evil in her heart.

"What's that?" Mary Beth inquires.

"I filed a sexual harassment claim against the warden once I was released from prison. When I threatened to file a lawsuit against her dipshit husband for fifty million dollars, he quickly cut a deal with me for fifteen million dollars."

"So you got fifteen million dollars just like that?"

"Not quite. I had a little dispute with my shithead lawyer over his share of the settlement. Plus, I had to give the warden half of my settlement for lying in court. This was getting to be too costly so I had to do something about preserving my settlement award," Erica says with a venomous glare that now replaced the earlier smirk on her face.

"What did you do?" asks a curious Mary Beth.

"I went to see this dickhead lawyer who mentioned something about the IRS coming after me for bullshit taxes on the money. I was really getting pissed off with how this had turned out."

"What happened then?"

"I hired someone to take care of the problem."

"You hired another lawyer?" asked Mary Beth.

"Not quite. I hired someone to murder my shithead lawyer, the warden, and an IRS agent, who was a major source of agitation to me."

"You hired a hitman?"

"Actually, he was an undercover cop. He really had me fooled."

"Wow. That's some story," remarked Mary Beth. "You should have your story made into a movie or something."

"Right. I'll do it behind bars in my spare time. Care to share why you're in here," Erica asked her new cellmate.

"It's nothing as glamorous as what you did. I only schemed to defraud patients and the doctors I worked for," Mary Beth said ever so modestly. For the next fifteen minutes, Mary Beth explained in detail how she operated a criminal enterprise for approximately one year. To Mary Beth's surprise, her cellmate seemed to be captivated by the scheme.

"And you got seven years for that?" Erica asked.

"Yeah. Why?"

"Seven years seems like a pretty stiff sentence for someone who took a plea. I'm not a lawyer, even though I played one in court. But, seven years? You must have had a really shitty lawyer," Erica says.

"He lived in my neighborhood and had this reputation of being a big-time criminal defense attorney. Anyway, he made this big production of getting the prosecutor to reduce the sentence from like forty five years to seven years if I pled guilty."

"Who represented you?" Erica asked.

"Wallace Shadybrook," answered Mary Beth. "Do you know him?"

"He's the rotten son of a bitch I tried to have murdered," replied Erica.

Chapter 27

As Mary Beth and Erica got to know each other better, they felt a certain camaraderie that they shared so much in common. "We should do something together," Mary Beth said to Erica.

"Hey babe, we're in a federal correctional facility, not Club Med. I don't think the prison authorities are about to give us a weekend pass to go off on vacation."

"Erica, what I meant was that we should run some type of scam while we're locked up in this dump," replied Mary Beth. "Any ideas?"

"I know all about the IRS. We'll file tax returns," Erica suggested.

"You want to run a tax preparation service in prison?"

"That's not what I had in mind," remarked Erica.

"What then?"

"We file phony tax returns for anyone whose personal information we can get, like a social security number and date of birth. We'll set up offshore bank accounts using nominees and deposit the refunds in the accounts. The money sits in the accounts collecting interest that is not subject to US taxation. When we're released, we'll withdraw the funds as necessary."

"Erica, I don't think it's going to work. The IRS will eventually discover its error and come after us for the refunds," Mary Beth pointed out.

"Mary Beth, relax."

"What?"

"The IRS is swamped with people filing fraudulent tax returns. There's no way a bunch of intellectually challenged civil servants can catch up to us."

"Are you sure?" Mary Beth asked.

"It's guaranteed to work. Filing fake tax returns will make falsifying medical records and submitting fake insurance claims look like kid's stuff," declared Erica.

"OK. What have we got to lose?"

"Right. If we get caught, what's going to happen to us? We're already in prison."

****

"Say that again?"

"Detective, there is nothing left to do on the Boris Krushenko investigation. Close the case and move on to something else," Laverne Kressley is telling her homicide detective.

"What's going on? I haven't wrapped it up yet."

"Actually, you have. I have been ordered by the police commissioner that we are to close the Krushenko case and give everything we have to the FBI. Apparently, the DA has worked something out with the US Attorney and this is now a federal case. The feds will take over the investigation and Boris will be their problem. Your work is finished."

"It sounds like the feds want to take credit for convicting

Boris."

"From what I've been told, the US Attorney is going to have Boris enter a plea."

"But how can Boris do a plea bargain if he hasn't been charged with specific crimes as yet?"

"Just close the case and box up your files so we can send it to the FBI. As of now, Mr. Krushenko is the federal government's problem."

****

Sitting in his chambers and looking out the window as snowflakes fall onto the ledge, Judge Barton pauses to reflect on the mess that has now engulfed his judicial career. The judge has learned that an investigation has commenced to determine his competency to decide cases in light of a number of highly controversial rulings.

To further complicate matters, Judge Barton is convinced that his late father accepted a bribe. Racked with guilt that his father committed a crime, Judge Barton contemplates what steps he should take. Unable to discuss this dilemma with anyone, the judge decides that whatever he does, it must repair the harm he has inflicted on everyone concerned.

Confident that the IRS will file appeals with respect to those cases in which he ruled in favor of the petitioners, the judge is satisfied that the harm that he caused the government will eventually be nullified. While the decisions may be reversed on appeal, the expense of further litigation is a cost to be absorbed by both sides.

Next, Judge Barton assumes that the petitioners whom he

unjustly ruled against most recently will also file appeals and eventually be rewarded with favorable decisions. Again, in these instances, both sides will have to deal with the expense of litigation. In Judge Barton's mind, while regrettable, this is part of the cost of going to trial.

However, of greatest concern is what the judge should do with the proceeds resulting from the bribe he believes his father accepted. If he refuses to accept the money, Barton is validating the accusation leveled against his late father. Should Barton keep the money, he is now part of the problem.

Unmarried and without children, the judge is not anxious to go home. Tonight, the judge will sit behind his desk and contemplate what needs to be done. For the next several hours, Judge Barton will reflect on his personal dilemma.

By the time Judge Barton has reviewed his options, he has decided that merely resigning his position as a federal judge will not suffice. Stepping down from the bench may alleviate the concerns expressed by the IRS, but it will not provide him with peace of mind. Nor does the possibility of anonymously giving more than four hundred thousand dollars to those individuals who were deprived of justice in his courtroom appear to be a viable option.

Having considered his options, Judge Barton has concluded that the only viable alternative to his dilemma requires a complete cleansing of his soul. Not yet forty years of age, the judge reflects on what life would be like as long as he derived a financial benefit from an illegal act.

Content that he has no desire to share in any ill-gotten gains, the judge takes pen in hand and composes a letter which will serve as the foundation for his obituary. For the next hour, Judge Barton recounts the many academic and professional accomplishments in his life. Not having a great deal to say about growing up in foster homes, Judge Barton declines to go into detail about his personal life. However, the judge does acknowledge his deep affection and love for his biological parents and concludes by saying how much he misses them.

With the letter finally completed, Judge Barton closes his eyes and takes several deep breaths as if he is about to jump off a cliff to a certain death. The judge has reached the point where he is about to consume a full bottle of sleeping pills. However, before he swallows the pills, the judge decides to have three or four glasses of scotch whiskey. The following morning, Judge Barton's cold body will be discovered by his clerk.

The final irony to this tragic situation is that Judge Barton will have died thinking his father did something wrong. This will be the last thought the judge remembers in his final moments.

****

Wallace Shadybrook is either the most popular criminal defense attorney in town or the only lawyer who is foolish enough to accept certain undesirables as clients. Given Wallace's unseemly reputation, it is the latter.

Wallace has been hired by Ralph Elwood to handle his legal defense. What this really involves is negotiating a plea bargain on Ralph's behalf. This is something that Wallace can do without much effort because any plea bargain in this case will be done on the prosecutor's terms. Wallace has no problem with that because he isn't going to litigate this case under any circumstances.

Once the District Attorney transferred jurisdiction of Ralph Elwood's case to the FBI, it didn't take long for the US Attorney to indict Ralph for murder-for-hire, solicitation of violence, mail fraud and witness tampering. Stunned that the feds were going after him, Ralph threatened to file a lawsuit against everyone in the federal government, starting with the President of the United States.

Meeting his new client in a federal detention center, Wallace asks about the information that his client has promised the US Attorney in exchange for his freedom.

"I have enough dirt on Boris Krushenko to bury him. But before I give the prosecutor anything, I want a deal that allows me to walk. I want a new identity and a new life. I want financial security. I want to be able to live in a nice climate without anyone knowing who I am. I want ...."

"Ralph, you're not playing a TV game show. It doesn't matter what you want. What matters is what the government is willing to do for you," Wallace cautions his sleazy client.

"I've got a lot of poop on old Boris. What I have to say should be worth an awful lot to the feds."

"Let me get this straight. You planned to have two witnesses murdered in order to cover up an embezzlement scheme. The prosecutor has you cold on the murder-for-hire charge and you want the key to the city?"

"Yeah."

"OK. It's never too late to dream. I'll pass your demands along. First, tell me what you have that's so valuable."

"For the better part of the past decade, I handled Boris Krushenko's books. Boris operated a number of illegal enterprises. Drugs, prostitution, the rackets, you name it. Boris had his hands into everything. I know all about it because I participated in the drugs, prostitution and sports betting. As a matter of fact, I lost my shirt gambling and went into debt to the tune of ten million dollars. The only way I could pay off my gambling debt was if I could steal the money from my clients."

"OK. Let's get back to the businesses that Boris operated," Wallace said.

"Let's say you wanted to own a deli somewhere in downtown Baltimore. If you wanted to operate a deli on Charles Street, you had to see Boris about obtaining the permits and licenses. It wasn't the city government that you had to worry about. It was Boris."

"Boris demanded a bribe?"

"To Boris, it wasn't a bribe. It was more like insurance. The pay-off was to ensure that you got the permit to operate a deli. If Boris wasn't paid, you weren't going to be awarded a license to sell food."

"So, as I understand it, Boris is an intermediary in the licensing process?" Wallace asked.

"Exactly. Only it doesn't end there. Boris takes a percentage of your gross. That's his fee for allowing you the privilege to operate a deli."

"I take it that this money is then laundered. Did Boris have you launder it for him?"

"Boris had me do two things to disguise what he's done. First, he had me record the payments as a business expense so he could deduct it on his tax returns. I'd bury it under licensing fees, insurance, office supplies, whatever, on his company books. Once the entries appeared on the General Ledger, it would look legit. Then, Boris would have me wire transfer the money to an offshore account under an alias. The money collects interest that is not subject to US taxation and the principal grows each year. The feds have no idea what Boris has stashed overseas," Elwood exclaimed.

"That's just racketeering and tax evasion. The prosecutor's

not going to offer you much for that info," Wallace noted.

"I have more. Lot's more."

"OK."

"Boris ran a phony company that promised homeowners protection from having their homes foreclosed on by the banks. For a nominal fee, he offered to guarantee their mortgage payments," Elwood said.

"What?"

"Here's what Boris did. He charged an upfront fee of three thousand dollars to cover your mortgage payment. If you defaulted on your mortgage, Boris claimed to make the payment for you and would then work out a re-payment plan so that you could pay him back later. Only that never happened. If you missed the payment, Boris walked away from any liability. Here's the punch line. You lose the house and your money."

"How did Boris get away with this?"

"He paid off his flunkies in the government. But that's not all. Do you remember that Ponzi scheme that Adolph Gerstung supposedly ran?"

"Yeah," answered Wallace.

"Well, Boris was really behind it. Boris owned a commercial office cleaning business where he cooked the books. Boris had me inflate sales revenue to make it appear that the business had a lot of clients. Only it didn't have any clients," boasted Elwood. "Boris then had me prepare a phony financial statement so he could entice a group of gullible investors to purchase the company.

"Adolph was named principal corporate officer, shareholder and director. Boris used Adolph as the front man on the deal to conceal his actual ownership and control.

"When the business was sold for ten million dollars, Adolph was charged with fraud. Adolph didn't have any of the money because it went into a secret foreign bank account that Boris set up in the Cayman Islands," explained Elwood.

"Didn't Adolph point the finger at Boris?"

"He had planned to, but was convinced otherwise when Boris had one of his goons talk to Adolph."

"You can prove all this?" Wallace asked.

"I have copies of records. It's available for the right price."

"What makes you think the prosecutor will want to deal with you?"

"Wallace, I'm holding all the cards," Elwood said with a smug look on his face as he turned his palms up, confident that he would soon be a free man.

Chapter 28

"You tell that dirtball client of yours that there's no deal."

"C'mon Evan, you need his cooperation to convict Krushenko."

"There is no deal. What part of 'there is no deal' do you not understand?" replied Evan Horan, the assistant United States Attorney who intends to add Ralph Elwood's name to his fast growing list of high-profile convictions.

Evan Horan joined the US Attorney's Office out of law school, where he finished in the top five percent of his graduating class. Although Evan has been with the US Attorney's Office for less than five years, he has already amassed an impressive number of convictions in court. In appreciation for his outstanding accomplishments, Evan has been assigned the Ralph Elwood case.

Standing slightly less than six foot tall and possessing the slender physique of a competitive swimmer, Evan moves about the office much like a panther stalks its prey in the jungle. Catlike quick, Evan can glide from office to office without making a sound. Sitting across from Wallace, Evan decides to play a game of cat-and-mouse with the idiot facing him.

"What's the problem with my client cooperating in exchange for a break on sentencing?" asks a clueless Wallace.

"Your client hired the local neighborhood thug to murder two witnesses who can testify that he embezzled eight million dollars from his clients. We have the thug on an armed robbery charge. We have your client's conversation on tape. We have your client paying the guy one hundred thousand dollars to murder two people. Ralph Elwood deserves to go to prison."

"But Krushenko's crimes are far worse."

"Are we comparing the merits of which criminal acts are less objectionable? From my point of view, Ralph Elwood's criminal behavior is every bit as bad, if not worse than Boris Krushenko's criminal behavior. They both deserve to rot in prison. But giving Elwood a get out-of-jail pass isn't going to happen," said the AUSA.

"I can't believe you're not going to cut a deal with him. Don't you want his cooperation?"

"I don't need it."

"It would make sending Krushenko to prison that much easier," Wallace asserted based on the assumption that Boris would be convicted in court. However, Wallace's assertion fell flat.

"Wallace, what makes you think Krushenko is going to trial?"

"For crying out loud, he's a criminal who belongs in prison!" Wallace exclaimed.

"That's true," the prosecutor said as he nodded his head in agreement. However, what Wallace didn't know was that Boris Krushenko had already made a deal with the US Attorney. In return for his cooperation, Boris would get a reduced prison sentence. With Boris as the cooperating witness, Ralph Elwood would soon be finding himself doing a stretch in prison for a period of time longer than his ex-client.

When Wallace met with his client in detention later that

morning, he relayed the gist of his conversation with the prosecutor. This did not go over well with Ralph.

"Are you serious?" asked Ralph.

"I couldn't get to first base with him. He won't deal with you."

"Why not?" asked Ralph, to which Wallace shrugged before answering.

"The assistant United States Attorney doesn't like you. He used words like despicable and reprehensible to describe you. He perceives you as ethically challenged and finds your character to be morally deplorable. I believe he even used the word 'evil' in characterizing you."

"Wallace, I resent that. These accusations are morally offensive. I'll sue him for defamation, slander, libel and whatever else I can think of. Make a note to file a lawsuit against him when you get back to your office. "

Ignoring what his client just said, Wallace says, "You plotted to have two witnesses murdered after they discovered that you stole eight million dollars from your clients. Is this registering at all?"

"Look, Wallace. I made a mistake. I exercised poor judgment at a time in my life that was full of upheaval and emotional duress."

"Really? What was going on in your life?"

"I can't remember. I could have been going through a divorce or something," Ralph says even though he has never been married. "Maybe my mother died. I don't know. But I made poor decisions which I now deeply regret. This is something that you should tell the prosecutor. Go back to him and get me a deal." With Wallace dismissed, Ralph had the guards escort him back to his jail cell.

Later that morning, Wallace returned to his palatial office in order to catch up on some house-keeping items. When Wallace checked his voice mail, he learned that Richard Cahill had been indicted. It took CID only a few weeks to wrap up its criminal investigation and refer the case to the Justice Department. The US Attorney quickly accepted the case for prosecution and had Cahill indicted on several criminal counts.

Wallace was now delighted that he had a case that he thought was ideal for a plea bargain. If he couldn't get Ralph Elwood a deal, Wallace was confident he could broker a plea for Richard Cahill. Wallace was so determined to cut a deal that he intended to do so even under the worst terms possible.

Chapter 29

Erica has taken it upon herself to tutor Mary Beth on how to file a phony tax return. "We start by using the name and social security number of someone who recently died. We're going to create a fake W-2 and show a lot of withholding tax credits," explained Erica.

"Wait a second. Won't the IRS be able to match the withholding taxes and the income from the fake W-2?"

"We'll file the return right at the start of the new calendar year. The IRS will issue the refund before authenticating the W-2 information. When the IRS finally gets around to matching the W-2 information, it'll be too late. By then, we'll transfer the funds to an overseas account in a tax haven country. We'll always be one step ahead of them," Erica declared.

"Are you sure?" asked Mary Beth, who was still somewhat skeptical that this scheme could work so easily.

"Babe, how easy was it for you to bamboozle the insurance companies and the five stooges you were working for?" Erica asked.

"It was simple."

"And you think that this is going to be any more difficult?"

"I guess not. It just seems too good to be true," replied Mary Beth.

"It's better than robbing a bank. We do everything using a computer and there's no paper trail. Trust me, I know what

I'm doing," said Erica.

****

Several decades ago, Mary Loder made a name for herself as an IRS trial attorney who successfully litigated a number of high-profile political corruption cases in the United States Tax Court. The US Attorney was so impressed with Mary's reputation that when his office needed another AUSA, he personally recruited her.

Somewhat bored with civil tax cases, Mary thought that doing white collar criminal cases might re-invigorate her. For the next twenty years, Mary has prosecuted a number of white collar criminals with near spectacular success. The next target in her sights is Richard Cahill.

Wallace is aware of Mary's reputation and has been told that she is anxious to prosecute Richard Cahill. On the other hand, Richard Cahill is neither anxious to go to trial, nor is he receptive to going to prison. The moment has now arrived for Richard Cahill to attempt to strike a deal.

Having surrendered his passport and required to put up one million dollars as bail, Richard Cahill has insisted that he accompany his lawyer to meet with the assistant United States Attorney. The tennis pro has decided that he wants to open the contest with the ball in his court. This is evident from the outset of the pre-trial conference.

"Mrs. Loder, I appreciate given the opportunity to meet with you and I want to express my sincere desire to cooperate," Cahill says in trying to get off to a positive start.

"Mr. Cahill, this is a pre-trial settlement conference. We are past the stage of cooperation because you never really cooperated with the government throughout its investigation. Your attorney was invited to meet with me to discuss the terms of a plea," stated Mary.

"Right. That's what I really meant to say. I want to enter into a plea," said Cahill.

"So you're willing to plead guilty to all criminal charges?"

"Yes."

"Good. Then we can move on to sentencing recommendations. My office will agree to recommend a sentence of eight years, with time off for good behavior," the prosecutor replied.

"Wait a minute. I was hoping to get probation," Cahill stammered.

"You can hope all you want, but you're not getting probation. You're doing prison time."

"But, I can give you names," Cahill offered in exchange for leniency on a prison sentence.

"Excuse me?" says Mary.

"I can give you names. I can tell you who else accepted appearance fees and didn't report the amounts on their tax returns. I know of others who pocketed appearance fees and tanked matches so they could go off and play other tournaments. I wasn't the only one who did this."

"And how is it that you know that some of your fellow tennis pros did not report these amounts on their federal income tax returns?"

"Huh?" Cahill asked.

"How do you know for an absolute fact that these amounts weren't reported to the IRS?"

"Well, you see ...." Cahill stammers again.

"No, I don't see. Unless you happened to prepare the tax returns in question, how do you know that these payments were not reported?" Mary demands to know.

"Perhaps my client misspoke," Wallace interjected.

"I think your client is blowing smoke. He doesn't know his ass from his elbow. The offer is eight years. If you decline, the next time I speak with you, the offer will be nine years. If you decline again, the third and final offer will be ten years. If we go to trial, I'm going to ask for twelve years when I get your client convicted."

"You actually think you'll win?" asked Wallace, without any conviction in his voice.

"I'm seriously looking forward to seeing you in court. Good day gentlemen."

As the defense attorney led his client to the elevator, he wondered how he could get out of this case. There was no way he was going to trial and there was no way his client would agree to a plea bargain if he had to do eight years behind bars.

"The prosecutor seemed pretty confident that she would win. What do you think?" Cahill asked his lawyer.

"I think you shouldn't go to trial."

"Why not?" asked Cahill.

"There are too many things that go against you."

"Like what?"

"Like the facts. All she has to do is lay out the facts and you can kiss your ass goodbye. By the way, in case you didn't notice, that Loder woman is a shark," remarked Wallace.

"She didn't really seem interested in my providing incriminating information on others, did she?"

"Not in the least. She either doesn't care or doesn't need it. As a witness, you don't have much credibility. Also, unless you know for an absolute certainty that your fellow tennis pros didn't report the amounts as income on their tax returns, your testimony is suspect," offered Wallace.

"So what do you propose?" Cahill asked once again of his lawyer.

"If you want to go to trial, hire another lawyer. Otherwise, I'll call the prosecutor in the next day or two and tell her you'll plead if she's willing to consider eight years."

"What if she won't give me eight years?"

"Then you'll do nine years," replied Wallace.

Chapter 30

"Ladies and gentlemen of the jury," Wallace says as he rises, buttons his dress suit and makes his way towards them. "You have been selected to decide a man's fate. It is an awesome responsibility which I know all of you will take seriously," Wallace says, suspecting some jurors could care less whether a defendant is convicted and sent to jail. "Indeed, it is such a serious matter that it requires your complete, absolute and undivided attention," the elderly lawyer adds for overkill.

The case of the United States of America v. Ralph Elwood, Jr. has started in federal court. While Wallace offered every excuse possible to be recused, the trial judge refused to do so. In each instance, Wallace complained to Judge William Smulyan that it wasn't fair to him or to the defendant. When every excuse offered was rejected, Wallace simply said, "Judge, my mind's not into this case. I don't think I can bring my 'A Game' to court."

In response to this, Judge Smulyan replied, "I think that if you spent your time focusing on defending your client rather than dreaming up reasons why you should be allowed to withdraw from representation, you could argue this case with the utmost eloquence. I'm sure you'll do fine once your mind is clear. I can sense your 'A Game' is on your fingertips."

Wallace is now stuck. With the prosecutor not willing to entertain any offers for a sentence of less than seventy five years, Wallace must take this to trial. Of course, having Wallace appear in court to argue a case is like trying to get a vampire to attend Sunday morning church services. Appearing in court is one thing. Actually arguing the case is an entirely different matter.

The opening statement in a trial is limited to outlining the facts of the case. This is each side's opportunity to depict the theory of the case to the jurors, explain the criminal charges that are the grounds for the case, and provide a general road map as to where this trial will take them. Each party is entitled to say who their witnesses are, explain their relevance, and provide an insight into their testimony under oath.

For Wallace, he will have none of this. This is because Wallace does not wish to participate in this legal proceeding. In essence, Wallace is going to make a half-hearted attempt at providing the bare-bones minimum he can get away with in court, without being subject to sanctions.

"I would like to introduce my client, who is the defendant in this case," Wallace says as he points to Ralph to let the jurors know that Ralph is the target of the prosecutor's wrath. As Wallace points in the defendant's direction, Ralph appears to be either bored out of his mind or is pretending to be bored out of his mind. The bored look is not very effective because the jurors can sense that Ralph is guilty of the crimes for which he has been charged and could very well be guilty of far more crimes that he has not been charged with having committed.

While Ralph is conservatively dressed in a white button down cotton dress shirt, stylish silk tie and dark blue business suit that is appropriate dress attire for court, he still looks like the guiltiest person in the courtroom. Perhaps it is because of his slender physique which is screaming for nourishment. With beady eyes, a tongue that seems to dart in and out of his mouth too often, and slicked back hair, Ralph could pass for anyone who is wanted for having done anything immoral, illegal or unkind to his fellow human beings.

"I know from experience that when you use the word

'defendant,' some people automatically assume that person is guilty. If someone has been charged with doing something wrong, they must be guilty, right?" Wallace asks rhetorically as he extends his arms and places his palms up in the air as if he were delivering a sermon in church.

"Well, our criminal justice system isn't supposed to be like this, but it often is the case from an emotional standpoint. Typically, citizens such as yourselves may view someone as being guilty because that person has been arrested by law enforcement officials. It doesn't necessarily mean people are biased. It's merely a part of our normal thought process due to the fact that they haven't heard the facts and evidence in question.

"That is why our judicial system provides that a defendant is presumed to be not guilty until proven otherwise. In this respect, in criminal cases, the burden of proof requires that the prosecution demonstrate the defendant's guilt for each element of the crime beyond a reasonable doubt. As you will be instructed by the trial judge, a reasonable doubt is considered synonymous to a moral certainty."

Wallace is pleased with what he has just said and decides to make eye contact with each juror. Looking into the eyes of each juror without making it too obvious that he is gawking at them, Wallace adds, "Because the burden of proof rests with the prosecutor, my client is not required to prove his innocence. This right is guaranteed by the 5th Amendment, and as such, all that my client is required to do is argue that the prosecutor has failed to meet his burden."

Pausing for a moment to shift gears, Wallace turns and says, "I would like to say a few words about my client." As he says this, Wallace makes it a point to wink at the female jurors, who do not bother to wink back.

However despicable Ralph Elwood is, Wallace feels that he must humanize the defendant as a person, regardless of his character flaws. "My client's a certified public accountant who at one time, worked as an agent for the IRS. When my client started his own accounting practice, he didn't have the luxury of being selective when it came to choosing clients. He unselfishly agreed to perform accounting work for any client who hired him. At first, most of his clients were relatives, friends and neighbors. Over time and as his practice grew, my client performed work for clients who expected more than just tax planning, the preparation and filing of tax returns and setting up record-keeping systems," Wallace adds.

"One such client in particular expected far more from my client. During this period, my client did things that he now deeply regrets. This goes to the question of character and my client readily admits that he failed in this regard," Wallace says with a sigh and makes a face that suggests deep humility and sorrow for the defendant.

"My client could justify moments of weakness by saying that there was trauma in his life. Of course, we all experience trauma from time to time. It's a part of everyday life. However, most of us usually don't do things that we deeply regret.

"Working long hours to provide the highest level of accounting and tax advice to his many clients may have taken a toll on my client, which resulted in a serious lapse of judgment on his part. I'm not a psychiatrist so I can't offer a medical explanation as to how this happened. However, the reality of this is that it did happen.

"In getting to spend quality time with my client, I can say that I truly believe he is a man who genuinely cares for others," Wallace says with a great deal of insincerity. Upon hearing this, the jurors must wonder how quality time can be spent with someone who is behind bars.

"My client is a man of profound integrity," Wallace continues.

"And that's what makes this trial so tragic. I believe in my client's innocence and trust that by the end of this trial, you will also believe in his innocence."

With nothing else to say, Wallace takes his customary bow as if the jurors were royalty and returns to the defense table where he takes his seat next to the psychopath who is his client.

"Mr. Horan?" Judge Smulyan says, as if the prosecutor needed a personal invitation to speak.

As the assistant US Attorney stands, he shakes his head for the benefit of the members of the jury and says, "I'm not quite sure what I just heard." Walking slowly in the direction of the jurors, the prosecutor says, "I think counsel for the defense has admitted mistakes in judgment by the defendant. Now, we don't really know exactly what these mistakes are because opposing counsel hasn't elaborated on them. We'll get to that during the trial. But in the meantime, I would like to briefly give you an overview as to what the government has alleged these mistakes are."

Making subtle eye contact with each juror to try to gauge their attention, Evan pauses just long enough to let the moment in time build. The prosecutor then says, "One of the purposes of an opening statement in a criminal case is to address the charges that have been filed against the defendant. Whereas defense counsel has characterized the criminal offenses as outrageous and unfounded in fact, he has neglected to specify the exact criminal violations for which his client has been charged. The defendant has been charged with hiring someone to murder two witnesses to his having stolen eight million dollars in client funds. The criminal offenses constitute murder-for-hire, solicitation of violence and witness tampering. In addition, the defendant's embezzlement scheme constitutes mail fraud. By my count, that's a lot of criminal offenses. Twelve counts to be exact," said the AUSA.

"Included in these alleged criminal offenses is social security fraud, identity theft, money laundering, and filing false tax returns. The money that the defendant generated from these schemes went into offshore bank accounts under fictitious names.

"If you're wondering why the defendant did this, it's simple. The defendant had lost ten million dollars gambling. To pay off most of his gambling debts, the defendant absconded with eight million dollars of client funds which his clients had designated for remittance to federal and state tax authorities. The defendant failed to remit any of these funds to any governmental agencies.

"When several of the defendant's clients discovered that their money had not been remitted to the appropriate tax authorities, they complained to the defendant and threatened to file suit if he did not return the money. We know that the funds were not repaid by the defendant and in response to the intended lawsuit, the defendant conspired to have those clients killed. According to the police, the defendant paid one hundred thousand dollars to have these two individuals murdered.

"I would agree with opposing counsel that the defendant had a lapse of judgment. However, this lapse of judgment apparently went on for about a decade. Throughout this period of time, the defendant recklessly participated in sports gambling, knowing full well that he did not have the financial resources to wager to this extent. This was not a momentary lapse of judgment.

"This is a case about greed and attempted murder. As jurors, you are going to be asked to listen to the testimony of witnesses, evaluate the weight of evidence presented and reach a verdict based on such testimony and evidence. I'm confident that by the time you have had an opportunity to do this, you will find the defendant guilty of the offenses for which he has been charged. Thank you for your attention and for performing your civic obligation by serving on this jury."

Before Evan had an opportunity to take his seat, the defendant stood at attention and exclaimed, "I don't want this idiot defending me," as he pointed with his left hand in the direction of Wallace. What Ralph should have added to this statement was that he didn't want Evan Horan prosecuting him.

"Mr. Elwood, please sit down," ordered Judge Smulyan.

As Ralph took his seat, he continued by saying, "Judge, I don't want him as my lawyer." Ralph made it a point to exclude the idiot reference this time, much to the appreciation of the judge.

"Mr. Elwood, do you wish to represent yourself?" inquired the judge.

"Yes, sir," declared a very excitable defendant who had no reservations playing lawyer in his own defense.

"Gentlemen, let's take this up in my chambers. The jury will return to the deliberation room and court is recessed for fifteen minutes," announced Judge Smulyan as he tapped his gavel on the bench.

Having escorted the lawyers and the defendant to his chambers, Judge Smulyan didn't bother to take his robe off. Placing one hand up in the air to silence anyone from speaking, the judge waited until his stenographer was ready to transcribe. When the stenographer nodded to the judge that she was ready, Judge Smulyan didn't waste any time.

"Would you like to tell me what the problem is?" he asked the defendant, as the opposing lawyers sat at opposite ends of the sofa.

"Judge, I didn't like what my lawyer," Ralph says with a

sneer, "had to say about me in his opening statement. He admitted that I made serious mistakes. The prosecutor jumped all over it and painted a picture of me as a master criminal. This picture is now hanging in your courtroom for all twelve jurors to see. Looking in their eyes, I can see that they've already convicted me. Either give me a new trial or let me defend myself."

"Your Honor, granting a mistrial at this time makes no sense. No one has testified and no evidence has been presented. At the very worst, the defendant's character has been called into question for having a lapse in judgment, whatever that means," argued Evan. "I would like to point out that defense counsel did not specifically elaborate on what this lapse of judgment involved."

Before anyone in the room could offer a thought on the subject, Evan added, "The jurors have the right to hear the criminal charges and at no time did Mr. Shadybrook say that the defendant was guilty of any of the criminal offenses," asserted the AUSA.

As Wallace was perfectly content to sit this out, he did not bother to express his thoughts on the subject. Hopeful that he will be recused, Wallace merely sat on the judge's sofa like an elementary school student is told to sit on a bench outside the principal's office.

Curious as to what Wallace had to say on the subject, Judge Smulyan turned to the defense attorney and said, "Would you care to participate in this discussion, Mr. Shadybrook?"

Wallace merely shrugged his shoulders at the invitation, as if to say that he didn't want to be bothered and let his hands fall to his lap.

"Mr. Elwood, I'm not going to grant you a mistrial. There was nothing that was said by Mr. Shadybrook in his opening statement that would lead the jurors to believe that you are guilty of the criminal charges. As a matter of fact, your attorney repeatedly stressed your innocence of the criminal charges. If necessary, I can have the court stenographer provide you with a transcript as to your lawyer's opening statement."

"Judge, I was there and heard every stupid word he said. I wasn't impressed," retorted Ralph.

"Mr. Elwood, should you wish to personally handle your defense, I would caution you against doing so."

"Judge, he didn't do what I wanted him to do," Ralph exclaims as he points an accusing finger at Wallace. Given the defendant's annoyance with his lawyer, there is little likelihood that these two will be functioning as a well-oiled machine in and out of the courtroom. The underlying bitterness for this rift is premised on the fact that Wallace failed to do what was asked of him.

While Wallace and Evan know exactly what is being alleged, Judge Smulyan does not have knowledge that Ralph's demand for a plea agreement was not considered by the prosecution. "He was supposed to cut a deal for me and he didn't!" Ralph practically screams. "I shouldn't even be here now. I should be in a federal witness protection program."

"Can someone please fill me in on this?" a confused Judge Smulyan says.

"Judge, it was my client's desire to plead guilty to the charges and negotiate the terms and conditions of a plea that would not involve incarceration. In exchange for his cooperation, my client would provide the US Attorney with information that would incriminate others of far more serious crimes. I was told that the US Attorney was not interested in negotiating a plea agreement." This is about all Wallace intends to say.

"I see," said the judge.

"That's not fair. I want a deal. I'm entitled to a deal. The last time I checked, this is the United States of America. It's my constitutional right to get a deal." Now pointing at the prosecutor with an accusatory finger, Ralph says with another sneer, "He never offered me a deal. What kind of a lousy criminal justice system is this?

"He," Ralph says now jabbing his finger in the air to emphasize contempt and disdain for the prosecutor, "never gave me a plea bargain. What is this, some Third World Banana Republic?" Ralph says in anger while he goes off on a tangent that he should have been granted a pardon in exchange for providing the prosecutor with information as to crimes committed by others.

"Mr. Elwood, the prosecutor is under no obligation to offer you a deal. Whether you are offered a plea bargain is solely within the discretion of the US Attorney. I don't have the authority to compel the US Attorney to offer you a deal."

"You're the judge. If you don't want to hear this case, can't you tell the US Attorney to negotiate with me?" asked Ralph.

"As I just said, entering into a plea agreement must be done with the consent of the prosecutor's office. There are certain terms and conditions to a plea agreement that must be agreed upon by the government. If Mr. Horan does not wish to offer you a plea bargain, that is his prerogative."

For the next several moments, there is complete silence in Judge Smulyan's chambers. Finally, Ralph breaks the silence by saying, "That's not right. I should get a deal."

With the exception of the defendant, it is clear to all in the room that the prosecutor is not interested in cutting a deal with Ralph. With nothing further to be accomplished by pursuing this subject, the judge says, "As it's clear that Mr. Horan is not receptive to entering into a plea agreement with you, you have two options. You can either amend your plea to guilty and we can proceed to the sentencing stage or you can go forward with your trial, which is your constitutional right to do," replied the judge.

"I'll go to trial."

"Fine. Before we go back to court, we need to address the matter of your desire to represent yourself. I'm reluctant to grant you permission to represent yourself, even though it is your legal right to do so. I believe that you will need legal advice as the trial progresses, particularly since this is a criminal case with serious ramifications. Therefore, I'm going to appoint Mr. Shadybrook as your legal advisor for this trial. As such, Mr. Shadybrook will be of counsel to you on procedural matters and points of law as situations arise. In addition, Mr. Shadybrook may also assist in examining witnesses, should you feel it is necessary.

"You have the right to question witnesses and pose legal objections as to the admission of evidence. I would hope that you rely, in part, on Mr. Shadybrook in this regard."

"What about my opening statement?" asked Ralph.

"What about it?" responded the judge.

"Don't I get a 'do-over'?"

"Your Honor," Evan says in exasperation as he extends his hands in the air. "He can't be serious." However, the judge merely waves his hand in the air as if to dismiss the objection.

"Mr. Shadybrook, did you inform your client as to the content of your opening statement?" asked the judge.

"No, judge. I did not. I did not disclose what I was about to say."

"OK, Mr. Elwood. I'll grant you a brief opening statement. This opening statement will serve as a general overview as to what this trial is about. As I said, your statement is going to be brief and to the point. You may refute the criminal charges and say what you intend to argue at trial. You have the right to introduce your theory of the case. However, you are not going to make wild promises to this jury that are speculative and without basis in fact. Nor can you jump right into the facts before any witnesses have been called. In addition, you are prohibited from mentioning anything about not being offered a plea agreement. There will be no references to this. If I hear anything inappropriate, I will immediately cut you off. Are we clear on this?" said the judge.

"Yes, sir," Ralph nodded. "I'll deliver an opening statement in my 'do-over' for the jurors that will knock their socks off. I have one question though."

"What is it?"

"Can I deny everything my lawyer said?"

Upon hearing that, Judge Smulyan merely placed his left hand to the side of his head as if he wanted to massage his temple. After he asked everyone to return to court, the judge opened one of the drawers in his desk and removed a bottle of extra strength aspirin. Chugging down several aspirin with a glass of water, the judge stood, shook his head, and wondered once more why he didn't go to medical school.

Chapter 31

Court is back in session, much to the chagrin of Judge Smulyan, who has a sinking feeling in the pit of his stomach that this trial could be the worst judicial proceeding he has ever presided over. That is saying a lot since the judge had to deal with the infamous Erica Whitman on more than one occasion.

Before Ralph is allowed to deliver what he terms his "do-over," Judge Smulyan has explained to the jury that the defendant has been granted permission to take a more active role in his defense. "While Mr. Shadybrook will serve as a legal advisor to the defendant, it is the defendant's desire to personally question witnesses. As the defendant intends to act as his own counsel, he has been granted an opportunity to make a brief opening statement. Mr. Elwood, you may address the members of the jury at this time," announces Judge Smulyan.

As Ralph stands, he feels it is incumbent on him that he button his suit coat and wipe an imaginary piece of lint from his sleeve. For good measure, Ralph also decides to adjust the knot in his tie before he is about to speak. Unsure as to where he should stand when he delivers his opening statement, Ralph checks to see if there are any marks on the floor as clues as to where to stand. Staring at the floor for far too long, Ralph looks up at the judge and with a puzzled look on his face, inquires as to where the judge would prefer that he stand.

"Mr. Elwood, you may stand where you are when speaking to the jurors. Please deliver your opening statement so that we can proceed," the judge warily instructs the defendant.

"My name is Ralph Elwood. I'm telling you my name because if you didn't know who I am, you'd mistake me for Al Capone," the defendant says to the jury members, who already know who he is and the criminal offenses for which he has been charged.

"You see, with all these criminal charges that the US Attorney has filed against me, I should be the nation's most wanted criminal. I wouldn't be the least bit surprised if my mug shot is posted in every post office in the United States," Ralph adds.

Before the defendant can continue on this tangent, Judge Smulyan interrupts his train of thought by reminding the defendant that his water is about to be turned off if he continues down this path.

"Right. I forgot," Ralph says to the judge as if they had a secret agreement.

"OK. Here's what I'm dealing with," acknowledges Ralph. "I've been charged with mail fraud, trying to have witnesses murdered, and so forth. These are truly bad crimes, and if I were guilty of this, I should go to prison. However, I didn't commit these crimes.

"Earlier, you heard from my attorney and he briefly alluded to certain mistakes that I made. It's true that I have made mistakes throughout my professional career. As a former IRS agent, I was trained to audit tax returns, find mistakes and get taxpayers to pay more in taxes than they would like to do. Now, as a CPA, I try to do my very best to ensure that my clients, whom I value as dear friends, do not have to pay more in taxes than they legally owe. It's not an easy job and there were times when I suffered lapses in judgment.

"As I look back and reflect on events, I will be the very first to admit my shortcomings. However, at no time did I engage in criminal behavior," Ralph says as he accusingly points his index finger at the prosecutor as if he could shift the guilt to the AUSA. "While Mr. Horan would have you believe that I stole money from my clients and paid someone to have them killed, I find the allegations to be without foundation and blatantly false. These accusations are malicious, reckless and are intended to destroy my reputation as a practicing CPA. It's mean spirited and untrue," Ralph says as he glances around the courtroom while wondering whether he left anything out.

However, Ralph is not finished. "I am deeply offended by the false charges and cannot fathom why the federal government intends to persecute me." Attempting to look contrite, Ralph says, "Sorry, I misspoke. I meant to say the word 'prosecute' although I suppose the word 'persecute' is also applicable. The real question you should be asking is why isn't the federal government going after the many criminals who are operating criminal enterprises and doing awful things? I just don't get it. Hopefully, you will be able to undo the horrible mistake that the federal government has inflicted on me."

Ralph has decided to pause in order to collect what little thoughts are left that need to be said. Pleased that he has delivered what he perceives to be an overpowering opening statement, Ralph makes a mental note to pursue a legal career once he is acquitted of the criminal charges. As if he could read Ralph's mind, Judge Smulyan gives him a stern glare that does not require much interpretation.

Instead, Ralph ignores the look he is given by the judge and continues by saying, "As members of this jury, it is up to you to ...."

Before Ralph can finish his thought, the judge's gavel can be heard pounding on the bench. "That's enough, Mr. Elwood. It is not up to you to tell the jurors how to perform the task at hand. I'll do that at the appropriate time. As far as I'm concerned, you've covered everything that needs to be said. Please take your seat," said Judge Smulyan, who was sensing that this trial will be the ultimate test of his patience.

Chapter 32

The direction this trial was headed was made clear to everyone at the outset. When the first prosecution witness was called to the stand, the defendant immediately objected with a loud, "Judge, I object to this witness."

"Mr. Elwood, the witness has not been asked a question as of yet. On what grounds are you objecting?" inquired Judge Smulyan.

"Confidentiality."

"I beg your pardon?" replied the judge.

"I'm referring to privileged communications between an accountant and his client."

"Objection, Your Honor," Evan said as he stood. "Federal law rejects the idea of an accountant-client privilege like that which exists between lawyers and their clients."

"Judge, I respectfully disagree," countered Ralph, who added the word 'respectfully' only because he believes it is what lawyers typically say in court for the benefit of the trial judge. "Federally authorized tax practitioner privilege is a limited evidentiary privilege available in federal tax law. The privilege is defined in an amendment to the Internal Revenue Code." Obviously Ralph had thought that by citing confidentiality between a tax practitioner and a client, he could prohibit all of his clients from testifying against him.

"Your Honor, I renew my objection. Privilege does not apply in this instance," replied the prosecutor.

"Oh, but it does," responded Ralph, who continues by saying, "if the prosecutor had researched the law, he would know this." Ralph is not shy about insulting Evan and plans to take several more shots at him before the trial is over.

"With respect to tax advice, the same common law protections of confidentiality which apply to a communication between a client and lawyer will also apply to a communication between a client and any federally authorized tax practitioner to the extent it would be a privileged communication," argued Ralph.

"Your Honor, once again I renew my objection. This privilege does not apply in any criminal matters," Evan said.

"Mr. Horan's right," the judge remarked to the defendant.

"But judge, Maryland is one of the states that enacted legislation which creates privilege for accountant-client communications. The last time I checked, this courtroom was in Maryland. Therefore, I have statutory accountant-client privilege and as such, I'm entitled to have this witness and for that matter, any and all of my clients barred from testifying," asserted Ralph.

Before the prosecutor can object under the grounds that this trial is in federal court, Judge Smulyan declares, "This trial is taking place under the jurisdiction of the United States District Court. You do not have statutory privilege in federal court, and even if you did, it would not apply because this is a criminal trial."

"Your Honor, I wish to renew my objection to your ruling," stated the defendant. "My work product is confidential. The advice that I provide to my clients regarding the likely outcome of tax audits is a privileged communication. It would do irreparable harm to my reputation if prospective clients knew that confidential communications could be disclosed at the request of the government."

With the palm of his hand supporting the weight of his head, Judge Smulyan rolls his eyes at what he is hearing. "The answer is no. Your objection to have this witness and for that matter, any other witnesses barred from testifying against you on grounds of confidentiality, privilege, or accountant-client communications, is denied. This issue will not be raised, addressed or argued in this trial again. Have I made myself clear, Mr. Elwood?"

"Fine. If I'm convicted, I'm going to file an appeal citing judicial error on your part, judge." Ralph Elwood has finally annoyed Judge Smulyan to no end. In the meantime, Wallace Shadybrook is observed resting his head on the palm of his hand and periodically yawning in apparent indifference to his client's ill-planned legal strategy.

In less than two full days, the prosecution has presented its case. Evidence that the defendant diverted his clients' money to pay off his gambling debts was introduced without contradiction. In addition, the thug who was paid one hundred thousand dollars to murder two of the defendant's clients testified as a government witness. Particularly damning was the tape recording that was played in court when the defendant met with the would-be-killer to pay him the final installment.

A number of local law enforcement and federal agents were called to the witness stand as prosecution witnesses. By the time the prosecution had completed the presentation of its case, Ralph had the dubious honor of being compared to the most despicable person in the nation.

Turning to the defendant, the judge inquires as to whether he is ready, to which Ralph replies, "Ready for what, judge?"

"Mr. Elwood, the prosecution has announced that it has rested its case. It's your turn to present your case. You may proceed," Judge Smulyan announced for the benefit of the defendant.

"Judge, I have no witnesses that I can call because by calling witnesses, I would be invalidating my right to confidentiality. I would rather go to prison than breach this most sacred of legal principles," announced Ralph. It remains to be seen whether Ralph is ready for prison.

"I see. Well, that's your prerogative. Gentlemen, we'll take an early lunch at this time. Closing arguments will start at 1 PM," instructed Judge Smulyan.

As the spectators in the courtroom make their way to the exit door, Ralph decides that it is time to have a word with Evan. "I want to talk to you," Ralph says in a tone of voice that a boss would use to a subordinate before firing that person.

Unruffled, Evan replies, "Did you want me to meet you in your office?"

"I don't need sarcasm from you."

"What is it that you want to say because I have things to do?"

"I want a deal. If you can't give me a deal, tell your boss to offer me a deal," Ralph instructs the AUSA.

"For the last time, I'm not offering you a deal. There is no deal on the table and you're in no position to demand that my boss give you a deal. Let me give you a word of advice. If you haven't prepared your closing argument, I suggest that you get started," Evan cautioned the defendant as he turned and left the courtroom.

At 1 PM sharp, the trial resumed, with the prosecutor delivering his closing statement. Evan was methodical and concise as he summarized the government's case against Ralph Elwood. In less than fifteen minutes, Evan had effectively made a compelling argument that Ralph should spend the rest of his life in prison.

Glancing down at the defense table where Wallace sat to the

right of Ralph, Judge Smulyan inquired as to who would be giving the closing argument. Fearful that it would be Ralph, the judge cringed when Ralph replied, "Since my lawyer didn't do such a great job with the opening statement, I'll take a shot at this."

A closing argument is the culmination of a jury trial. It is the final opportunity to communicate directly with the jurors. If properly done, the closing argument will have a lasting impact on each juror. In Ralph's case, his closing argument will hardly be proper, but will most definitely have a lasting impact on each juror.

Making his way to where the jurors were seated and reminded by the judge not to go beyond that point, Ralph begins by declaring his innocence. "How many times have innocent people been charged with crimes they didn't commit? A lot," Ralph said in answering his own question.

"And how many times have innocent people been sent to prison? A lot," Ralph answered his own question again. Apparently Ralph liked the idea of asking questions that only he could answer. Believing that he was good at this, Ralph now regretted that he didn't pose questions to himself when he had the opportunity to do so. Ralph then made a mental note to employ this strategy in the unlikely event he is found guilty and has to file an appeal for a new trial.

"What does that tell you?" Ralph rhetorically asks the jury. "It tells me that the worst thing you can do is send an innocent defendant like me to prison," he answers once again in case the jurors don't know the answer.

"So how do you deal with this dilemma? It's quite simple, really. You vote to acquit me of all of the false and malicious charges brought by an overzealous prosecutor who is determined to send me to prison," said the defendant who sensed he was generating momentum for a speedy acquittal.

"Only you can give me my freedom," Ralph implores the

jurors. "You have the power to do so. By acquitting me of these ridiculous charges, you can stand up to the federal government and say, enough is enough! We don't want you sending innocent, hard-working citizens to prison."

Wallace has maintained a relatively low profile throughout this circus. Eager to avoid the spotlight for fear that this fiasco will tarnish his sterling reputation, Wallace did not utter a single word in court after his underwhelming opening statement. However, Wallace must have offered some advice to his client when the time came for Ralph to take his seat. These words of advice probably related to throwing in a curtsy to the jurors at the conclusion to let them know that he is deeply respectful of their power to either find him not guilty or send his sorry ass up the river without a paddle.

As Ralph finally takes a bow and returns to his seat, Judge Smulyan massages his neatly trimmed beard and wonders why he gets stuck with mentally unbalanced defendants who have lost touch with the real world. Looking at his watch, the judge decides that if he sends the jury to deliberate now, he should have a verdict with enough time remaining in the day so he can play nine holes of golf.

****

Judge Smulyan's instincts are spot-on. In less time than it takes to read the better comics in The Baltimore Sun, the jury has the bailiff inform the judge that they have reached a verdict. Once everyone has returned to the courtroom, the verdict is read, at which time Judge Smulyan is pleased that the criminal justice system works. Judge Smulyan is also pleased that he has time to get in a late afternoon game of golf and is about to exit the courtroom once he announces a date for sentencing.

Before the judge can do so, the defendant turns to the AUSA and announces that he wants to see him to discuss a plea, to which the judge rather sternly instructs him to be quiet. It is the prosecutor's hope that Ralph Elwood will soon be escorted from the courtroom in shackles and never heard from again. Unfortunately, this will not be the case because Ralph Elwood is determined to work a deal.

Outside the federal courthouse, members of the press have gathered like hungry sharks circling a pool of smaller fish. In view of the fact that Evan can take the elevator to his office, he doesn't have to engage the media by saying something silly such as, "It was a hard fought trial and the government is grateful to the members of the jury who so diligently undertook their civic obligation to serve. The government is pleased with this verdict and is satisfied that justice has been served."

The only thing that was hard fought about this trial was keeping Ralph under control. Had the jurors returned a verdict other than guilty, they would have been charged with dereliction of civic duty, if such a thing is possible.

When Wallace finally exited the courthouse, the press descended on him like bees on honey. Wallace, who is always willing to accommodate the press, decides that he should offer his thoughts on what happened in court.

Careful not to refer to the defendant as his client, Wallace makes it a point to call the convicted felon by his last name. This will enable Wallace to distance himself from Ralph. To emphasize this point, Wallace will start by saying, "As you know, I did not actually serve as Mr. Elwood's lawyer in court. The judge appointed me to act as his legal advisor and provide guidance when needed. I am sad to say that Mr. Elwood insisted on taking an active role in his defense to such an extent that he was not receptive to any suggestions on my part as to sound legal strategy that might have been beneficial to his defense."

Taking a moment to survey his audience to see how many television news stations would be filming this impromptu news conference, Wallace decided to be assertive. "As a strong advocate of our criminal justice system, I believe that there are certain cases that are better off not going to trial. In this case, I strongly believe that it was the wrong decision to force Mr. Elwood to go to trial. In this respect, the blame should be placed squarely on the US Attorney.

"I am deeply disappointed that this case had to go to trial. I attempted without success to convince Mr. Horan that it was in the best interests of all concerned to allow Mr. Elwood to plead guilty in exchange for his cooperation in assisting the federal government investigate other criminal matters of far greater impact. Sadly, Mr. Horan declined to accept Mr. Elwood's offer.

"Although I cannot say with absolute certainty why Mr. Horan declined to allow Mr. Elwood to enter a guilty plea, I am of the opinion that Mr. Horan may have done so in order to further enhance his reputation as a crusading prosecutor driven to marking one more notch on his belt." Although Wallace's accusation will not endear him to the prosecutor, he is determined to press his point, which is entirely self-serving.

"As strongly as I feel about the ruthlessness by which Mr. Horan proceeded to prosecute an emotionally traumatized Mr. Elwood, I also find Judge Smulyan at fault for permitting this trial to continue. Mr. Elwood was clearly not in the proper frame of mind to act as his own attorney. Nor was Mr. Elwood receptive to anything I had to say. This should have been readily apparent to Judge Smulyan during the trial. In light of these circumstances, it was patently unfair to let this trial continue. I would think that this serves as grounds for an appeal," adds Wallace, who couldn't care less if Ralph received a new trial.

Ironically, Wallace has had far more to say to the reporters than he had to say in court. Comfortable in front of the cameras, Wallace rambles on for fifteen minutes, saying nothing of importance. As the members of the press start to walk away, Wallace is left with only one reporter to ask him questions.

Apparently Wallace doesn't seem to mind that the press conference has been a waste of time. This is because Wallace already collected a substantial non-refundable retainer from Ralph prior to trial for which he has performed minimal legal work. As Wallace says goodbye to the last reporter, he can't help but wonder why he hasn't found more clients like Ralph Elwood.

Chapter 33

Much to the chagrin of everyone in the courtroom, Ralph Elwood is back in court. Although dressed in a conservative business suit for the sentencing hearing, Ralph still looks like a cross between a rat and a snake.

The Department of Justice has spent more time than it would have liked to spend on its sentencing recommendation. With a maximum sentence of seventy five years on the twelve counts in which the defendant was found guilty, the prosecutor has recommended that Ralph serve seventy five years in prison. If sentenced to the maximum term and with time off for good behavior, Ralph should be close to one hundred and ten years of age when he is eligible for early release.

In view of the fact that Judge Smulyan is compassionate and fair in handing down sentences, he has reduced the term of incarceration to seventy years, with credits allowed for good behavior. Accordingly, Ralph could be released before his one hundred and fifth birthday.

To no one's surprise, Ralph does not take this news well. After announcing that he intends to file motions challenging the verdict and sentencing, Ralph once again insists that the prosecutor offer him a deal. "I'm entitled to a deal. It's my constitutional right. You owe this to me. I have time so we can talk now," Ralph says just before he is escorted from the courtroom by several armed guards who would like nothing more than to put a bullet in the back of Ralph's skull.

Evan merely shakes his head in disbelief that Ralph could continue with his insane behavior that he is entitled to a plea bargain following a conviction on all twelve charges. In contrast, Ralph is of the opinion that the AUSA is simply playing hardball and will eventually offer him a plea agreement so that Boris can be sent to prison in his place. This is very much wishful thinking.

Noticeably absent at the sentencing hearing is Wallace Shadybrook, noted legal advisor and shameless publicity hound. Having recalled his well-publicized diatribe in front of the media when he called out the prosecutor as being ruthless and cold blooded, as well as criticizing the trial judge as lacking the intestinal fortitude to stop the trial, Wallace decided that it would be in his best interests to stay away. This is one of the better decisions Wallace has ever made.

****

Ralph has endured the long bus drive to a federal penitentiary that does not have a swimming pool, tennis courts and a golf course. Nor does this fine facility have a shuffleboard deck, sponsor co-ed volleyball games or badminton. The only social activity available to Ralph will consist of lifting weights in a sweaty exercise room with very large angry looking men covered in tattoos who would have no qualms whatsoever in kicking the snot out of Ralph for any reason, or for that matter, without a reason. This is not what Ralph had in mind when he boarded the bus.

Ralph has been subject to the mandatory strip search and body cavity exam that borders on sexual assault. The last highlight of Ralph's first day in his new home involves meeting his cellmate, a rather large African-American male whose last name rhymes with lojack. Ralph was so intimidated by the sheer size of his cellmate that he didn't catch Reggie's first name.

The two cellmates soon discovered that they shared a common interest. Neither is happy with the legal profession and both men despise the lawyers who failed them in their hour of need.

"I'd like to kill the lawyer that I had," Reggie says with indignation for the legal profession.

"I'd ask you to murder my lawyer but I'm not really good at having people whacked," acknowledged Ralph.

"Yep, you already told me. That's why you're here," Reggie says while wondering why a reasonably intelligent CPA could be so stupid to have stolen millions of dollars from his clients and not have expected to be caught.

****

Ralph's second day in prison is almost as eventful as his first day. While enjoying a highly nutritional meal in the dining room, Ralph meets two of his fellow prisoners, Stan Lustman and Dean Pappas. After the introductions have been made and the three inmates have engaged in the normal bullshit, Ralph inquires as what horrible crimes his new friends committed.

When told that they pled guilty to tax evasion, bank fraud and a variety of other crimes, Ralph asked, "Is that it?"

"Actually, there's more in my case. While in prison and in a moment of weakness, I exercised poor judgment when I decided to have an FBI agent, the prosecutor, judge, an IRS agent, and my lawyer murdered," admitted Dean Pappas.

"Jesus," Ralph muttered. "So what happened?"

"The feds had me cold so I had this stupid prick of a lawyer negotiate a plea bargain for me but I later found out that he didn't do jack shit in terms of actual negotiations," said Dean.

"You don't have to tell me about shitty lawyers. I know all about them," Ralph quickly agreed.

"How about you?" Dean asked.

"I was found guilty of stealing eight million dollars from my clients so I could pay off my gambling debts to a notorious Russian mob figure. My clients went to the FBI, the IRS came after me for tax evasion and I got caught hiring someone to murder two witnesses who had planned to testify against me. I wanted to do a plea bargain but my asshole lawyer couldn't get to first base with the prosecutor," Ralph says while shaking his head in disappointment that things have come to this point.

"Why didn't you hire another lawyer?" asked Dean.

"It was already too late. The trial had started, so I took over my own defense. I figured I couldn't do any worse than the shyster who was supposed to defend me in court," said Ralph. "All he had to do was cut a deal with the prosecutor and I'd be in a federal witness protection program and never be heard from again. But, that dumb bastard couldn't get the prosecutor to listen to a word I had to say. Instead of trying to have my clients killed, I should have put a contract out on Wallace," remarked Ralph.

"Did you say Wallace?" asked Dean.

"Yeah."

"Wallace Shadybrook?"

"Yeah. Do you know him?" asked Ralph.

"He's the shithead lawyer who represented me," remarked Dean Pappas.

Now, Ralph and Dean share a common bond. They were each represented by Wallace Shadybrook, a lawyer who neither believes in taking a case to trial nor hammering out a plea bargain that is in the best interests of his client. Each one will have a long time to reflect on the wisdom of having hired Wallace.

Sitting at a nearby table are two inmates who are having a quiet conversation. Neither has picked up what Dean and Ralph have in common. For that matter, neither Richard Cahill, who is doing a nine year stretch in prison, nor Fred Lawson, who is a guest of the facility for the next seven years, are aware that Wallace Shadybrook happened to be their lawyer. They will have plenty of time to discover this as well.

****

"I read your Exam Chief's recommendation. What the hell was he thinking when he wrote this memorandum?" said the Commissioner of the IRS to Ken Holland, the Assistant Commissioner of the Examination Division.

"I warned him about this position of his," replied Ken Holland, who was about to distance himself from a proposal that was too radical an idea even if it could save the IRS billions of dollars.

"I can't advocate this proposal. Instruct Collins to explore other alternatives," ordered the commissioner.

"I've known Tom for a number of years. If he believes strongly in something, he won't change his mind," Ken said. Anxious to bury the hatchet in his subordinate's back as a result of an incident that took place a long time ago, the A/C added, "Tom's a free spirit. I suppose it's attributable to growing up in California where he spent his youth surfing."

"Are you saying that he's not a company man?" said the commissioner.

"I'm afraid that Tom has never been a company man," Holland brazenly lied.

"That really surprises me because his people have consistently been the best field agents in the country. I've always attributed their excellent work to Tom's leadership qualities," the commissioner remarked.

"That has hardly been the case. Those agents don't require his guidance and direction. I perceive Collins as a problem because he's trying to promote his own agenda. What do you want me to do with him?"

"If Tom's not on board with how I want this agency to function, you should have a face-to-face meeting with him to explore alternatives."

"Alternatives such as......?"

"Placing him into another position," suggested the commissioner.

"At this time, I don't have an open position for him. I would have to create a new position somewhere in the organization and that could look suspicious."

"You could have him go back to section chief," suggested

the commissioner.

"That's true. I could do that but it might create so much ill will that the repercussions could come back to haunt me."

"Is he eligible for retirement?"

"No. He's several years short on age and years of service."

"Too bad. If he were eligible, you could persuade him to retire."

"What if I persuaded him to resign?"

"Why would he want to resign?" asked the commissioner.

"We can't have a high ranking official at this level thinking outside-the-box. He's not executive material. In fact, he's taking up a position that someone with executive potential should be in so that person can advance within the agency. Let me talk to him about his future," said Holland, who is now plotting to bury the hatchet so deep in Tom's back that it's not coming out. The A/C sees this as his opportunity to finally settle a score and he is not about to let this moment pass him by.

"To tell you the truth, I really don't want to see Collins resign," said the commissioner. If you can't place him in a comparable position, bump him back to section chief. If there's fallout from any of this with his people, it's your problem."

"I'll take care of it."

Shortly after Tom was promoted to section chief, Ken Holland was instrumental in placing a personal friend into a front-line management position that reported directly to Tom. From the start, Cathy Ballard was ill-equipped to be an audit manager and proved it with her actions. Cathy antagonized the senior male agents in her audit group and became such a source of agitation that one agent in particular decided that he could no longer tolerate her as his boss.

In order to get this miserable woman out of his life, Louie Lipschitz made a telephone call to his brother-in-law, who at that time, was the president's chief-of-staff. With Louie's brother-in-law in a position of immense power, he directed the Secretary of the Treasury to instruct the Commissioner of the IRS to have someone under his chain-of-command immediately terminate Louie's tormentor.   This was accomplished with great swiftness because Ken Holland was warned not to intercede.

While Ken Holland did not hold Tom Collins directly at fault for his friend's dismissal, he considered Tom indirectly to blame because Tom knew that Louie's brother-in-law worked in the Oval Office and yielded the power to do whatever he wanted. Thus, if Louie were assigned to work for Cathy, it was only a matter of time before Louie would have Cathy terminated. Consequently, Ken was of the opinion that there was complicity on Tom's part in wanting to see Cathy gone.

With Tom advocating an extraordinarily controversial position on a subject fraught with problems, Ken decided that it was now time to exploit this dilemma so that he could pay Tom back on behalf of his friend. The A/C was practically salivating at the prospect of forcing his subordinate to quit.

That afternoon, Ken advised Tom that it would be in the best interests of all concerned if Tom tendered his resignation. As Tom had not met the eligibility requirements for retirement under any possible circumstances including disability, his options were limited to either resigning or being subject to dismissal by reason of a bogus insubordination charge. Even if Tom could delay termination by challenging his dismissal, he knew that he could not extend the process until he reached eligibility for retirement.

Given three days to make a decision, Tom decided to discuss

the matter with his wife and no one else.

"Let me get this straight. The IRS is trying to get rid of you because you came up with a bold idea that could save the federal government billions of dollars each year?" asked Tom's wife.

"Not really. My boss is using my controversial recommendation as an excuse so that he can get rid of me for my role in the dismissal of a friend of his quite a few years ago," replied Tom.

"Is he that petty?"

"It's called revenge. People in senior management do this all the time."

"Unbelievable," remarked Tom's wife, who just shook her head in puzzlement that this practice existed among supposedly mature adults in positions of authority. "The people running our government at the highest levels do this? This is just incredible!"

"I think I should resign," concluded Tom.

"Good for you. But promise me you'll find a job so we don't have to live in a cardboard box under some bridge and ask for handouts from strangers."

****

On the final day in which a decision was expected, Tom submitted his letter of resignation to Ken Holland, who immediately accepted the resignation, effective within thirty days. Within thirty minutes, news had spread throughout the Federal Building so quickly that it was reminiscent of the moment FDR announced that the United States had entered

World War II.

Louie is usually among the first to hear about personnel actions. As soon as he heard, he went straight to Tom's office and asked, "What in the hell did you just do?"

"I'm flattered that you would be disappointed that I'm leaving," remarked Tom.

"Seriously, I'm not that disappointed so don't be flattered. It's taken me how many years to get you trained to do your job and now you want to leave?

"I'm touched by your concern."

"Just between us, what's going on?" Louie asked.

"I think it's time that I left this agency."

"Bullshit! Not only do I know what bullshit looks like, but I can smell it. What gives?"

"Louie, it's not something that I want to get into now," replied Tom.

"OK. If you're not going to tell me, I'll tell you what I think it is. It's about this business of putting e-returns on a vacation plan. I had a feeling that the suits wouldn't be on board with this because it's not politically correct," Louie said. "Let me guess which one of the suits put the butcher knife in your back."

Pausing for a moment, Louie says, "That would be Kenneth Holland, A/C extraordinaire who couldn't find his way out of a paper bag even if given a set of AAA instructions, a road map, a state-of-the art navigational system and travel guide. How am I doing?"

"You're very astute."

"Yes, I am. And why is Holland going after you? Because

of your perceived role in the dismissal of Cathy whatever her last name is."

"Ballard."

"Right, Ballard. Well, it was my idea to get rid of Ballard, not yours. And this business with the e-returns?" said Louie. "I may have pushed you in the wrong direction so it's not your fault."

"No. I have to take full responsibility for that decision. You worked under my direction and you did what I wanted you to do. Do not take the blame for me," Tom instructed Louie.

"I don't think so. I'll talk to Dan and see what he can do for you."

"Your brother-in-law doesn't work in the Oval Office anymore. He doesn't have the kind of clout that he once had. Dan can't get my job back for me," Tom said.

"You might be surprised as to what Dan can do. With a couple of well-placed phone calls, he could have you reinstated and possibly put Holland out of a job. Better yet, maybe you'll be offered Holland's job."

"I wouldn't want Ken Holland's job. I don't want to deal with the D.C. traffic going to and from the office. I could do without having to rub elbows with people I can't stand. I don't want to spend all my time sitting in meetings pretending to be interested in what a bunch of imbeciles have to say about subjects they know nothing about. Need I say more?" Tom asked.

"No. Would you be happy finishing out your undistinguished career here?" Louie remarked with his typical sarcasm.

"With or without your constant bickering about the working conditions?" Tom said with a grin.

"I don't bicker."

"Yes you do."

"No I don't," argued Louie.

"You just proved my point. Don't let the door hit your ass on the way out. Please give Dan my best regards whenever you talk to him."

"I plan to talk to him soon," Louie promised.

As Louie was about to leave, he turned back and said, "Boss, if you leave, are you going to take your plants with you?"

Tom Collins is fixated on having large plants. Apparently Tom believes that large plants symbolize authority. Tom often compares the plants in the offices of other IRS executives. While Tom generally doesn't make it a practice of carrying a tape measure on him, he is very good at approximating the height of other peoples' plants.

In order to ensure that his plants outgrow rival plants, Tom has his secretary meticulously water and feed his two oversize plants on a regular maintenance schedule. There are young children in underdeveloped nations who only wish that they could receive the same care and attention.

"Why do you ask?" Tom is curious to know.

"I was just thinking that if you bail out and don't take your plants with you, I'd like to have them," replied Louie.

"The last time I checked, you didn't have a private office. You have a desk that is in a small cubicle. Where could you possibly put these plants?" Tom asked.

"I'd put them in a private office."

"But you don't have a private office," countered Tom.

"Actually, I was thinking that with you gone, management could temporarily fill your position with another manager and then back-fill that position. Once that's done, there would be an opening for an audit manager. That would open up a slot for me. Then, I'd have an office," Louie said.

"Your thinking is somewhat flawed. You might have an office, but no group manager has an office large enough to accommodate plants this size," Tom remarked.

"I wasn't finished," Louie shot back. "Once I'm promoted to group manager, I could be detailed into your old section chief position for up to one year. After one year in service as a group manager, I'm automatically eligible to apply for section chief. If I'm acting section chief for almost one year, I would be a lock to get the job. That means, I would get your old office and the plants."

"My body isn't even cold and you're already plotting to take my former job, my old office and the plants that I cherish more than life itself. That's cold," acknowledged Tom.

"I think it exemplifies my managerial potential," replied the little guy.

"I think it illustrates your talent to be a scavenger, eager to pick apart the discarded carcass of your fallen leader."

"That too," admitted Louie.

****

"Louie, I don't have that kind of clout anymore."

"Don't you have a rolodex with every bigshot's name in the federal government?" Louie asked his brother-in-law.

"My rolodex is impressive but I don't know the Secretary of the Treasury all that well."

"What about the Commissioner of the IRS?"

"Not really. I may have met the man once or twice. Look, the players have all changed since I left the government. It's a new cabinet now. I'd have to work the phones to connect with the right people in order to get access to those at the top."

"What about your former boss?" Louie inquired of his brother-in-law.

"Are you referring to the president?"

"No, I was thinking about the cleaning person who empties the trash bins in the White House."

"Very funny. You want me to put a call into the former president and ask him to talk to either the Secretary of the Treasury or the Commissioner of the IRS on Tom's behalf?"

"You're still tight with the ex-prez?"

"I believe that I am still tight with him," Dan Goldman replied in all sincerity.

"Good. Make the call and get back to me," Louie said as he hung up the phone.

Chapter 34

Dan Goldman is still in the ex-president's tight circle of friends and confidants. Dan's advice in various matters of government was always highly-regarded by his former boss. As such, Dan is one of the few people with unfettered access to the former president.

Dan made the phone call that was asked of him. Once Dan had explained the circumstances for the predicament that Tom was in, his former boss said, "I'll be happy to make some phone calls on his behalf. Perhaps I can even pave the way for this Holland person to be asked to leave."

"Thank you sir," replied Dan, who knew that nothing further needed to be said. If his former boss is true to his word, Louie could expect to see some fallout very shortly.

****

"What's happening at the IRS?"

"What do you mean?" the Commissioner of the IRS asked his boss, the Secretary of the Treasury.

"Anything I should know about?"

"As far as I know, it's business as usual," answered the commissioner.

"Let me ask you something, then. Does business as usual

always involve purging the management pool of talent as a result of a personal vendetta?"

"Purging management? A personal vendetta? What are you talking about?"

"I got a telephone call from Stephan Thompson, who relayed information from Dan Goldman, his chief-of-staff. Goldman's brother-in-law is a hot shot IRS agent," said the Secretary of the Treasury.

"That would be Louis Lipschitz. I'm familiar with Agent Lipschitz's reputation. From what I've been told, he's probably the best field agent in the country," replied the commissioner.

"Well, it seems that Agent Lipschitz was at the center of a controversy surrounding the termination of Cathy Ballard a number of years ago. More precisely, it was Dan Goldman who interceded on Agent Lipschitz's behalf and had Ms. Ballard forced out."

"That incident took place prior to my becoming commissioner."

"But you're familiar with the story?"

"Yes. I've heard an account of this story."

"There is an A/C in your employ who happens to be a personal friend of this Ballard woman. He did not appreciate what was done to her. According to information that has been passed on to me, your A/C held Ballard's direct supervisor responsible for her demise. The supervisor at that time was Tom Collins."

"And you think there's a personal vendetta at play here?"

"Collins has advocated delaying the issuance of all refunds with respect to e-filing until the IRS can verify all third party source documents. What he's arguing for makes perfect sense except it will not be legislatively enacted. Ken Holland has jumped on this as a foolish proposal and ridiculed Collins for thinking outside the box."

"I did agree with Holland that the idea is not politically viable," admitted the commissioner.

"I don't have a problem with your decision to reject the proposal. What I have a problem with is Ken Holland strong-arming Tom Collins into resigning."

"He did what?" exclaimed the commissioner, who was taken aback by the news that Tom Collins was forced to resign.

"Holland forced Collins to quit. What did Holland say to you about this?"

"Absolutely nothing," answered a visibly shaken commissioner who was outraged that a popular senior official could be forced to resign because of a perceived personal vendetta from years ago.

"Stephan Thompson was a very popular president with many friends in high places. He has taken an active interest in this matter because he feels that a good man has been wrongfully punished. Goldman is also someone with many friends in high places. These two men are a very formidable team even if they no longer run the country. I don't need people as powerful as Stephan Thompson and Dan Goldman upset with me. Do you catch my drift?"

"You want Tom Collins to remain in his position. I will arrange that," replied the commissioner.

"I think you should also do something with Holland."

"Such as?" asked the commissioner, who suspected that the answer is dismissal. However, he wanted to hear this directly from his boss.

"I'll let you use your imagination. Just make sure Holland is no longer an A/C. Either send him to a sub-office in Anchorage or tell him it's time he left. I don't really care but I want him removed as an A/C. The sooner it's done, the better," advised the Secretary of the Treasury.

"Consider it done by close of business today."

Chapter 35

"You wanted to see me?" Ken Holland said as he entered the commissioner's office.

"That's right. We need to talk," said the commissioner.

"What is it?" asked the A/C who was not advised in advance as to the subject of this meeting.

"Do you recall the recent conversation that we had regarding Tom Collins?"

"Yes, I do."

"Do you recall what actions you were going to take?"

"I told Tom that his proposal was in conflict with IRS policy. I asked him if he would agree to return to his old job, which he immediately refused to do. We seemed to be at an impasse so he agreed to resign."

"That's not the version that I heard," remarked the commissioner.

"I don't understand," said a visibly flustered Ken Holland.

"I have been provided with an account of your meeting with Tom Collins. According to the information that I was given, you threatened Tom by telling him that if he did not resign within three days, you would fire him."

Shaking his head to emphasize that this was untrue, Holland declared, "I don't recall having said that."

"Maybe you're experiencing selective memory loss," hinted the commissioner.

"This doesn't make sense. I wanted to place Tom in another position within the organization," Holland lied.

"No you didn't. What you told me was that if you demoted him to section chief, the consequences of such a move could have serious ramifications with the workforce," stated the commissioner.

"Right. I remember that."

"So I told you to place him in another executive position, if possible. I seem to specifically recall having said that if you could not find another comparable position for him, you would bump him back to section chief and deal with the consequences," said the commissioner. "Do you recall this?"

"Vaguely. Look, I didn't have a job vacancy for Collins."

"You forced him to resign when you could have moved him back to section chief. You threatened him," the commissioner said.

"I thought that's what you wanted me to do," Holland replied.

"That's not what I told you to do."

"Well, it's too late now. Collins has tendered his resignation and I've accepted it. He's out of your hair."

"Actually, Tom's not leaving. I've asked him to rescind his resignation and he's agreed to do so," remarked the commissioner.

"What!"

"I think the real thorn in my side is you. It's time that you left."

"You can't be serious!" exclaimed Holland.

"I am. And I checked."

"Checked what?"

"You have been eligible to retire for more than seven years. I want your papers on my desk in fifteen minutes. If you haven't submitted your paperwork by then, I'll terminate you for cause."

Thirteen minutes later, Ken Holland had submitted his retirement papers. By next week, he will be joining Cathy Ballard in her latest business venture, "Flowers R Us."

****

After Cathy Ballard was unceremoniously dismissed from her job, she started a house cleaning service in her neighborhood. Unwilling to actually get her hands dirty, Cathy hired a group of teenagers to do the grunt work such as cleaning the bathrooms and kitchens. Most times Cathy was not on site to supervise her crew so her employees removed anything of value in the homes they were supposed to clean.

Cathy's clients complained that jewelry, electronics, kitchen appliances, computers and televisions were missing. Insisting that her employees would not steal such items, Cathy suggested that young teens in the neighborhood had probably broken into the homes during the day when no one was home. Irked that Cathy was not responsive to the problem, the neighbors filed police reports, alleging theft.

When the police investigated the allegations, they discovered that Cathy's crew consisted of gang members with long criminal records for breaking and entering, armed robbery and other felonies. Once they were apprehended and some of the valuables were recovered, Cathy decided to cease business operations and start a new venture.

Over the years, Cathy has started, operated and closed more than sixty different business activities. Her most recent failure involved breeding miniature ponies.

Cathy has been operating a flower shop for almost one month. Her business, "Flowers R Us" will soon be filing for bankruptcy protection. With Ken Holland on board to provide his managerial expertise, the flower shop will soon be on life support.

Once Louie heard about "Flowers R Us," he made it a point to pay a visit to the business. Seeing Louie walking along the isles to look at the various plants and flowers sent chills down Cathy's spine.

"You over there, can I get some help here?" Louie said loud enough for everyone in the shop and along the sidewalk to hear him.

"Lois, can you wait on that customer while I tend to some business in the back?" Cathy said to her assistant so that she wouldn't have to deal with Louie. Cathy made a hasty retreat to her office and stayed there until long after Louie had left.

When Cathy returned, she asked Lois, "Did that customer purchase any flowers?" to which her assistant replied, "No. He said he didn't see anything he liked but promised to come back another time."

Once word had gotten out that Ken Holland was now selling flowers, Louie made a return visit to the flower shop. Pretending to make a selection, Louie yelled out once again, "Hey, can I get some help over here?"

When Cathy and Ken saw Louie prowling the isles, they both took off for the office in the back of the store and waited until

Louie had left. "I wonder how much longer that munchkin's going to keep doing this," said Cathy.

"Don't worry about it. He's jealous that you have a successful business and he's just a pencil pushing grunt," remarked Ken.

By next month, the terminally ill flower shop will cease to exist. In addition, Cathy will be notified by the IRS that she is being held personally liable for tens of thousands of dollars in unpaid trust fund taxes that she never bothered to remit to the IRS for several of her failed businesses.

Chapter 36

"No way!"

"I'm not jerking your chain. I used the same lawyer as you," said Richard Cahill.

"Wallace Shadybrook? The guy who looks like he's a hundred years old, with this big nose and oversized ears," said Fred Lawson.

"Don't forget the beady eyes."

"Right, how could I forget the beady eyes? I saw the way he checked out my wife, Mona. Like he was trying to put the moves on her," Fred said.

"Freddy, that's the same guy. He sold me out just like he did you. That prick took my money and didn't do jack shit for me on my tax evasion case."

"Well, if it's any consolation to you, at least I stiffed him on his legal fees. That check I gave him for his retainer bounced like a bungee cord."

"Good for you," Cahill remarked. "What's so important you wanted to talk about?"

"I overheard a couple of the guys talking about running this scam behind bars. I think it's got the potential to be a real moneymaker," said Fred.

"Who did you hear talking about it?" inquired a curious Richard Cahill, who is anxious to start making some serious money behind bars since his professional tennis career is effectively over.

"I don't want to reveal their identities. I'm a firm believer in confidentiality. I wouldn't want to disclose someone's name when it could come back to haunt me," replied Fred.

"Good point. What were they talking about?" asked Cahill.

"Using personal information of people in order to file phony tax returns," said Fred. These guys file the tax returns before the IRS can verify the income and withholding taxes claimed. Once the refunds are direct deposited into offshore bank accounts, there's no paper trail. One of the guys said that they expect to clear millions of dollars in less than three months."

"Jesus Christ."

"Yeah. That's what I said. We should pool our talents and do the same thing," urged Fred. "I figure that by the time I'm out of this dump, I'll have at least twenty five million dollars in an overseas account. Mona and I can then retire to a tropical island and get sloshed every evening while we watch the sun set."

"Count me in partner."

Chapter 37

When Dean Pappas and Stan Lustman learned that Ralph Elwood had once worked for the IRS and had operated a financially lucrative accounting practice, they gravitated to him like flies to horseshit. Once the parties had agreed on how much Ralph would receive, they all shook hands to seal the deal. Ralph was now officially the managing partner in Stan and Dean's criminal enterprise. In Ralph's mind, he was a rock star. However, to Dean and Stan, it was strictly a business relationship with someone they neither liked nor trusted.

****

"We heard what you guys are doing," Dean Pappas said to Fred Lawson while they were paired together in the laundry room.

"What have you heard?" asked Fred as he sorted out the towels among the items that he pulled out of the oversize dryers.

"You know," Dean said with a smirk as he placed the linens in a separate bin.

"No, I don't know. If I knew, I wouldn't have to ask you what it is that you heard," replied Fred.

"We know what's going on," intimated Dean, who moved on to the prison jumpsuits that were in the wash and ready to be placed into the dryer.

"I'm glad you know what's going on. Care to share it with me."

"Why? You already know," Dean hinted with a sly grin on his face.

"No, I don't know," answered Fred as he folded the underwear and socks with a blank expression as if he had no idea what Dean was talking about. Fred merely shrugged his shoulders as he went about folding clothes.

"C'mon Fred. You can't keep secrets in prison. You and the tennis pro plagiarized my plan. Stan and I are actually quite flattered that the two of you are following in our footsteps."

"Plagiarized your plan? What plan?" asked Fred, who had now figured out what Dean was alluding to and attempted to play dumb.

"As if you didn't know," replied a cynical Dean. "I just want to know how much you and the tennis pro have grossed so far."

Having accepted the fact that Dean knew what was going on, Fred replied, "Four million three hundred thousand dollars in less than two months. "How about you?" he asked Dean as he started to unload more clothes from another washing machine.

"With the three of us filing tax returns around the clock, we're at ten million and change in just under three months."

"Jesus. I was going to take bets that we could beat you guys but you're way ahead of us. What's your secret?" asked Fred.

Not anxious to reveal their secret weapon, Dean ignores the question and says, "We could do a friendly wager. We'll even give you a handicap since its three against two," offered Dean, who started to empty more clothes into another dryer.

"I'll take it up with my partner. Getting back to my question which you neglected to answer, how is it that the three of you can crank out that many income tax returns?"

"I have access to a virtually unlimited database of names. Plus, we've got Elwood on our side!"

"The CPA who looks like a rat!" exclaimed Fred. "I wouldn't trust that leech to hand me a bar of soap."

"I wouldn't either. But that SOB can prepare a phony tax return in the time it takes to order a combo meal at Burger King. You have to respect somebody with those skills!" Dean said with a huge grin on his face.

"How about combining our resources?" suggested Fred, who stopped folding clothes to take a two minute break.

"Why? We're making a lot more money than you. If we merge operations, the three of us are giving you and the tennis pro a portion of our hard earned money. That's contrary to how capitalism is supposed to work."

"Hey, I'm not trying to cut into your profits. I just thought that we could pool our talents," replied Fred.

"If you want us to combine our operation with yours, you'll have to buy-in."

"Buy-in?"

"That's right. You'll have to make a sizable capital contribution for the privilege of working with us and sharing in our pool. I'll talk to my people but the buy-in is going to be steep," Dean advised.

"We're practically brothers. Can't we just work together while we serve our sentences?" Fred pleaded.

"No. While we're here doing time, my people intend to make as much money as they can. We aren't operating a charity. And this isn't a hobby. You want in, you'll have to pay for the privilege. Think of it as having to pay an entrance fee to gain membership in an exclusive country club," Dean said.

"How much?" asked Fred.

"At least five million in cash, maybe more," suggested Dean. "I'll take it up with my people and get back to you."

****

Most people do not go to a beauty salon before they go off to prison. It would seem that the logic behind not undertaking a make-over is because there is no need to do so. Nobody holds beauty contests behind bars and extra credit is not awarded to those who look the best in bright orange jumpsuits with the word "PRISONER" in bold capital letters on the back. The only thing a nice appearance will do is bring about unwanted attention.

Shortly before Mona Lawson was to enter a federal correctional facility where she will undergo five years of rehabilitation in order to re-enter society as a much better person, she splurged on a full body make-over. This was done after Fred had left for the Big House. Mona rationalized that, if nothing else, a make-over would make her feel better before she goes off to prison.

When Mona made her debut in the dining hall, she was instantly noticed by Erica and Mary Beth, who had already become very good friends.

"Well, who is that?" Erica asked with lust in her eyes, as if Mary Beth would happen to know.

"How should I know," Mary Beth replied.

"Find out and get back to me on that. There's a shortage of fresh meat in this dump and someone who looks that good should be in our club," Erica instructed her flunky.

"We don't have a club. It's just the two of us."

"Mary Beth, if you have two people who share a common bond, that constitutes a club," advised Erica. "That hot looking bitch doesn't know it yet but we are going to induct her into our select little club."

"What if she doesn't want to join our club?" Mary Beth wondered aloud.

"She will," Erica said with absolute certainty in her voice.

****

Just as Mona was about to set her tray on one of the dining tables several rows from where Erica was sitting, Mary Beth approached her with an invitation to sit at Erica's table. When Mona looked over to see Erica, she was rewarded with a warm smile that betrayed Erica's true intentions.

With her food tray in both hands, Mona slowly walked to where Erica was sitting and introduced herself. Once all the introductions were made, Mona started asking a lot of questions about life behind bars and whether the inmates have social activities. Rolling their eyes in disbelief that Mona is either incredibly naïve or just plain stupid, Erica and Mary Beth explain that prison is generally not a place for social interaction but can have its fun moments.

Curious as to why Erica and Mary Beth are behind bars, Mona asks the obvious question and is provided with a detailed account of their crimes. When asked to reciprocate, Mona does so and is pleased that Erica and Mary Beth are impressed with her lack of integrity and morality.

"We should do business together," Erica says.

"In here?" asks Mona, unsure what Erica is talking about.

"Mary Beth and I have a very profitable venture that we're working on. It's quite lucrative and we could use another person to help out." Erica says this as if she's operating a fast food franchise and is in need of an assistant manager.

"What is it?" Mona inquires.

"We'll fill you in later," Erica says. "Mary Beth and I prefer to shower after dinner. Meet us in the shower room in ten minutes and we can go over everything there."

"What about the guards?" asked Mona.

"The guards are okay with us showering after dinner. Sometimes, they'll even join us. Just tell them you're expected."

"Great. I could use a good scrub down in this filthy place," Mona added.

"That's exactly what we had in mind. A good scrub down," Erica whispered to Mary Beth as they got up from the table to head in the direction of the showers.

Chapter 38

As a general rule, when convicted felons attempt to negotiate a business deal by themselves, the words "ethics" and "integrity" do not come into play. When five crooks sit down to work a deal, the more likely probability is that they will try to screw each other out of something.

Dean and Stan had argued as to who should negotiate on behalf of their team, with both men of the opinion that their criminal accomplishments were greater than the other's.

"I cleared fifty million dollars a year tax-free until I was convicted of tax evasion. How about you?" Stan said.

"Not only was I convicted of tax evasion, but I was also guilty of bank fraud to the tune of sixty million dollars. And let's not forget that while I was rotting in prison, I tried to have my tormentors murdered. Throw in murder-for-hire and I've got you beat."

At the same time Dean and Stan were trying to decide who the bigger crook was, Fred and Richard were embroiled in a similar discussion.

"I ripped off tennis promoters, sponsors, tournament directors, and so many others I lost track. If the feds hadn't nailed me for tax evasion, I'd still be working three scams all at once," Richard said with pride.

"That's kid stuff to what I was able to do. I finagled twenty five million dollars out of Chase and almost got away with it. On top of that, I fleeced that shithead lawyer out of his legal fees," Fred countered.

"OK. I'll give it to you because you screwed that old fart, Shadybrook."

With Dean taking the lead for his team and Fred the spokesman for his side, the talks are going nowhere. Fred has expressed displeasure with a buy-in of almost six million dollars and has countered with a buy-in of three million dollars, which has been summarily rejected.

"What do you really want?" Fred asks, hoping to cut to the chase.

"Six million dollars."

"I asked you what you really wanted. That means I want to know what you're willing to accept," Fred says as a matter of clarification.

"Six million dollars. That's what I'm willing to accept," was Dean's terse reply.

After several hours of not getting anywhere, the leaders for each group return to their respective cells, with no further talks planned. However, Fred has only just started to formulate an alternate plan which he hopes to implement very soon.

The following day, Fred is assigned to laundry duty with Ralph. While Fred regards Ralph as a snake who cannot be trusted, he recognizes that Ralph is the key to making millions of dollars. Recalling something about there being no honor among thieves, Fred decides to initiate a preliminary inquiry that lacks any honor.

"Ralph, what's happening?" Fred asks not out of interest in hearing what is new with Ralph but to get the lines of communication open for a frank discussion.

"You tell me," was Ralph's noncommittal response.

"OK. I suppose Dean told you that negotiations have broken down. We're not going to merge our operations," Fred said as he started to load the clothes into the first of the washing machines.

"You couldn't pull the trigger," Ralph said to intentionally needle Fred.

Trying to remain calm, Fred replied, "My partner and I didn't want to overpay. We're making money on this scam."

"You're not making what we're making and you stole the idea from me. So don't complain to me," Ralph remarked while he filled up one of the washing machines and started it on the first rinse cycle.

As painful as it is to say, Fred knows that he must say it to appease Ralph. "We know that you're the genius behind this scam. My partner and I want you on our team. I don't see why we have to pay your partners when we can pay you to be on our side," Fred said in hopes of appealing to Ralph's ego and greed.

"It's always good to be appreciated."

"And we appreciate your brilliance," replied Fred as he started the rinse cycle on the next load.

"How much?" asked Ralph.

"Are you referring to a cash payment or a percentage?" Fred asked.

"Both."

Upon hearing that, Fred raised an eyebrow, to which Ralph declared, "I don't work cheap. You guys want me to play on your side of the street, it's going to cost you."

"OK," Fred said as he extended his arms above his head in mock surrender, fully aware that Ralph was in a position of dictating the terms of his compensation.

"Look, here's the deal. "First, you'll have to entice me with a cash offer. I require a cash payment of two million dollars to get things started. In addition, I get fifty percent of the tax refunds. The remaining fifty percent gets split up between you and the tennis pro. How you want to do it, I seriously don't really care. The important thing is that I get two million upfront and fifty percent of the refunds," demanded Ralph. "Are you down with that?"

"I'm down with that," Fred said as they shook hands after dumping the last of the soiled underwear and socks into the washing machines.

Immediately after a two million dollar cash payment had been deposited into one of Ralph's secret offshore bank accounts and it was agreed that Ralph would receive fifty percent of the tax refunds, Ralph switched teams much to the dismay of Dean and Stan.

"How could he do this to us?" Stan asked. "Ralph was like a brother to me."

"Stan, he was lower than the poop that settles to the ocean floor. I couldn't stand the guy and that's saying something because he helped make us rich."

"How are we going to manage without him?"

"Stan we really don't need him anymore. We already have the mechanism in place. We know how to stay several steps ahead of the IRS. We have nothing to worry about. Plus, we don't have to share the money with him. This is what we call addition by subtraction. And most importantly, that snake is somebody else's problem."

****

With Ralph as the team leader, Fred and Richard are now making money hand over fist. At this rate, by next month they will have recouped the two million dollars that they had to pay Elwood. Ralph is also pleased with the arrangement because he is earning more than what he would have in his former partnership.

It would seem that these five felons have made the best of this situation. However, sometimes the best laid plans can sometimes go astray.

Like Fred, Ralph enjoys laundry duty. The laundry room is where Ralph likes to transact business such as negotiating deals. If only Ralph could have asked Evan Horan to meet him in the laundry room of the federal penitentiary. There, Ralph could have worked his magic and sold the AUSA on a plea bargain. Ralph often reflects on his missed opportunity and wonders how he can make a compelling argument that he is truly deserving of a pardon.

Today, Ralph is slated to spend the entire morning in the laundry room. As Ralph dumps the first load of soiled clothes into the one of the washing machines, he is greeted by another inmate assigned to laundry duty.

"Hello Ralph. It's so nice to see you," said the inmate. However, the voice and heavy accent seemed to take Ralph by complete surprise.

When Ralph looked in the direction of the person who greeted him, he instantly froze with fear and said nothing. Blinking his eyes repeatedly, Ralph was hoping that this was just a bad dream.

"I hope the prison authorities are treating you well," said Boris Krushenko in a deceptively menacing tone of voice that brought about a distinct chill in the air.

Boris, who was broad shouldered and thick in the neck and upper back, now stood several feet from Ralph. Most importantly, Boris blocked Ralph's path to the exit doors. The sight of Boris Krushenko standing only a few feet from him was a total shock that left Ralph absolutely terrified.

"Mr. Krushenko, what a surprise it is to see you here," Ralph finally stammered as if he were choking on bullshit.

"Ralph, what's with the Mr. Krushenko? It's Boris. Please, we're old friends. I insist you call me Boris."

"Of course, Boris. What are you doing here?" asked a terrified Ralph.

"Laundry. I'm supposed to be doing the laundry."

"No, I meant in the prison."

"Ah, the prison," Boris said with a hearty laugh. "Well, my friend, that's a long story. You see, I had law enforcement at all levels after me. Local police, state police, Interpol, the FBI, you name it. Everywhere I went, I had law enforcement all over my back. Do you know what that's like, my friend?" Boris says with a wave of his meaty hand. "Anyhow, the FBI had so much dirt on me that I had to cut a deal. You know what I'm saying?"

"I do."

"Yes, my friend, I suppose you do. I think you know all about making deals. Isn't that what you wanted to do?"

"I swear I didn't make a deal. The feds prosecuted me without ever offering me a plea bargain."

"But, you wanted to cut a deal. In the worst way, I understand," replied Boris, who was incredibly well-informed.

"No, it's not true."

"Ah, but I think it is true. You wanted to sell me out so you could avoid all this," Boris said as he extended his arms in the air.

"No, I swear. I didn't rat on you," Ralph pleaded.

"Ralph, my dear friend. I know you didn't rat me out, as you say. But, you wanted to rat me out. As a matter of fact, you would have sold me out if given the chance. That's not what friends do."

"That's right. Friends don't betray each other. I swear I never betrayed you."

"I am so pleased to hear you say that, Ralph," Boris said as he took one step forward to extend his hand in friendship.

When Ralph saw Boris extend his hand, he knew that he had to offer his hand as a gesture of friendship. As Ralph weakly put his hand out, Boris pretended to shake his hand but, at the last second, grabbed Ralph's extended hand with his left hand and bent it back at the wrist while pulling in an upward motion, thereby breaking the wrist. Boris then used his right elbow to deliver a clubbing blow to the left side of Ralph's temple, which left Ralph dazed from its impact.

In extreme pain from having his wrist broken, and now pulverized by the elbow strike to the head, Ralph is about to collapse to the floor. However, Boris managed to grab the back of Ralph's skinny neck with his left hand as he kneed Ralph in the groin several times. The pain that was now centered in Ralph's groin left him bent over as if he were about to heave his guts.

Delighted that Ralph was convulsing uncontrollably, Boris then grabbed Ralph's earlobe and yanked him over to one of the dryers. Standing practically on top of Ralph, Boris whispered in his ear that the end is in sight. Ralph could feel the hot breath from Boris' mouth and winced in pain as Boris repeated, "My friend, it's almost over."

Boris was careful not to leave any noticeable bruises on Ralph's body. He did not want it to appear that Ralph was involved in an altercation with another inmate so he deliberately directed strikes to those areas of the body least likely to show evidence of a physical assault.

"Get in," Boris ordered Ralph.

Openly defiant that he would not voluntarily comply, Ralph said, "No." However, the word "no" is a word that is generally not said to Boris so he encouraged Ralph to get into the dryer by yanking once more on the earlobe.

When Ralph inquired as to why Boris was doing this, Boris merely shrugged his shoulders and replied, "Because I want to."

With one more very forceful tug on Ralph's earlobe that resulted in pain so intense that it caused him to scream at the top of his lungs, Ralph reluctantly agreed to get into the dryer. "OK. OK. I'll climb in," said Ralph, who was now crying. However, this appeared to be taking longer than it should, which started to annoy Boris because Boris had a full plate on his schedule now that he was running a number of business ventures from prison.

Growing impatient with Ralph, Boris simply picked him up and dumped him inside the dryer and set the dials to start the drying cycles. To make sure that Ralph fulfilled his part, Boris stayed to watch through the glass door in the front of the dryer.

Once Ralph showed no signs of life, Boris stopped the drying cycle and removed the dead body from the dryer. Careful to avoid getting any blood that had drained profusely out of Ralph's eyes, ears, nose and mouth on his bright orange prison jumpsuit, Boris positioned the body just where he wanted it to be discovered. Placing Ralph's corpse up against the dryer, Boris turned and left the laundry room, satisfied that the head of the snake has been cut off.

It was not until twenty minutes after Boris had left the laundry room that Ralph's dead body had been discovered by the inmate who was supposed to work that morning in the laundry room. However, the inmate was instructed by one of the guards to start his shift one hour later than normal. When the prisoner asked why, the guard merely said, "Just be ready to start at 9 AM instead of 8 AM. You're getting an extra hour off so don't complain."

Chapter 39

"What do you mean Ralph's dead?"

"Fred, I just overheard the guards talking about it. Ralph was murdered in the laundry room," said Richard Cahill, who was standing off to the side with his business partner in the prison courtyard while their fellow inmates lifted weights, played basketball and made threatening hand gestures in the direction of certain inmates they wanted to murder.

"You think either Dean or Stan killed him?" Fred asked.

"I don't know. Do you think they could have been that bitter about Ralph making a deal with us behind their backs?"

"I have no idea," said Fred.

Just as Fred said this, a rather broad shouldered man with a thick neck and Russian accent moved closer to them. "What is it that you don't know?" their fellow inmate asked.

Apprehensive as to who was talking to them, neither one replied. "I asked you a question," the prisoner said in a harsh tone of voice which indicated that a reply was expected.

"I don't know," Fred said.

"If I heard you correctly, that's the second time you said that."

"C'mon man. Just chill out, okay," Richard uttered with false bravado.

"You are the tennis pro?" Boris Krushenko asked.

"And you are?" asked Fred, who attempted to say this in an assertive tone but failed.

"My name is Boris Krushenko. Your late friend, Ralph Elwood was an acquaintance of mine. A dear friend for so many years," Boris said with a sigh, "until he tried to betray me. Then, Ralph was no longer my friend."

"What is it that you want from us?" asked Richard.

"I am a businessman. I have many business ventures. One such venture involves filing tax returns. I enjoy filing tax returns. Do you know why?" asked Boris in a soft spoken voice.

When Fred and Richard simply shook their heads to let Boris know that they did not know, Boris said, "Because it makes me a lot of money. If you kind gentlemen continue to be my rivals, you are cutting into my profits. The way I see it, you're taking away money that rightfully belongs to me. That's stealing. Do you know what I do to people who steal from me?"

Neither Fred nor Richard could utter a word and again, merely shook their heads.

"They wind up like Ralph."

Fred and Richard allowed their eyes to wander to see if anyone in the courtyard would be coming in their direction. However, the other inmates must have been told to keep their distance because there was no one near the three of them.

Growing up in Russia, Boris learned how to be a thug at a relatively young age. By the time Boris had turned thirteen, he had been arrested for breaking into liquor stores and stealing merchandise. Not satisfied with just stealing liquor, Boris graduated to stealing cars, armed robbery and assault. By the time Boris had turned sixteen, he had earned a graduate degree in murder.

Trained by his uncles and cousins to murder people on behalf of the mobsters who employed him, Boris took great pride in being a highly efficient and cold-blooded killer. One of the first things Boris was taught was to never allow a murder to be personal. His uncle Vladimir often said to Boris in what he considered to be a teaching moment, "It's all about business."

While Boris decided that Ralph had to be murdered for attempting to betray him, he allowed this to be an exception to his rule and made it very personal. Boris then decided that he would use Elwood's death to intimidate his competitors.

Boris is very astute when it comes to closing a business deal and made it a point to say, "No help is on the way. In here, I run this place. The guards take their orders from me. Any inmate that I want to have put on ice, is put on ice. Now, what I want you two gentlemen to do is assemble everything you've done as of today, put it in cardboard boxes that the guards will be giving you, and bring it to my cell by 4 PM today. The guards will come for you a few minutes before 4 PM and escort you to my cell. I want all of the tax returns that you've prepared, your offshore bank accounts and anything else that relates to what Ralph was doing."

"But ....you're putting us out of business," Fred complained.

"True. But I'm also allowing you to live because if you don't give me what I have asked for, you will suffer the same fate as your former business partner."

"Does this mean you don't want us filing any more tax returns?" Richard asked.

"You must have been hit in the head by one too many tennis balls. If I even suspect that you were thinking about filing another tax return, I will personally cut off your dick and shove it down your throat. Then, I will slit your throat from ear to ear. Have I made my intentions clear?"

"I believe so," said Richard. Fred merely nodded in tacit acquiescence because he was too scared to move his lips.

****

Erica, Mary Beth and Mona are now the best of friends and partners in crime. Mona has been quickly indoctrinated into what Erica calls her "club."   The three make it a point to shower together every evening after dinner. It is readily apparent to Mona that her trip to the beauty salon has paid dividends.

Erica has taken Mona under her wing and provided her with one-on-one instruction in the art of filing phony tax returns. Although Mary Beth appears to be somewhat jealous of the personal attention that Erica has bestowed on Mona, she has wisely kept this to herself.

Mona has proven to be a surprisingly quick study and has enthusiastically embraced Erica's scheme to defraud the federal government. In fact, Mona is so taken with the idea of fleecing the federal government out of its tax revenue that she plans to continue doing this once she is released from prison. Mona has concluded that this is something that she and Fred could do together as a family activity and turn into a lucrative part-time business.

When Erica learned what Mona has planned to do following her release, she advised Mona that before she could do this, royalties of some sort would have to be paid, to which Mona replied by saying, "Huh?"

"Look, babe. This business venture was my idea. I brought you into this as a favor. You can't just go out and start your own business that you've copied from my business model. That's infringement. It's like I wrote a best-selling novel and you plagiarized it. You can't do that. It's criminal. So, if you want to do this after you're released from this dump, you have to first obtain my permission," explained Erica.

"OK. Do I have your permission?" Mona asked nicely.

"No. You need to purchase a franchise from me," Erica remarked in all seriousness.

"A franchise?"

"That's right. It's like McDonald's. You want to open a McDonald's? You have to first pay a franchise fee to the people who own the McDonald's name."

"Are you kidding me? You're running a criminal enterprise from prison. How in the world could you have gotten a patent on this?" Mona asked.

"With lawyers, anything is possible," answered Erica.

Chapter 40

At 4 PM, Fred and Richard were officially out of the tax preparation business. However, that still left Dean Pappas and Stan Lustman as rivals of Boris Krushenko.

Boris, who like the late Ralph Elwood, enjoyed transacting business in the laundry room, used his influence with prison authorities to have Dean and Stan assigned to the laundry room that afternoon. As the two partners in crime were busy dumping linens and towels into the washing machines, Boris entered the room without being noticed. Casually strolling over to where Dean and Stan are sorting out the towels, Boris asks if they know his name.

"Why would we know your name if we don't know who you are?" replies Stan.

"You sound like a lawyer. Are you a lawyer, Stanley?" Boris asks.

"How did you know my name?" asks Stan.

"I know all about you and your partner, Dean," responds Boris. "You two have quite a reputation in here."

"Yeah, I guess we do," Dean replies with pride, as if being recognized in a federal correctional facility is a badge of honor.

"You were partners with Ralph Elwood, now deceased. Is that right?"

"How did you know?" asks Stan.

"It's my business to know everything that goes on in here."

"And you are?"

"My name is not important," he says followed by a dismissive wave of his hand as if he is about to perform a magic trick. "I was a former business acquaintance of the late Ralph Elwood. Unfortunately, Ralph went from being a trusted associate to a traitorous competitor. That wasn't a good career move on his part."

"You had Ralph killed?" Dean asked.

"No. I didn't have him killed," Boris says as if he had been insulted by having been asked that question. "I murdered him myself. There's a difference between having someone do something for you and doing it yourself."

"Why are you telling us this?"

"Because you are stealing money from me by filing tax returns that I should be doing," said Boris. "I can't have that. So, this is what we'll do. You're going to stop filing my tax returns right now or I'm going to deal with you just like I dealt with the late Mr. Elwood."

"Wait a minute. I've been filing phony tax returns for the past six or seven years and now you're telling me I can't do it anymore?" Stan feebly protested.

"Stanley, had I wanted you to enlighten me as to what you've been doing for the past six or seven years, I would have asked you to do so. But I didn't. That's because I don't really care how long you've been filing phony tax returns. What I do care about is what you plan to do today," Boris says without any rancor in his voice. Pausing for a moment and waving his index finger back and forth at Stan, Boris says in a far more menacing tone, "You'll stop right now or you'll be carried out of this prison in a box before I sit down to have dinner."

"Why can't we co-exist as friendly rivals?" Dean asks while trying to control the stutter in his voice.

"My dear friend, there is no such thing as friendly rivals. We are either good friends who do not have competing business interests or you will die very painful deaths. Which do you choose?"

"We would like to be your good friend," replied Stan.

"Good. The guards will deliver cardboard boxes to your cell this afternoon. Fill the boxes with all of your tax forms, include the lists of your offshore bank accounts and anything else I need to have. You'll bring everything to my cell at 8 PM sharp. If you don't show up with the boxes, I'll make arrangements to have both of you buried in the courtyard first thing in the morning. Do we understand each other as to what will happen?"

"Perfectly," Dean and Stan said in unison.

"Well, I don't want to take you away from your laundry duties. Don't forget what I said. I always say what I mean and mean what I say." Having made his intentions clear, Boris turned and exited the laundry room, leaving Dean and Stan to consider their fate. Boris had other business to transact and with meetings taking place for the next several hours throughout the prison, the kingpin wondered whether he should hire an administrative assistant in order to help plan his busy schedule.

Once Boris left the room, Dean and Stan looked at each other in utter despair. They have now been forced into giving up a very profitable enterprise. Now they wondered how they could supplement their income behind bars.

"Supplement our income? Anything we try to do, Boris will order us to stop," Stan said.

"Jesus, what the hell are we supposed to do in prison if

we can't operate a legitimate criminal enterprise?" Dean complained.

"Hey, maybe we should talk to Boris about an early release," Stan suggested.

"An early release?" exclaimed Dean. "He's an inmate just like us. Do you honestly believe that he has the juice to get us paroled?"

"Let's ask him when we visit with him tonight," said Stan.

Chapter 41

As word spread that Tom Collins will not be leaving Club Fed, Louie has made it a point to embellish upon the part that he played in saving Tom's job. "Louie, you made one phone call. How is that instrumental?" asked Tom.

"It was that one phone call that put everything into motion," answered Louie.

"No. It was Dan who put everything into motion. I think you've inflated the minor role that you played. However, I am truly grateful for what you did."

"I take it you want to show your gratitude by putting me in for a Special Act Award." In terms of dollars, the Special Act Award that is bestowed upon Louie will pay no more than two hundred dollars, which is considered insignificant as an award. However, it is recognized as an important award in the sense that the employee did something above and beyond that person's duties and responsibilities. When competing for a promotion, someone who has received a Special Act Award is generally given preference over someone who has not.

"No. I want to show my gratitude by ordering you back to work."

"OK. OK. But before I go, did you want to hear about what I just learned?"

"Is this related to work?"

"It is. It's about your e-filing project," replied Louie.

"What is it?"

"Before I begin, did you want to hear about the latest medical breakthroughs with penile implants, a subject that is near and dear to your heart?" Louie teased his boss.

"No, I do not!"

"You should.   According to Harvard medical school researchers, significant strides have been made in ...."

"Lipschitz, I don't want to hear another word about your stupid implants," exclaimed Tom.

"Wouldn't you want to do this for your wife? Doesn't she deserve ...."

"That's it. If I hear one more word from you on this subject, I'll have you cleaning the restroom floors in this building with a toothbrush. When you're finished with the floors, you'll use the same toothbrush on the toilets. Have I made myself clear?"

"I think so," responded Louie, as he gave Tom a puzzled look which did not fool his boss at all.

"Good. Now tell me what's going on with your project."

"I detected certain trends with these fraudulent e-filings. I was able to get our IT people to cross-reference certain bogus tax returns where the same mailing address was used. Our IT people also cross-referenced the same offshore bank accounts where the refund checks were deposited. Thousands of refunds were issued to people who had recently died."

"These offshore accounts.......... What did you find out about these accounts?"

"The names used for the offshore accounts are bogus. These accounts were set up using fake foreign trusts. We were able to identify the owners of these trusts by tracing all of the bank account applications."

"And?" Tom asked.

"The owners of a block of offshore accounts consist of Dean Pappas and Stan Lustman, who are currently incarcerated in a federal correctional facility for tax evasion and a myriad of other crimes. If you recall, that Pappas prick tried to have me murdered," Louie exclaimed with anxiety in his voice.

"If my memory serves me correctly, a number of our fine, upstanding citizens tried to have you murdered. Let's see, I recall Erica Whitman, Billy Joe Berman and Stanley Scherr off the top of my head. Have I left anyone else out?" Tom inquired.

"Isn't that enough? Getting back to what I found out, there's a second group that consists of Richard Cahill and Fred Lawson. Cahill was sent to prison for tax evasion while Lawson was convicted of bank fraud. According to the warden, Pappas and Lustman are cellmates."

Before Louie could finish what he was about to say, Tom interjected. "As are Cahill and Lawson, I presume."

"You are very astute, My Holiness," Louie remarked.

"I'm really not all that surprised," acknowledged Tom, "that we have criminals in a federal penitentiary operating a criminal activity that involves the filing of fraudulent income tax returns."

"There's more. The most fraudulent returns in this sampling have been traced to Ralph Elwood. Does that name ring a bell?"

"Jesus Christ! Elwood's behind this?"

"Why wouldn't he be? Elwood's in the same penitentiary as the others...... Correction, he was in the same prison until he turned up dead in the laundry room. I wouldn't be the least bit surprised if the five of them had formed their own little gang behind bars. Picture this," Louie says as he extends his arms for effect. "Lunch and learn, sponsored by Ralph Elwood, a disgraced former IRS agent and CPA," Louie says.

"This is absolutely unbelievable," mutters Tom.

"Wait, there's more," Louie says as he points his forefinger in the air. "Detective Reed had been investigating Boris Krushenko's criminal enterprise until the feds took over the investigation. It seems that Boris is the owner of a handful of foreign bank accounts where tens of millions of dollars in fraudulent tax refunds have been deposited."

"I don't believe this," Tom says as he gently massages the side of his head.

"Hold on, because I have more on this subject," Louie says as he begins to pace back and forth. "Our IT people have identified several million dollars in deposited refunds to another offshore account that is in the name of a foreign trust. This is where things really get interesting."

"We have another criminal behind bars filing bogus tax returns?"

"In a sense," Louie replied as he nodded his head, although the response seemed a bit vague to Tom.

"Do we know the identity of the person who is the owner of this foreign trust?" Tom pressed Louie.

"The owner of the trust is named Deborah Macht."

"That name sounds familiar. Do you know who she is?" Tom asked.

"As a matter of fact, I do. It just so happens that Deborah

Macht is a highly respected federal prosecutor. She's an assistant United States Attorney in the Justice Department's Criminal Tax Division."

"Are you kidding me?"

"I am not kidding you."

"What in the hell is an AUSA doing filing bogus tax returns?"

"She's not," said Louie. "Debbie Macht was the prosecutor in the Timothy Bell case. If you recall, Bell had entered into a plea bargain with the Department of Justice where he pled guilty to all of the charges in exchange for a reduced sentence. Bell later became a cooperating witness in an unrelated case ......"

"Where he claimed to have incriminating information that could be used in the criminal prosecution of our beloved former president, who is no longer with us because he blew his brains out on national television," Tom interjected before Louie could finish what he was saying.

"That's right. Bell had the Justice Department amend its plea agreement on the basis of his promised material cooperation. However, when I eventually discovered that Bell falsified financial records that undermined the pending criminal investigation, Debbie Macht filed a motion with the court to have the amended plea agreement set aside. Debbie was victorious in court and when Bell was taken away, he grumbled something about getting even with Debbie. I was later told that he said something to the effect, 'You haven't heard the last of me,' when he was being led out of the courtroom."

"He got even by depositing several million dollars in an account in her name. I wish he would have gotten even with me," Tom joked. "What do you intend to do with this information?"

"I put a call into the Deputy Attorney General's Office at Justice to let him know that Debbie has been set up by Bell. Our IT people have put together the records that would support what I've told you. In addition, I think someone at Justice should be looking into filing charges against everyone involved in the filing of fraudulent e-returns. There's probably hundreds of millions of dollars in offshore bank accounts that we should be recovering."

"You said they're using the names of dead people?" Tom asked as he tried to comprehend all this.

"They're using the names of dead people as well as the names of millions of taxpayers who filed state income tax returns," Louie replied.

"How in the hell did they get the names of people who filed state income tax returns?"

"They hacked into the records compiled by the State Comptroller's office. The state hasn't officially disclosed this but I have it on very good authority that millions of tax records which should have been encrypted are no longer confidential. That information has been leaked to our criminals who can't file these bogus e-returns fast enough behind bars," Louie added.

Tom seems to be mulling this over for several minutes when he finally says, "Can you draft a memorandum that summarizes everything you've just told me and reference this by corroborating documents?"

"Of course."

"Do it. I want it on my desk before you leave today."

"My Lordship, what pray tell are you going to do with this?"

"I'm going to give it to our Public Affairs Officer and ask her to forward it to the Justice Department for release to the press. Once the press runs with this story, it should put more pressure on Congress to act."

"Great. Just make sure you don't use my name on it," Louie said as he was about to make his way back to his desk to compose a factual account of a story that no one will believe.

"Wait a second, Louie. I'm curious as to how you were able to link Elwood, Pappas, Lustman, Cahill, Lawson and Krushenko."

"I worked from a list of people who had recently died. There was one name on that list that was used by everyone. That was the common denominator."

"So these guys had access to the names and social security numbers of anyone who had passed away within the last year. And they passed that information amongst themselves. Whose name were you able to link to everyone?" Tom asked.

"M.L. Barton," replied Louie.

"The M.L. Barton, the Tax Court judge who recently committed suicide?"

"That would be correct," Louie remarked.

"That's very clever," Tom said.

"Thanks," Louie said somewhat surprised that Tom would be so quick to bestow praise on his work. "It isn't often that you praise my brilliance," Louie said.

"I wasn't talking about you. I was referring to our criminals. Using Barton's name was a stroke of genius and irony."

"I'm glad you admire the brilliance of the many criminals who were able to bamboozle the IRS out of millions of dollars," Louie said as he left to go back to his desk, not having given up on the thought of becoming the next supervisory agent with a large office and oversized plants.

Epilogue

One week later, the Justice Department issued a news release to the press that soon made the front page of The New York Times. Senior executives at the IRS and Treasury were asked to comment by members of the press who jumped on this story like bees are attracted to honey.

Expressing shock and dismay that criminals locked away in a federal penitentiary could outsmart the IRS by collecting hundreds of millions of dollars in illegal tax refunds, government officials declared that this problem will be fixed immediately. This is typical of federal officials declaring that whatever the problem is, all appropriate steps will be undertaken to prevent the problem from ever happening again. When asked what steps will be taken to correct the problem, IRS executives referred the media to Treasury while Treasury officials suggested that the members of the press ask the IRS what it intends to do.

Although Tom Collins served as the impetus for the public announcement, he preferred to keep a low profile on this politically controversial topic, stay in his current job and let his prized plants continue to grow in hopes that they will eventually reach the ceiling in his office.

The public outcry over the rampant abuse of e-filing has finally registered with the country's politicians, who referred all questions to IRS and Treasury officials, who in turn, suggested that the press ask these questions of Congress. When it comes to choosing not to answer questions out of fear that whatever is said is wrong, officials in the federal government do not take a back seat to anyone.

The controversy eventually was resolved when the president took time out from his busy schedule to meet with a classroom of third grade students in an elementary school in Iowa. When an eight year-old girl suggested to the president that the IRS not issue refunds until it could verify the income and withholding tax credits being claimed, the president replied, "Why young lady, that's a great idea! How in the world did the IRS not think of this? As soon as I get back to Washington, I'm going to ask Congress to implement your suggestion."

With that being said, the problem that had plagued the IRS for so many years had been solved by an eight year-old child.

Meanwhile, FBI agents were assigned the task of conducting a criminal investigation of Boris Krushenko, Dean Pappas, Stan Lustman, Richard Cahill and Fred Lawson. At least the agents would know where to find these less than upstanding pillars of society. Given the information that was developed by the IRS, criminal charges would soon be filed.

What to do about Timothy Bell is another matter. When Debbie Macht was told what Bell had done, she immediately asked to be named lead prosecutor once criminal charges had been filed against Bell. In light of the fact that Debbie may be a material witness against Bell, another AUSA will be handling this case, much to Timothy's disappointment.

When Louie was given the assignment to address the e-filing problem, he decided to submit an employee suggestion in order to receive a monetary award. For years, the IRS has brazenly flaunted its Employee Suggestion Program as part of a marketing campaign to let employees know that they are continually encouraged to submit ideas that could save the federal government money. If an IRS employee submits a suggestion that will save the federal government money, that employee is entitled to receive a cash award based, in part, on a percentage of the cost savings to the IRS. However, this is like a television game show that is rigged because the IRS makes it a practice not to pay cash awards to its employees, often citing a variety of lame and bogus excuses.

Louie is cognizant of the IRS's track record in not living up to its commitment and has decided to show what the cost savings is based on the actual numbers as determined by the Office of the Inspector General. By doing so, the IRS cannot challenge Louie's cost savings estimates.

Louie then made the argument that the methodology used by the IRS in processing tax refunds is flawed and must be corrected by a verification of third party source information. An automatic suspension period of ninety days would be required to implement this procedure.

With Congress now supportive of the very recommendation that Louie has made, the little guy is calculating his soon-to-be vast wealth. "I'm guessing my cash award will be in the neighborhood of about three hundred million dollars," Louie tells his wife, Lucy.

"I wouldn't go out and spend the money just yet, dear," the little woman cautions her wishful thinking spouse.

What Louie hasn't taken into account is that the IRS can impose a limit on the cash payment. This limitation is substantially less than three hundred million dollars. There is something else that Louie has not considered. The IRS will not act on his suggestion during Louie's lifetime.

Once the IRS actually considers Louie's suggestion, a team of analysts will be tasked with the responsibility of finding a reason not to approve the suggestion.

If Louie were to weigh the likelihood of ever collecting a cash award for his employee suggestion, the odds would be greater in Boris Krushenko being granted a presidential pardon or Timothy Bell being invited to The White House to have dinner with the president and first lady. By the same token, Dean Pappas, Stan Lustman, Richard Cahill and Fred

Lawson would all be paroled well before Louie is given his cash award.

"Louie, I think the odds are better that you would be the next section chief, sitting in my former office and admiring my plants," Tom has reminded Louie whenever the subject of his cash award is raised.

"The thought of you with all that money turns my stomach," Dave Darick adds. "You would be absolutely unbearable."

"Louie's already unbearable without all that money," JW decided to chime in for good measure.

"When I get the money I so richly deserve, I will hire a publicist, a business agent and a lawyer to represent me in my future dealings with the IRS. I'll stage a propaganda campaign for promotions and when I do take over as section chief and occupy your old office with the oversize plants that need to be pruned, I will personally make your miserable lives even more miserable," Louie shot back.

"You already do a pretty effective job of making us miserable. I can't imagine it being any worse," Dave replied.

"Oh, it can be much worse, trust me," Louie promised.

"While we're on the subject of money, did you hear about Emma Gordon?" JW asked.

"Who the hell is Emma Gordon?" Louie wanted to know.

"She's the eight year-old kid in Iowa who told the president what to do. I read in the paper that the president was so pleased with the advice that she gave him that he personally donated one hundred thousand dollars to a trust fund for her college education and asked her to consider a career as a civil servant upon graduation from college," said JW.

"That is unbelievable," Louie said while shaking his head

and shuffling off to see someone else to complain about the working conditions in the Federal Building.

"Did you really read about that in the paper?" asked Tom.

"Are you kidding? I just made it up to bust the little guy's balls," admitted JW.

"Well, I don't want to be around when the little bugger finds out it's not true. You know how he can get," remarked Dave.

"Don't we all know it," agreed Tom, who simply nodded with pleasure that his beloved oversized plants were doing so well.